Be True to Me

ALSO BY ADELE GRIFFIN

The Unfinished Life of Addison Stone

Tighter

Picture the Dead

Where I Want to Be

ADELE GRIFFIN

Be True to Me

ALGONQUIN 2018

Published by
Algonquin Young Readers
an imprint of Algonquin Books of Chapel Hill
Post Office Box 2225
Chapel Hill, North Carolina 27515-2225

a division of
Workman Publishing
225 Varick Street
New York, New York 10014

First paperback edition, Algonquin Young Readers, May 2018.
Originally published in hardcover by Algonquin Young Readers in June 2017.
Printed in the United States of America.
Published simultaneously in Canada by Thomas Allen & Son Limited.
Design by Colin Mercer.

LIBRARY OF CONGRESS CATALOGING-IN-PUBLICATION DATA
Names: Griffin, Adele, author.
Title: Be true to me / Adele Griffin.
Description: First edition. | Chapel Hill, North Carolina :
Algonquin Young Readers, 2017. | Summary: Told in two voices, Jean, a rich girl, and Fritz, an outsider, compete for the affection of handsome newcomer Gil during the summer of 1976 at an exclusive Fire Island enclave, and discover their competition has higher stakes than either can imagine.
Identifiers: LCCN 2016053858 | ISBN 9781616206758 (HC)
Subjects: | CYAC: Friendship—Fiction. | Dating (Social customs)—Fiction. | Love—Fiction. | Wealth—Fiction. | Fire Island (N.Y. : Island)—History—20th century—Fiction.
Classification: LCC PZ7.G881325 Be 2017 | DDC [Fic]—dc23
LC record available at https://lccn.loc.gov/2016053858

ISBN 978-1-61620-808-0 (PB)

10 9 8 7 6 5 4 3 2 1
First Paperback Edition

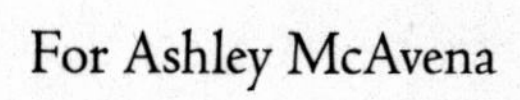

For Ashley McAvena

But I was used to finding something deadly in things that attracted me; there was always something deadly lurking in anything I wanted, anything I loved.

—John Knowles, *A Separate Peace*

Be True to Me

PART ONE

My breath pitched and fell rough as the water itself. I'd always been a strong swimmer; for as long as I'd been alive, I had connected with the flow of every sport I'd ever tried. But this wasn't a sport; this was nature. Nature had its own rules, and the ocean was against me.

I wouldn't make it. I wasn't going to make it.

But I couldn't believe it, either. I didn't lose at these things.

"Gil!" I called over my shoulder.

It never occurred to me that he wouldn't be there.

JEAN

. . . the truth itself seemed like a tiny detail.

My older sister had the face I always wanted. Elegantly elfin, with a nose like a Valentine silhouette. But she didn't stop at pretty; Daphne also looked decisive. You could see at a glance that here was a girl who had strong tastes in shoes and music and what should be poured into a flask before a tailgate party during Homecoming Weekend.

Ever since I was little, I'd thought that if I looked more like Daphne, people would understand what I was all about. Because I was every bit as sure of what I wanted. I just never came across that way.

Tonight, I'd been sprawled across her bed, watching her pack for Barcelona. Shoulders back, chin tilted, frowning slightly, she'd hold a dress against her lanky frame and then I'd wait for her firm yes or no. I was in charge of taking the noes back to her closet. Sometimes she'd ask my opinion, as if it counted.

"Does this match my hair?" Daphne's hair: a drop of strawberry in straw-gold blond. Parted clean, cut neat to the chin.

This was a nautical mini dress with large covered blue buttons.

"Yes. It looks perfect on you. You can wear it on the Fourth."

"They won't be celebrating that in Spain. Anyway, the buttons are tacky." She tossed it to me. "Mom's taste, of course."

Did Daphne act the way she looked or did she look the way she acted? I picked up her toiletry kit, precisely organized with her shampoo and roll-on, her bottle of Nair depilatory and her pots of Magic Gloss. There was also some loose jewelry, including my earrings.

"Hey, Daph. These are mine."

She snatched up the kit and slapped me away. "Jean, don't be pesky. I bought those earrings at campus crafts fair last semester. Now go get my quilted wraparound."

I slid off the bed. Daphne's wardrobe took up the extra closet in the hall between us. By the time I'd returned with the skirt, she'd screwed in the earrings. My chest constricted. Daphne was already a knockout. I was the one who needed killer earrings—at least for tonight, when everyone would notice us together and compare us.

Now I saw myself reflected in Daphne's bureau mirror, my hair a dark blond cloud, my face doughy and uncertain—I favored the Danielsen side, my mother always sadly decreed, blaming her Nordic bloodline, although she herself had managed to escape its curse of a thick waist and eggshell-pale skin.

"I can't believe you just put those on."

"They're *mine,* Jean."

My heart raced with the unfairness. "When you're asleep," I said, "I'm going to sneak into your suitcase and take them back."

She flicked her fingers at me. "Go ahead. And then I'll check for them in the morning, and if they're gone, we can fight about it. And Mom and Dad will get upset and make one of us fork them over. But either way—you'll know you were wrong. And eventually, your stupid behavior will upset you, and you'll call me one night in Barcelona, probably way too late and waking me up, apologizing, trying to get me to believe it was an honest mistake."

My face went hot. That did sound like me. "You don't know anything."

"I know you spend half your time doing stuff that you spend the other half regretting."

My sister's voice was lower and sharper than mine. It made the things she said sound too important.

"I'm sick of being your handmaiden," I said, and slammed out.

But I regretted this move immediately. My own room looked so empty after Daphne's, which was always such a fun, popular-girl party of Dingo boots and silk scarves and *Vogue* magazines and ticket stubs. I searched my closet halfheartedly for something to wear tonight. Not that it mattered. All eyes and ears would be on Daphne and her glamorous summer plans for studying in Spain.

The Cool one or the Other one? The Pretty one or the Other one? The Foxy one or the Other one? Everyone said it. Maybe they didn't say it to my face. But the comparison was always in their eyes. I was glad my sister wasn't coming with us to Sunken Haven. Even when we got along, we were siblings, officially positioned and divided as rivals.

A whole summer of no Daphne felt too good to be true.

Changed into a fresh dress, the one I'd worn to Bertie Forsythe's senior spring formal at Choate, I still wasn't any match for her. I was the plainer, heavier Other Custis Sister.

And it was cruel of Daph to take my earrings. It was like she was saying I didn't deserve them.

The doorbell buzzed. The first guests had arrived. I heard the caterers sweeping in and out of our kitchen, circulating trays. Dad put on a jazz record, and Mom was squealing *hellos* and *darlings*. There was a soft click next door as Daphne sailed out. I stayed hidden with my paperback copy of *Looking for Mr. Goodbar* for another half hour or so. Then I crept unnoticed into the living room, where the bon voyage was in full swing.

Friends and neighbors were scooping hors d'oeuvres and speeding through Chablis. Mom was holding court by the living room windows. Dad poured highballs at the bar cart.

From a passing tray, I took the single glass of white wine that my parents let me have at cocktail parties, and I stayed on the edges. I watched my earrings twinkle, hypnotic, in Daphne's ears. It burned me up. I should do something. I gulped the wine and gave it a couple of minutes to buzz through me.

Good grief, maybe I would do something!

Lightheaded, I plunged through the crowd.

"Oh, my gosh!" My voice broke through to Daphne and her group of admirers, including my godfather, Carpie Burke, damply overheated in his summer suit. "You found my earrings!"

Daphne's smile went stale. Her finger touched an earlobe. "Jeanie has been hounding me about these."

"They were in my Christmas stocking," I explained, though nobody had asked, "and they *mysteriously* disappeared the same day."

"Santa would want us to share. Listen, you can borrow them anytime, okay, Sis?" Daphne's glib party voice only made me madder.

"Ha, now that's interesting. Borrowing my own jewelry!"

"I don't think we've been introduced." The young man standing next to Carpie had a Southern accent and an amused tone, as if I were saying charming things that made him want to get to know me better, instead of barking accusations at my sister.

"This is my goddaughter, Jean," said Carpie loud and quick. "And Jean, I'd like you to meet my nephew, Gil Burke. In fact, this is why I brought him out tonight. To get to know some of the young Sunken Haven set."

"How do you do, Jean?" The direct, unexpected lock of Gil Burke's eyes on me turned my mind blank with surprise, as he extended his hand. "Nice to meet you."

"Hello." I tried not to stare. I felt dizzy. Why'd I drink that wine so fast? Carpie's nephew? Yes, I saw that. But Gil was the handsome, athletic version. His eyes were the warm brown of Dad's favorite bourbon, and his skin glowed like he'd just stepped out of the sun. He looked like a person who'd be happier in general to be outdoors.

Shy as I felt, I didn't stop staring. Beside me, Daphne laughed. I was acting awkward—but I couldn't help it.

"Gil's done some good work at the firm this spring. Next week, he's coming out to Sunken Haven, and he's staying at the house with Weeze, Junior, and me. You'll show him how we do things there, won't you, Jeanie?"

"Oh! Sure!"

Gil hadn't let go of my hand. Once I'd read that party handshakes were icy because in moments of social stress, the blood flow pumped into more important organs. But Gil Burke's hand was all heat. I was sorry when he finally let go. "If you're Carpie's nephew, then why haven't we met before?" I asked. "The Burkes are practically family."

"I'm on the hillbilly branch of the Burke family tree." Was he being serious? His lips held a jokester's quirk.

"Gil's and my birthdays are the same year, four days apart," said Daphne. That meant Gil was nineteen—a new nineteen, because Daphne's birthday was last month. I'd turned seventeen in December, so Gil wasn't too old for me—but he was also fair game for Daphne, and if she wanted him, I'd never get him.

I hoped Gil knew she was leaving tomorrow for Spain.

"You better give those back before you leave for Spain tomorrow for the whole, entire summer," I said. Then I reached over, my hand raised like a slap, and batted at an earring.

Daphne squealed and hopped. Her fingers cupped her ears.

"Jeanie, my girl," said Carpie. "Fighting is for sandboxes."

When I made another snatch for them, Gil's laugh and "Easy" as he caught my arm stopped me. But his smile was kind. "You're a wild card, huh?"

"Daphne's a liar."

"Oh, please, Jean. I really—I can't handle your childish impulses tonight." With a parting glance of pitying contempt, Daphne left us. By then, Carpie had also smoothly redirected himself across the room, probably in search of more adult company.

"She pushes my buttons," I confessed to Gil once we were alone. "I don't know what comes over me."

"Except *you're* the one Uncle Carp wants to teach me the straight dope on Sunken Haven, am I right?"

"I guess so." Only because Daphne would be abroad. I didn't say that. I was conscious of how hard we were staring at each other.

"I need to split, go get a real dinner," said Gil. "Want to join? Can you recommend anywhere?"

"Oh! Sure." My heart tripped at the unexpectedness of his suggestion. "How about Hollander's?"

"You and me? Hollander's? That bar is legend." Gil's voice dropped. "Think you can get us in?"

"Easy." Could I? I'd never gotten in without Daphne.

"Then let's bust outta here."

"I'll check with Mom." Quickly I glanced over at the other side of the room, where Mom and her friends were still close to the windows. "They're spying on Baryshnikov."

"Who?"

"Mikhail Baryshnikov. He's that ballet dancer who defected from Russia. Now he lives across the street. Every night he walks his poodle." I turned. "She'll say I have to be home by ten thirty."

"You can go *anywhere* in the city, so long as you're home by ten thirty?"

"I'm not going anywhere *bad*."

"Right. Just *illegally*, into bars. 'I must file this under Crazy Pastimes of Young Citizens of New York.'" Gil had switched into a Russian accent. "'You are not merely cute girl. You are valuable KGB information source.'"

"Buy me a beer, and I'll spill all my secrets." *Cute girl*? Did Gil Burke really think I was cute?

I was glad Daphne was on the other side of the room, so she didn't see us leave. But once we were in the elevator, I could hardly look at Gil. My throat felt dry with nerves. On the curb, Jimmy, the doorman, whistled for a cab and then slammed us inside it.

This was a date, right? Wasn't it? I didn't have much to compare. My school-year social life was meet-ups at Lexington Candy Shop or the Regal Theater. My summer social life was Bertie Forsythe, who otherwise I only saw when I attended his boarding school's formals weekends.

Tonight felt completely different from any of those excursions.

Gil seemed relaxed. "The life of Miss Jean Custis!" he said. "The Upper East Side apartment. Happy summers at this mysterious Sunken Haven. Let me guess: You have a ski pad, too?"

I laughed. "Just a time-share in Stowe. You make us sound too glamorous! My parents are the last word in dull."

"Oh, Mumsie! Oh, Daddykins! So very ho-hum!" Gil flicked my arm. My skin tingled at the mark.

"Where are you from, anyway?" I shifted down in my seat to stare at Gil at an uptilt. My Dalton friends and I had practiced our cab angles on each other. It had been decided that I looked cutest on an up-tilt. "I mean, where is your accent from?"

"Elmore, Alabama. I'm a transplant."

"How recent?"

"I came up to City College this year. Let's just say Uncle Carp's taken an interest since I got straight *A*s. Found me a job clerking at his firm, and now he wants to transfer me into his alma mater, Columbia. He's been like family."

"Well, probably because he *is* family! Do you get along with Junior?" I couldn't help but make a face. Junior Burke was Carpie's awful son, a year older than I was. The Burkes had tried and failed to fix up Daphne or me with Junior for years, but no dice. Gil was a whole other story. The Burkes would be able to set up Gil with any girl in a heartbeat.

How lucky that I'd got to him first!

"Funny thing about Junior," said Gil, "but I haven't even met him yet. Last week, he went straight from Syracuse to a week of sailing camp. I'll meet him when he gets back."

"But isn't Junior your first cousin? That's pretty close family, I'd say."

"I never met any of the Burkes till I moved here."

"What? In your whole life?"

"My folks and Uncle Carp don't get along."

"Why not?

Gil's expression was complicated. "Uncle Carp hasn't had much to do with us, is all I meant."

"It's funny, because for us, the Burkes have always seemed like relatives."

"Funny," Gil repeated, but it was clear he didn't think so. I'd blundered.

Thursday night at Hollander's. Through the windows, the bar looked packed. Kids were pressed around the outside entrance as usual, hoping for the magic nod from Jack Hollander that would admit them.

"I'm not dressed right," said Gil. "I look uptight in this suit."

"You look cool." Though among the shaggy-headed boys in

their summer khakis and sockless loafers, Gil did look formal in his button-down and blazer.

"If we need to take off," he said, "I know a diner in Hell's Kitchen where the batter-fried onion rings—"

"Just you wait." I was on my tiptoes, waving to Jack, who was outside working the door. "His dad owns this place. He'll get us in." I was betting Jack's crush on Daphne would carry us. When Jack saw us, he smiled. "No sister, Jean? Look at you, Miss All Grown Up!" On his all-powerful signal, Gil and I bumped to the head of the line and shot through.

We pushed past underage girls lined up at the bar. I saw a clump of graduated Dalton seniors. I felt like a cat, sleekly sliding past them, Gil in tow and no Daphne to steal my moment.

In the dining section, Gil and I slid into the last empty checked-cloth window table, where a waitress took our order.

As Gil explained how he wanted his burger, I let myself enjoy a long look at him. He was a real Ryan O'Neal type, with those wide-spaced features and that polished, winning smile. When he shrugged off his blazer and hung it on the back of the chair, I noticed a stitched monogram at the shirt pocket—C.G.B.

"You're wearing Carpie's shirt?"

"Yep. He's Carpenter Gilroy, I'm Christopher Gilroy. And he's strict as all hell about how I show up at the firm. But I'd wear a tutu and toe shoes if that's what he wanted, he's been that solid to me since I showed up in New York."

"Oh, yes. Carpie's the best. But soon all you'll need are Polo shirts and tennis whites. Sunken Haven's so relaxed."

Gil took a first sip from the beer that had been set down. "You sure? Aunt Weeze went ahead a few weeks ago to 'open the house.' What's that even mean?"

"It's not glamorous, if that's what you think! It's about clearing out the mouse droppings and scrubbing the salt off the windows, airing the beds and sweeping out the sand and the pine needles. My family's house is right on the ocean. You can smell sage and bayberry all the way up South Beach."

Gil was looking at me deeply. I'd never had anyone look at me like this. Not even Bertie, who always had a smile for me. "Your eyes shine when you talk about this place. You must love it."

"Oh my gosh, I do! I've spent every summer there since I was born. It's a shelter island, you know. One side's ocean and the other's the Long Island Sound. Our cottage, Lazy Days, is right on the ocean. And it's . . ." I was about to say *my first summer without Daphne.* But it seemed petty. "It's going to be so fun," I said instead, truthfully. *So fun without Daphne.*

"Carpie said kids work," said Gil.

"They do. We do. We all have jobs, for pay or volunteer."

"Volunteer?" He quirked an eyebrow.

"It seems corny, but everyone pitches in somehow."

"So what are you *volunteering* to do there?" His smile was teasing.

"Well, June and July it's nothing but tennis," I said. "See, I lost the Junior Girls Singles championship last year, and my parents went ape." Even after a year, my tennis fiasco humiliated me. "I'll be on the court day and night."

Gil looked amused. "I'm teaching swim classes and waiting tables at the yacht club. Guess I'll be the boy fetching your ice-cold Yoo-hoos and Winks."

"No, no, it's not that way! Kids always work at the club. We wait on one other, we babysit one another, we teach the little ones to swim!"

He laughed. "I didn't mean to rile you."

"I don't want you to think I'll be having this la-dee-da summer, while you're toiling away."

That made us both laugh. "It does sound pretty cushy," said Gil. "I've helped at my stepdad's hardware store since I was knee-high. Now, that's some dull work."

"There's loads of kids on payroll who still have fun. Mrs. Walt—you know Walt's Chocolates? Well, that's her family—but at Sunken Haven, she's just the sweet old lady who runs the thrift shop, and I worked there last year." I was rambling, I blamed the wine and beer and not quite knowing how to act around a boy who made me feel so giddy. "All I'm really saying is it's busy, you know . . ."

Gil's eyes were warm on me. "It's cool how you're so serious about everything. You're a funny princess."

"No, no! I'm not," I answered sincerely.

He laughed. "Especially when you don't mean to be funny."

But I'd meant that I wasn't a princess.

Our burgers arrived, distracting us as we squirted ketchup and loaded the buns with lettuce, onions, and pickles. Led Zeppelin was on the jukebox. "What sort of music do you go for?"

Now Gil leaned in on his elbows. I'd struck a nerve. "Clapton, Tom Waits, Lynyrd Skynyrd. But I dig most any rock-and-roll—me and my pal Kenny took a bus twenty-three hours to see The Who in Fort Worth."

"I've been to Madison Square Garden twice this year. Once for David Bowie and once for Elton John." This wasn't true—it was Daphne who'd gone. But I'd heard enough about both concerts. In the moment, staring at Gil, I wanted it to be true so badly that the truth itself seemed like a tiny detail.

"Elton John? That guy's a dud." Gil began to sing "Bennie and the Jets" through his adenoids.

My cheeks got hot. Daphne never did dud things! Or did she? What would Daphne say in this moment? "Well, I saw Elton's whole act, and it's a complete hoot!"

Gil shrugged. "Piano's good if Waits is playing it. I'm more into guitars myself." He molded his hand around an invisible neck, and with the other hand, he strummed air. "I used to mess around in a band—we called ourselves The Mindbenders. But that was B.C.—Before Carp. Now I'm at the firm day and night. He's got me in his focus—which I do appreciate," added Gil quickly. "Hope I wasn't coming off ungrateful."

"Have Carpie and your family mended fences?"

Gil paused, as if deciding how to frame this. "Matter of fact, one of the deals of my being here is, I can't contact my family."

"Why not?"

He smiled, guarded. Sipped his beer and shrugged in answer.

"But that's family politics for you," I said. "Anyway. I'm glad you told me. I'm always here to listen if, you know—" I floundered "—you want to tell me more."

Now Gil eyed me in a way that burned up my cheeks. "I want to know more about you."

"Oh, okay. Me. Um. Like what?"

"Like . . . what do you love?"

"Love! Oh my gosh! Don't put me on the spot!" I hid behind my beer mug—only a few sips remained. I wouldn't order another. Even one drink made me too careless with my words. "I love tennis," I told him after a pause.

"Where I'm from, that game's for snobs."

"I never feel snobby when I play. I feel happy. Unless it's . . ." against *her.* "Unless it's too competitive."

"Have you got a shelf full of trophies?"

"Not exactly."

"Aw, you're stewing about something." Gil's voice was gentle. He tipped his head, watching me. "Cat got your tongue? Tell me."

"No. There's nothing to tell."

"Come on. Put it out there."

Fritz O'Neill. She was something real. She was something to put out there. But I wouldn't even speak her name out loud. Not tonight.

Fritz O'Neill, who last summer had entered the Junior Cup Tennis competition at the eleventh hour. Then she'd casually annihilated me. My loss had shocked the family. My mother's and Daphne's names were *both* etched into plaques that hung in Haven Casino's center hall.

But not mine.

"I'm training super hard for a tennis rematch that I lost last summer. I've been practicing after school and every weekend."

"Bet you'll do fine."

"There are other good players."

"Like who?"

"I guess I can't remember her name."

"Arrright, arrright." Gil popped his last huge bite of burger in his mouth. He ate too quickly, but his appetite also made him sexy, like a wolf.

When "Young Americans" came on, I clapped for it. "I love this song!"

"I'll get out there if you want."

Toward the far end of the room near the jukebox, kids were bouncing and shimmying and trying to look like they weren't working too hard on their moves.

"Okay."

Gil slapped a ten on the table to pay. "Let's go."

When I stood with him, he took my arm and led, turning me in and out easily, and then pulling me close. When he held me to his chest, I melted against the press of his body. Were Dalton girls watching? Was Jack Hollander? Would people talk about how smooth we looked out here? I felt expansive with all the possibilities.

And when the song ended and Gil stared down at me, for once my uptilt felt entirely natural. I'd never felt so radiant as I did in his gaze.

Gil leaned in close to my ear. "Hollander's. Bowie. You. At least I got one New York night exactly right."

We danced to a few more songs, then we left the bar, sailing into the warm, almost-summer night. We had enough time to walk uptown and still beat my curfew. Three hours ago, I hadn't even known he existed, and now here was Gil Burke, blazing bright as a comet through the center of my world. I was giddy with it, almost frantic with wanting to absorb and memorize every detail of each, shared moment.

"Kinda funny, remembering about earlier," Gil said, as if he'd been listening in on my thoughts. "When Uncle Carp first mentioned his goddaughter?" He took my hand and slid his fingers through mine. "For some reason, I pictured a little girl with braces and a hula hoop."

I sighed. "Carpie thinks I'm still a child."

"You're anything but." He said it sweetly. Not like a come-on. His fingers were woven strong through mine. Gil had seemed sure right from go that I was special—a fun-loving New York girl with connections to "It" bars. And now a brand-new thought overtook me.

First Gil had rescued me from my fight with Daphne. Then he'd sprung me out of the apartment and whirled me into this perfect evening. What if Gil had come here all the way from Elmore, Alabama, to Sunken Haven *for me*?

Could it be true? Instead of a summer playing handmaiden to Daphne, was I being delivered something entirely different—a summer in the spotlight? A summer starring Gil Burke and me? The idea, as it steeped, filled me with tense, panicky joy—it sounded too good to be true, like something a West Village psychic would promise for fifty cents.

Summer flings and sexy romances were Daphne's territory. Not mine. I was the one you *didn't* pick.

I swatted off my hope like a bumblebee, knowing it was too late. I'd already been deliriously stung.

FRITZ

FORT POLK, LOUISIANA

I'd had such a bad spring.

I spent my last day at home before Sunken Haven working a full shift on my feet at the PX. Ringing up shoe trees and salad spinners and whatever else was sale-priced low enough to send the army wives scrambling. An hour before I got off, a lady came in and ripped my head off because I didn't think she could return a knee brace she'd been using for about a month. Good thing it was only my fake birthday. If this were my real birthday, Jesus, I'd probably have burst into tears.

My parents were throwing me a month-early party. They did it every year, since they never saw me on my birth date, July fifteenth. I'd always compare the two dates—the one here, versus the real one I'd spend hanging out on Main Beach with Julia and Tracy, sunbathing and debating which parties to hit later.

In fairness to my parents, they made the night special in its own way. When I came out of my room, showered and changed for the evening, a haul of wrapped presents was displayed in a festive heap on the table. And foodwise, Mom had gone all out: iced vegetable mousse and her seven-layer spinach-crabmeat casserole. To be safe from pickier eaters, she was also heating up a couple of packs of Jimmy Dean pigs in blankets.

The heat in the kitchen was baking the whole house. June in Louisiana was even hotter than July in Sunken Haven. The best cooldown was to stick my head in the freezer, where my cake waited in its pink and brown polka-dot Baskin-Robbins box.

"Fritz, if you're ready, will you get your head out of there and go see who's at the door? Since your brother won't budge." Mom had made Kevin stay home tonight, but he was spaced on *The Six Million Dollar Man* in my parents' bedroom, the only room with an air conditioner.

"No problemo." I slammed the freezer shut and went to meet the Fowlers as they banged through the screen door and into the living room.

"Hi, Mrs. Fowler. Hello, Major Fowler!" Mrs. Fowler was a flow of Dashiki caftan and cigarette smoke as she wafted over to deliver my birthday gift.

"Oh, thank you, Mrs. Fowler."

"You're very welcome, Almost Birthday Girl. Though I'll tell you, the walk over just about did me in. Whew, this heat." She plopped onto our sectional and plucked a flowered packet of cigarettes from her purse, lighting the butt of her last cig to a fresh stick. Then she crossed her legs and patted the place beside her. "Now, come sit here by me. You all packed and ready? How many times have you been out to Fire Island now?"

"This is the seventh," I said. "I've been visiting Julia since I turned ten. It's basically the best place in the world. And my last shift at the PX was today."

"Well, that explains your big smile. Even if you couldn't pay me to visit a place called Fire Island." Mrs. Fowler fanned herself with the back of a hand. "You can fry an egg on my stoop as it is."

"Funny thing is, it's cooler there than here." And I'd be there tomorrow! Smelling the salted wind through the marsh grass. Feeling the sand between my toes, and Julia's shoulder jogged against mine, as we walked to the candy store.

Sunken Haven was as unlike a ten-hour shift ringing up layaway as you could possibly get.

"What's the connection again to this place?" asked Mrs. Fowler.

Mom arrived to set the cheese board on the coffee table. "My friend Patsy Tulliver and I were both pregnant in Fort Hood," she said. "Me with Kevin and Patsy with Dot. We did Lamaze classes together and got close, and so did our daughters. Even after Patsy's husband left the service, Fritz and Julia stayed friends, and they always spend summers together. The Tullivers are so generous about hosting."

"And Julia's my best friend," I added, sounding like a third grader. But I was so excited to see her that I wanted to say her name out loud.

"Our Fritzie needs a break. It's been nothing but double shifts since school got out." She ruffled my hair. "I have a good feeling about this summer."

She said it partly because she wished it, since I'd had such a bad spring. My breakup mopes, my speaker-blasting of "Crazy On You," my TV marathons—I wasn't my usual self.

"I'm ready for it," I agreed.

"You still feeling bad about that boy?" Mrs. Fowler asked when Mom had scooted back to the kitchen. She took a long drag on her cigarette, exhaling smoke through her nostrils like a mystic.

"What boy?"

"What boy! Fritz! You know what boy! Colonel Houlihan's younger son. The football player with the big ears who stole your smile."

"Oh, Scott."

"Oh, Scott! Oh, him! He was never right for you. Big ole show-off. I used to see him come into the rec center with the other boys on the football team."

"He dated me when I was a cheerleader, and he dumped me when I quit the team. So that was, you know . . . enlightening." I hated talking about it. Scott had been so cool—right up till the minute I realized he'd only seen us the way he wanted his friends and teammates to see us. "I was dumb about him."

"Breakups hurt," said Mrs. Fowler, "no matter how they happen. But the hurt doesn't stick forever. You'll heal, Fritz."

I smiled in answer, as if I agreed—even though I had no idea if that was true—and leaned forward to dip a carrot stick in onion dip. If I was supposed to be getting over Scott Houlihan, then leaving Fort Polk was a start.

Soon the party hit its groove. Neighbors never bothered to ring our bell, they just blew on through, delivering six packs, and gifts for me. The air was thick with smoke and Chique perfume, recently stocked at the PX, and the scent of choice this summer.

The gifts were fun, but Stephanie Ewart, my best on-base friend, had taken a babysitting job tonight, and once Mom put on the Donna Summer, the living room turned into a sad scene of adults in jumbo bell-bottoms all juking out, then quickly checking with me:

Fritz, do your friends do the hustle or is that only us old fogies?

I slurped down a slice of ice-cream cake. The air was roasting me.

When nobody was watching—not that anyone would have cared—I slipped to my room. The Junior Cup was balanced on my blue Samsonite. I was sorry to be returning the cup. I've been winning sports medals and pins and trophies since I was knee-high to a peanut, but I've never gotten to keep anything as grand as this old lady. Sterling silver.

All year, it had sat on my bookshelf, reminding me of summer.

But it wasn't mine. Then again, nothing on Sunken Haven was mine for keeps.

I turned up "Magic Man," the first track on *Dreamboat Annie,* which never left my turntable. Then I unwrapped my birthday gifts: portable hot curlers, a few albums, some color-change mood lipsticks, and three seventeen-dollar birthday checks.

By the time I pulled on PJs, the house had quieted. Only then did I let myself check in with my old diary, rereading this and that, and eventually, of course, I led myself back down the painful path of entries about me and Scott. Which led me to flipping back even further, to the well-read details from the two times we'd almost had sex. (Both almosts were at the Park & Rec, parked behind the picnic tables, in the back of Mrs. Houlihan's station wagon, which smelled like their cocker spaniel, Cookie. Each time, I'd had second thoughts. And so, instead of sex, we'd had a fight.)

I don't know why I always reread those parts. Maybe because it felt like I dodged a bullet? I knew some girls didn't care about it, but I had zero regrets that my first time hadn't been with a guy who ended up being not at all who I'd hoped he was.

Tomorrow, I was outta here, and I was leaving my diary at home. I was done with writing down every journal-worthy moment, preserving my emotions only to be humiliated by them. For the rest of this summer, Julia and I'd be together, earning tips and partying on the beach and enjoying all the usual fun. Maybe I'd remember everything, maybe I wouldn't. It didn't mean I hadn't lived it.

Fort Hood, Fort Lee, Fort Polk. Our family had moved onto

three different bases since I started spending summers with Julia. I was used to army living, but Sunken Haven was my childhood constant, the one place that pulled me in and held me, year after year, to its unchanging comforts. In some ways, it was the closest I'd ever had to a permanent home. I felt lucky every summer that I got to go back.

JEAN

SUNKEN HAVEN, FIRE ISLAND

"She's nothing to me."

We'd arrived three days ago. And every single day had been a slow, dragging, nail-biting torture, wondering when I'd see Gil again.

I had tried to keep myself distracted. There was tennis clinic in the morning and most afternoons, of course. I'd also reunited with my best friends, Sara Train and Rosamund Wembly, and we'd been as inseparable as ever, meeting up for light lunches and beach time and bike rides, rotating lazy visits to one another's houses, with nights reserved for the usual icy beers on someone's deck or out on the dunes. The rhythm of a summer season was so set, it was already hard to distinguish the days of this summer from the chime and dissolve of years before.

Except that this summer, all I'd thought about was Gil. He'd been one of the most tantalizing secrets I'd ever kept. A thousand times a day, sunbathing on Main Beach or ordering grilled cheeses at the club, Gil had been on the tip of my tongue. If only I could dare to speak about him! How my story could shake up this quiet afternoon, as Sara shellacked her toes alternating colors of bright yellow and purple while Rosamund made a chocolate-pudding Bundt cake—Lazy Days always had the best-stocked pantry, thanks to Mrs. Otis, who ran our home like an army general.

I imagined myself casually starting the conversation, about how I'd met and fallen head over heels for the handsomest, smartest, most charming guy in New York. City.

And he happened to be Carpie Burke's nephew.

And he'd be here, oh, any day now.

Then, while the girls squealed and teased and plied me with questions, I'd unspool every delicious detail—from that first rattle of my heart when he'd clasped my hand and said my name, to the moment we'd kissed good-bye.

"Here you go. Door-to-door service," Gil had said when he'd dropped me off at the apartment, his knuckles chucking me lightly under the chin. "What a change from my usual nights, hanging out with other interns. Thanks for a great scene." He'd hesitated. "Hope I didn't seem like too much of a hick, around all those prep-school kids."

"Oh my gosh, no!" I'd laughed. The idea that Gil could be insecure had seemed outrageous. "You're not serious, are you?"

He'd smiled. Then he'd taken my shoulders, tipped me back

slightly, stepped forward, and I'd softened into the sudden deep press of his mouth on mine and the glint of his eyes on me when he'd broken away. His voice had been low, for me alone. "But you'll be my coach, right? You'll tell me how it all works over there? Uncle Carp's not the only one relying on you."

"Count on me."

"I think we're coming into Sunken Haven a week from tonight."

"I'll be there."

There'd been no second kiss. He was too much of a gentleman. I'd watched him amble down the block, his jacket hooked over his shoulder, his stroll unhurried, as if the Upper East Side were merely another country road.

That was Thursday. Today was Sunday.

I glanced at Rosamund and Sara.

No no no. I looked down into the little plastic bucket I'd stuck in the sink. My task today was making a homemade deer repellent—just about the most unromantic chore I could think up. But like tennis, it was one of those mundane tasks that helped me get through the day without spilling a word. Because I couldn't. I didn't want the girls to know my heart's desire. What if Gil got here and had no interest in me, after all? What if he realized that I was nothing special?

What if I'd misunderstood everything? Too mortifying—it got me dizzy even considering it. I finished unwrapping a bar of lye soap, which I dropped into my bucket along with a few cups of water.

"Might rain," Rosamund mentioned in her dreamy voice that didn't care if it did or didn't. Her arm cranked the mixing bowl as she strolled past the windows, gazing out at the clouds hanging over the mackerel sea.

"Can't you get Mrs. Otis to do that?" Sara asked, without breaking concentration on her pedicure. Her square feet were up on our kitchen island—my mother would have screamed at the sight.

"Tabasco sauce makes her eyes itch. Deep breath. Here comes the hard part." I cracked the two rotten eggs.

The sulfurous stink was immediate—Rosamund, as she layered the cake's pudding filling, scrunched her nose. "I can't believe you're mixing up that dead farts smell while I'm baking a yummy cake!"

"I'll be done soon." Green-onion tops, garlic cloves. A splash of Tabasco so it tasted extra horrible for the rodents. It was darkly funny to watch all the creatures come up to gnaw on the pachysandra—and then scurry off after the first, terrible taste.

From the hall, the phone rang.

"I'll get it, I'll get it!" I galloped out of the kitchen, through the pantry and dining room, to the front hall.

Gil hadn't telephoned, but every time it rang, I hoped.

Mrs. Otis had beaten me. "No, I'm sorry," she was saying into the receiver, "Jean's not in."

"I *am* in, Mrs. Otis!"

With the flat of her hand, she gestured for me not to interrupt her. Mrs. Otis disapproved of social phone calls in general, for me in particular, and on Sundays most of all. She put a Sunday phone call in the same category as a fire extinguisher: for emergencies only.

My heart was slamming like I'd already finished a set of tennis warm-ups.

"Please, Mrs. Otis." I made a grab for it, caught it, and tugged hard. "Hello?"

"Jean?"

Oh, *Christmas!* That voice. It felt like an eternity since I'd heard Gil's drawl, with its deep, sleepy hint of Southern magnolia.

I sank into the hall chair, the receiver clamped under my chin. "Yes. This is she," I said in my best manners. Gil had seemed to like it when I upheld a certain society style.

"Gil Burke speaking." I could hear the *chatter-snicks* of typewriters in the background. "Sorry to trouble you on a Sunday."

I wound the curly phone cord around one finger; with my other hand I nervously rearranged the apple and pear in the bowl of plastic fruit that had sat on our hall console since forever. "No trouble at all!"

"So here's what. Uncle Carp wrapped up a case early. We've been finishing the paperwork over this weekend, and now he wants to come in Tuesday afternoon. He told me to get hold of Aunt Weeze, but she's not picking up. I got ahold of this Sunken Haven directory and I found your number and . . ."

Tuesday! Tuesday was two days away! "Absolutely. We'll get the message over to her. We see Weeze all the time."

"Aw, thanks. Then I'll cross it off my list. So, how're you keeping, Princess Funny? How's the tennis?"

"Super." My whole body was trembling. Should I ask Gil if I could meet him dockside Tuesday? It was a tradition, whenever the ferry sailed into harbor, that kids went out to greet the boat—the younger ones even jumped off the dock.

"See you soon," Gil spoke, undaunted, into the terrible static. "Sooner'n I'd reckoned, even."

"Yes! That's so nice!"

"Day after tomorrow."

"I'm looking forward to catching up," I said in a rush.

"Me, too. Been thinking about you. But I better go, I can't tie up the line."

"Of course, of course. Bye-bye."

Next thing I heard was the dial tone. My blood was lighter than air.

"Who was that, that you were dying to talk to?" Rosamund winked as I reentered the kitchen. "Was it our ever-faithful Bertie, inviting you to Punch Night?"

"No, it was Coach Hutch," I lied. Oh, but I'd messed up! I should have mentioned Punch Night to Gil! I ought to have invited him! *So there's this dinner dance at the club this Friday, and since you won't know anyone . . .* My fists clenched as I stared down at the bucket of repellant. I could have poisoned every critter in our garden right then, I was so annoyed with myself.

"But you and Bertie'll go, right?" said Sara. "You're such an old married couple."

I looked up. "We are not! We're more like friends!"

"Oh, Jean, please! I can't stand when you take Bertie for granted," said Sara. "He's got such beautiful gray eyes."

"Plus he's in love with you," added Rosamund.

I could feel my lips press into a line. It really wasn't my fault that Bertie had beautiful gray eyes and was in love with me.

"Did either of you girls see that bulldozer come in this morning?" Sara looked up from her toenails. "Which cottage is being renovated?"

"Snappy Boy, most likely," said Rosamund. "Isn't it always being improved?"

Even mention of the Burkes' cottage made me feel like a shaken can of soda about to be popped. I frowned, swirling the repellant with a wooden spoon. Maybe on Tuesday, if I was out strolling *near* but not *at* the dock—*Gil! I almost forgot you were coming in on this ferry! By the way, there's this thing at the club*—would that be all right?

No! Too forward, too desperate.

"The bulldozer is here to clear for a helipad near the firehouse," I told the girls. "Because of what happened to Tracy Gibbons-Kent."

"What happened to Tracy?" asked Sara. "Come to think of

it, she hasn't been over once yet. I miss her." She leaned up to stare out the window, to where the Gibbons-Kent house, Serenity, was visible a little higher up on the shoreline.

"Tracy's not here this summer," I said. "She came up with some friends this spring and got into a terrific mess. She did thirteen shots of vodka and passed out. When the Coast Guard finally arrived, she was having toxic seizures."

"*What?*" Rosamund whipped around, her mouth hanging open. "Does anyone else know?"

"Gosh, no," I answered. "Only my parents and a few others. If we'd had a helicopter here, it would have dropped Tracy at Mount Sinai in twenty minutes, instead of an hour." I was parroting everything Mr. Gibbons-Kent had said when he'd come over for an Executive Association dinner our first night here. There were ninety-six private homes here, but only a handful of families truly ran and knew everything. Our family was one of them.

"Jeez," said Rosamund. "I can't imagine summer without Tracy. She *makes* the scene, you know?"

"What about Tiger? Is he here?" Sara asked. Tiger was Tracy's big brother. Just about every girl in Sunken Haven had dated Tiger. This summer, Sara was crossing fingers for her turn. Which would never happen—and it wasn't only because of her acne. Sara was too rough, too blunt. Boys had been backing away from Sara since kindergarten.

"Tiger's coming in tomorrow," I said over my shoulder, as I

sloshed the bucket out to the mudroom to let it sit. "But Tracy's in a rehab center."

"That seems like extreme punishment for getting toasted," said Rosamund. "Now Tracy has to change her whole life?"

I shrugged a nonanswer. My parents had figured there was more to the Tracy disaster. They'd decided that it was all about a boy. "You mustn't tell anyone what I said." I snapped off my gloves. Tonight, with clothespins on our noses, Mrs. Otis and I would take paintbrushes and coat all the deer favorites—pachysandra, daylilies, and sarsaparilla—with the repellent. It was an old Sunken Haven recipe, and it worked.

"Tracy's such fun. Julia Tulliver and Fritz O'Neill will be especially bummed that she's gone." Sara leaned forward and blew on her toes.

"Now if only we could get rid of Fritz Oh-No." Rosamund popped in the cake with a bang of the oven door. "You should feed *her* repellent, Jean."

The girls burst into laughter.

"I don't have a grudge against Fritz," I said. "She's nothing to me."

"She's nothing to me, either," said Sara. "But I don't know what Julia sees in her. What do you bet by this time next year, Army Girl will have gotten herself pregnant by some soldier in her neighborhood?" She smirked.

"Fritz wouldn't do that. She only plays dumb." My voice was louder than I'd anticipated.

"True," said Rosamund. "She's such a fake happy-go-lucky."

"Did you see her and Julia at the clambake last night?" asked Sara.

"Yes," I answered. "I saw them. They stopped by before going to Cherry Grove to see *Jaws*." It had been nearly a year since I'd seen Fritz. I'd forgotten things about her, and last night had brought it all back into microscopic focus. Her catlike hazel eyes, her freckles, her shaggy, layered hair. Her raspy voice like she chewed gravel instead of gum. How overly, carelessly upbeat she was, and how easily people gathered around her for no other reason, it seemed, than to appreciate her backbends or cartwheels or whatever show-offy thing she was doing, usually in a pair of short-shorts. Fritz often had the effect of making me feel prudish, no matter how hard I worked not to seem so.

And it struck me as unfair that even during a summer where my sister wouldn't be around to take up all the attention, here was slinky, scrappy Fritz—who didn't even really belong at Sunken Haven—to remind me of my shortcomings in a whole different way.

"*I* didn't see her. I must be good at zoning Fritz out," said Rosamund.

"She always seems so trampy, without actually being trampy," said Sara.

"We've never really made a point to get to know her," I said.

I could feel the girls exchange a look, and I knew they were remembering about last year. How Fritz had beaten me so brutally at tennis.

But I wasn't in any mood to think about that. In fact, with Daphne so far away, I was glad not to be thrust into the heat of any competition, sports or otherwise. The sweaty, frustrated anticipation of a tennis rematch was not nearly as pleasant as imagining walking into Punch Night, my hand slipped through Gil's.

"Been thinking about you," he'd said. I could still hear his voice in my ear.

Tuesday couldn't get here quick enough.

FRITZ

SUNKEN HAVEN, FIRE ISLAND

It wasn't like I'd been trying for it . . .

"Incoming!" Julia's kid sister, Dot, was eleven years and eighty-two pounds of trouble lunging me from behind. Her arms wrapped around my neck.

"Quit it, you grape nut." I was sitting with Julia on the deck bench of the dock terminal, a saltbox with a dynamite lookout view. As in, we could see down, but nobody could see up.

"Whatcha doing?"

"Come on, Dot." I shook her off as best I could. Dot loved to follow me everywhere. "You almost choked my lights out."

"Why are you two up here?" Dot wedged herself between us on the bench.

"Go away!" Julia pushed Dot off so that she fell on her butt. I started to laugh.

"Hey!" Dot sprang right back up. "I was only seeing if you two were jumping."

"No, we're not. But look." Julia pointed. "Ferry's coming. Get down there or you'll miss it."

Dot bounced on the balls of her feet. "What are you two *doing?*"

"Something secret," I teased.

"Come jump, Fritzie! The water's perfect." Dot tugged my hand. "I know you want to."

"Thirteen years old is the last cool jump year," I said. "It's a kid thing."

"Liar! You love to jump. And I just guessed what you're both up to!" Dot whooped. "You're spying on that guy who Weeze Burke was telling Mom about. Her nephew from Alabama. Am I right or am I right?"

"For the last time! Get lost!" Julia reached out to smack her.

"Up your nose with a rubber hose!" Dot squeaked as she ducked Julia's hand, then pogo-hopped down the steps to the bay.

"Dot is a goon in a training bra this summer," muttered Julia. "Sorry."

"We were like that once." I slipped the binoculars from Julia's knapsack and focused in on the pier. A batch of kids was lined along the lip, flexed to plunge.

"Do you see him yet?"

"They haven't even thrown the line!"

"My eyes are sharper." Julia snatched the binoculars from me and stood.

"Sit! Or everyone'll know what creepers we're being." But then I started cracking up. Julia stuck out in any crowd, since she was so tall, almost six feet though she swore five ten, with hair pale as wheat and long enough that she could sit on it.

Now Julia was laughing, too. She shooed me off. "You're the worst spy ever! Go jump!" She ordered. "I can tell you want to! But be careful!"

I made a break for it. When I caught up with the dozen-plus kids at the dock, they all started up, whooping and cheering.

"Fritz!"

"I knew it!" Dot's eyes shone. "You can't resist!"

"Jump from the chair, Fritzie!" someone called, and then a booming cry of a "*Jump! Jump! Jump!*" was taken up.

Now I saw. Some joker had stuck a lifeguard chair at the end of the pier. It was stupid high, too high for almost anyone to risk it.

"Tiger Gibbons-Kent put it there," called one of the Shreve kids. "So far, he's the only one who's been mad dog enough to jump off."

"Come on, Fritz!" called Dot. "It's boys against girls! We're counting on you!"

I looked the chair over. Maybe it didn't scare me that much. I'd been raised on high dives at the YMCA, and I'd done an assisted parachute out of a C-130 when I was twelve years old.

"Arright, arright. This one's for you, Dot."

But it wasn't until I'd climbed all the way up, kids loudly cheering my every step, and my toes were curled tight around the edge of the chair, that I understood the stupid risk of it. I knew I'd have to push out—way out—to avoid hitting the bottom. Tiger must have done this at high tide. Now the watermark was low. I could see the boat crowd leaning over the rail on the fast-approaching Sunken Haven ferry.

Shoot. They were probably all watching me, too. The other jumpers were lined up at the edge of the dock. It was kind of a perfect moment, and too late to back down.

"Wooooooo!" I let my lungs carry my confidence as I leaped, leading the group, feeling the collective whoosh as all the kids below followed my cue and jumped off the dock. My splash was mammoth; I'd gone long and out, my feet brushing the soft mud bottom. I resurfaced to cheers and smacking applause from all around, as the ferry blasted its horn and propelled itself up alongside the dock.

The water felt good. I was in no big rush to leave it. I treaded and floated. It was fun to watch the families come in. First all those Hastys, bouncing down the boarding ramp, led by their brand-new setter puppy. Cute! The Hastys were followed by four generations of Knightleys, from ancient Mr. and Mrs. Knightley, to Chip's parents, to his married sister, who this summer was pushing a baby stroller, to Chip himself. I had to smile, watching him. Good to know Chip hadn't changed a bit. He was still a live wire, jumping around all over the deck, making air passes with his lacrosse stick, getting on everyone's nerves.

Next, arms linked and giggling, came Porter Todd and Mindy Tingley—best friends, Dot's age. Dot would be excited to see them.

Then I saw him. The new guy. Gil Burke. He was tall, in a straw hat, orange T-shirt, and funky gym-teacher shorts, ambling behind Carpie, who'd come strutting off the boat like he was leading the Easter Day Parade.

I sank lower, blowing bubbles through my nose, my eyes on Gil. I wondered what Julia could see. He cut a nice shape, long and lean. As soon as he was on the dock, he started taking some stuff off the baggage trolley. Item one, a beat-up nylon sports bag. Then a taped guitar case. Then a nice leather suitcase—luggage that had to be Carpie's.

Now he was holding too many things. He reminded me of a bellhop, the way he stood all straight and careful, and he didn't set down a thing until Carpie pointed him toward the hand-pulled wooden wagons used for carting luggage.

Gil might have had Carpie by a couple of inches, and he was at least thirty pounds lighter, but the way they stood, they could have been carbon copies of each other. What had Weeze Burke said—Carpie's sister's son. I'd never seen any of Carpie's relatives up here. Certainly no sister. Now suddenly here's the nephew, a dead ringer for his uncle. It seemed a little messed up that Carpie had never wanted to bring him out here, for the bragging rights alone.

I pulled out of the bay to sit on the edge of the dock, where I shook the water from my ears. Watching. "Gil Burke, you are hot stuff." I muttered it the same second that Gil dropped the bags in the wagon, and then turned to look down at me with a huge grin plastered on his face.

Yeesh, had he heard me? No way. He was only smiling at all the jumpers, all out of the water and shaking or toweling off on the dock.

I stayed put a little longer, breathing it out. The one-two punch of the jump plus Gil had succeeded in speeding my heart rate. I watched both Burkes as they moved along the walk, Carpie doing his usual strut and backslap as he introduced his nephew to everyone.

Once they got good and gone, I stood, wringing water from my T-shirt, and walked back to the lookout, where Julia was waiting.

"You get an eyeful?"

"Ohhh, yeah!" A grin split her face. This summer's Julia took some getting used to. Her braces were finally off, and her gorgeous, high-wattage smile now balanced her beaky nose. Julia had a new edge—I'd told her so. Ever since we were kids, we'd always privately, casually measured ourselves against each other. Like, I was the athlete, but she had the voice. She loved romance, and I was gung-ho adventure. She had the height, while I had some curves. She loved my hazel-green eyes, I'd have killed for her icy baby-blues. The only thing we'd ever jokingly decided that we tied for was boobs, although I had more perk and she had more heft.

We stretched out on the bench for a couple of minutes. "You're a real daredevil, Fritzie, jumping from the lifeguard chair," she said, with a light pinch to the top of my thigh. "You gave me a heart attack."

"Gil Burke's also about to have a heart attack, if he hasn't met Junior yet."

Julia snorted. "If I had to spend a whole summer under the same roof with Junior, I'd go bonkers."

Junior Burke was a jerk from way back. He was the kid who, a few summers ago, had fed refried beans to the nature center's aquarium fish, and then laughed while we all went ballistic, watching them die. To nobody's surprise, Junior had grown up to be the guy whose idea of a perfect day was getting wasted on the yacht club porch, playing quarters and rating girls' bods on a one-to-ten.

Nevermind that Junior himself was a four, maybe a six on his best day.

"I hope Gil is as fine on the inside as he is outside," said Julia, her hope echoing mine.

"Me, too." In some ways, this was already shaping up to be a decent summer for Julia and me. We'd only been here for four days, but we had started our jobs at the yacht club, and we had a whole new kind of privacy from living at the Morgue—the girls' dorm—instead of our old arrangement, sharing Julia's bedroom at Whisper, the Tulliver cottage. If we weren't waitressing or tanning ourselves to a crisp at the beach, we relaxed in our room, splitting cans of Duncan Hines chocolate frosting and watching soaps with the Bay Shore Community College girls, who sometimes handed down their older-girl wisdom, like how it felt to be on The Pill.

But we also missed Tracy. It was different here without her, and I wished she'd come back. I couldn't picture her spending the summer auditing classes at Smith. Trace had never struck me as the academic type. Privately, Julia and I had decided the story was bullshit, especially when we called to get her summer address and phone number, and Mrs. Gibbons-Kent told us in a tense voice that she was running out the door and we should ring back some other time.

All the other summers, Tracy Gibbons-Kent had been our third Musketeer. The Gibbons-Kents were one of those families who did things like fund Sunken Haven's rebuilding after Fire Island got knocked by a hurricane. Trace had been our girl in the know—she could tell us where the best parties were happening, or which families had easiest access to liquor cabinets, or whose parents were off-island that week, leaving only a babysitter in charge. Also, Trace never hoarded her information, like some of the other Sunkie kids, and without her lead, we'd lost some standing here. Just last night, the clambake had migrated from Barn Meadow to Little Beach to Great South Bay without anyone informing us. Julia and I got there so late that most of the chow was gone.

It wasn't like people were giving us a bum steer. It was more like they hadn't thought about us. Either way, the outcome was the same: We weren't in the loop.

Julia packed up the binoculars and together we took the stairs down. "Bet you've got a shot at Gil the Thrill at Punch Night."

"But you're the musical one," I reminded. "You guys could sing duets, fall in love, and become the next Captain and Tennille." I batted my eyelashes.

"So funny I forgot to laugh." Julia made a face. "Anyway, you know I'm into Oliver O. these days. If you and Gil connect, we're a perfect foursome. How fun would that be?"

"Maybe I've sworn off love forever."

"You can't escape it *forever,* Fritzie."

"Okay, but next time I fall for a guy, it won't be because people said we made a cute couple or because he's the quarterback. Next time, I want something real. Otherwise, I'm fine to be single all summer."

I'd been speaking to Julia's back as we trotted down the stairs. We rounded the bend to Bay Walk in time to see Dot cruising off on Julia's ten-speed.

Julia sighed. "Crud, all that brat does is kidnap my wheels. And it's not like I can use hers." We now considered Dot's bike, still in the rack, the nubby white tires and banana seat, the dinky pink-and-white daisy basket, the streamer handlebars. "Let me chase her down. Meetcha at the Morgue." She yanked Dot's bike out, straddled it, and pushed off into a daddy-longlegs pedal.

I unracked my own bike, also known as Mrs. Tulliver's rusty hand-me-down. Having a fine ride wasn't a status symbol here. In fact, you scored more points if you could freewheel a junker with some skill. I had to admit, I was proud to be in the second category. I could ride this rusty hunk with one hand tied behind my back better than Junior Burke could move his two-hundred-buck Raleigh.

About a quarter mile up, the path forked into three options; a right onto Ocean Walk, straight on the ridge, or a double-back to the bay.

It was on the ridge where I caught up with the Burkes.

Carpie and Gil had stopped right outside the post office. I reeled in, my right foot dragging, bumping to a brake just shy of where Gil was standing in the middle of Sunken Haven's tiny town center. To one side stood the business office, the grocery store, and the candy store. Across the paved bike path was the nature center. Dr. Gamba's office-home was around the corner, and the church was on the opposite side.

With a finger steady at the wagon handle, Gil waited for his uncle, who was walking into the post office. I watched Gil take it all in; the weathered gray-shingled houses, the light push of the wind through the long, wild grasses, the slivered breaks of white foam caps on the deep blue ocean horizon. The way Gil was staring was so sweetly bumpkinish, it kind of reminded me of my very first summer here. As in, was this perfect place for real?

I'd stopped closer to the grocery store, near some tennis-skirted moms sipping Frescas and smoking. I watched Gil drop the wagon handle and stroll over to inspect the fenced-in nature center, where kids kept their box turtles.

WE'VE GOT LIVE SCALLOPS! was chalked on their sandwich board.

I let my bike roll closer. Gil was thinner than Scott Houlihan. Taller, too.

Suddenly, his gaze focused me with an almost audible click. Like he'd known all along I was sneaking up on him. "Here she is. Queen of the jump."

"Yup." I laughed. "Guilty." My clothes had dried to the point where they weren't plastered to my body, but they still gave me away.

"That was amazing. You some kind of mermaid that only grows here?"

"Ha, I might be." The scrape in my voice that I'd hated as a kid, but had recently got me the school nickname "Stevie" after the cute singer in Fleetwood Mac, was working for me right now, I hoped.

"Naw. Not the way you talk." Gil reangled his funny straw hat to see me better. "You're nearer to where I'm from." His eyes were like dark honey in the afternoon light. "I'm Gil," he drawled.

"I'm Fritz. Florida born, Louisiana for now. My dad's in the army."

"I'm Alabama, born and raised. Glad to know it ain't just me filling the cracker quota." He was laying on his accent extra thick to make me smile.

"You're Carpie's family, right? You heading over to Snappy Boy?"

"Uh-huh." Gil glanced at the post office. "Say, which eleven-bedroom mansion are you camped out in? Bide-a-Way? Seaside?"

"Not me." I scoffed. "I'm barefoot and free, unless I'm doing a shift at the yacht club. And I sleep in the Morgue."

"Yeah? I'm working some club shifts, too. My start day is tomorrow."

"Cool. I'll be there, along with my best friend, Julia. We'll show you the ropes. Ninety percent of the orders are for Waldorf salad and a glass of white wine. And if you bring out the drinks quick and cold, along with extra buttermilk ranch dressing before they ask for it, you'll get a good tip."

"Cool. But you sleep in the *morgue*?"

I pointed to the candy store. "Just some bedrooms over the store. It's where they stored corpses during the winter in the olden days. Since the ferries didn't run off-season."

"In other words, it *was* a morgue?"

"Yes, but now it smells nice. Like girls." Was that flirty? Maybe. Gil's smile made me feel flirty. It sure made me feel chatty.

"Remind me what girls smell like?" Okay, if I was being flirty, he was being super-flirty.

"Sugar and spice? Wella Balsam and Lip Smackers?"

Gil's laugh was a treat. His eyes were drinking me up. Had I really just told Julia I was fine to be single all summer? I could feel some major butterflies. "So lemme ask you something, Fritz.

What's the straight up with these . . . Sunkies?" In his charming, wide-smiling face, his eyes were alert for my answer.

"What do you mean?"

"I mean, how do you get on with all these Yankee Doodle families that's been coming out here for thirteen generations of lobster rolls?"

"This place is a cinch." I flicked a hand. "You gotta be yourself. Like, just be happy being you. The rest will follow."

"Got it." But I could tell my answer—true as it was—had fallen flat.

"Also, over the years, I might have learned a trick or two." I dropped my voice and waggled my eyebrows. "If you want the scoop."

"Arright, *now* we're cookin' with gas." Gil's nod was a movement through his whole body as he listened. "Tell me."

"First thing is, I've got a skeleton key opens everything here. Second, I know how to get rid of Sunken Haven bed fleas. Third, I can tell you where's the best cup of chowder from Ocean Bay to Lonelyville. You need me to keep on?"

"Fleas? That a joke?"

"Nope. Standard sand fleas, and all it takes is a strong vacuum cleaner. And *my* bed's never had 'em. If that's a consolation." Two more flirty points for me. We were grinning at each other like simpletons. I eased my rear end higher up on the bike seat and rolled my wheels back. My eyes couldn't let him go. "But regular kids and Sunkie families get along fine. You'll do great. Even in those gym shorts." I couldn't resist a tease. They weren't exactly Sunkie style.

"But I *am* Sunkie family," Gil answered sharply, for the first time seeming a bit unsure of himself. "I'm a nephew."

"Gil!" Carpie's voice boomed from across the path. He was squinting at me, recognizing me by face if not by name—though of course I'd met him dozens of times over the years. "Let's move along. Cocktails at six."

"Yessir," Gil called. But then he lingered, his gaze spreading over me like melting butter.

"Gilroy!" Carpie's voice cracked the whip. Typical. Carpie liked to play the family man, but the minute anything didn't go his way, he threw worse temper tantrums than a six-year-old. I'd seen Carpie blow his stack regularly at Junior's regattas. And once, at the yacht club, he'd doused his dinner plate with a glass of water when his steak arrived overdone.

Sandwiched between Junior and Carp, it might be a tough summer for Gil. I hoped underneath all his Southern charm, he had what it took to deal with it.

"Catch ya on the flip, Fritz," he said now, with a quick salute and another heart-melting grin. "You gotta teach me that jump."

"Easy breezy." I'd never been so conscious as today of my accent sounding out of place on Sunken Haven. Army kids moved on base bringing local accents from all over the States. I hardly noticed. But Gil sure had heard mine.

"All right, then." That smile. Those shoulders. That slow

Southern stroll. Ha—not even Carpie's purple-faced impatience could make Gil pick up his feet. That boy didn't need any advice on how to be exactly himself.

Maybe Gil knew exactly how to stand up to those spoiled Burkes, after all.

JEAN

And in that shift, the universe.

Gil didn't call me Tuesday, the afternoon he was supposed to have docked. He didn't call me Tuesday night. But perhaps Tuesday was too soon? He might have needed to get his bearings, unpack, spend some time with Junior, all that. Or possibly he'd ended up having to stay in the city another night?

At dusk on Tuesday, I strolled the bay and the beach, hoping I'd "accidentally" run into him. My parents had gone off Sunken Haven for an overnight stay, visiting friends on Shelter Island, so I didn't have any inside lead on the Burkes' activities from them. It was so frustrating. I tried—and failed—not to think about it.

Wednesday, I stayed out all day, biking straight from tennis clinic to Sara's. The Trains were one of the only families at

Sunken Haven who had a swimming pool, and the plunge felt perfect on my burnt skin. Afterward, Sara's mother served lunch on the patio: cold chicken and fruit salad.

"Jean, did you know about Carpie Burke's nephew?" Sara asked, startling me as we resettled in lounge chairs with our bowls of mixed berries. "He came in yesterday, and he's here all summer."

So he *was* here. My breath immediately compressed in my chest. "Gil Burke, you mean? I met him in New York. I heard he'd be out here."

"But you never mentioned him once! And he's so hot! I ran into him this morning, down on the Bay. He was walking with Tiger to teach a Minnows class."

"He's cute, I guess." My spoon intently chased loose blueberries around the bottom of my glass bowl.

"More like gorgeous."

"If you say so." I didn't want to talk about Gil, and certainly not with Sara. It would happen today, I decided. Today, I'd go back home, and he'd have left me a message.

I returned to Lazy Days late that afternoon, giving Gil all the time he needed to call me. I stared for a long time at the black telephone, that blank telephone pad. Mrs. Otis might not like the phone, but she was scrupulous about leaving messages.

I could try to justify it, to believe what I wanted, but I knew better.

Thursday night, there was a Regatta Relays party on the North Bay lawn. It was casual, early enough that there were still lots of younger kids flying around, playing tag and slurping Popsicles by the time I showed up to meet Sara and Rosamund. I wore a pair of white flares and a ruby-red top. If by any chance Gil wanted to find me, he'd be able to spot me from a mile away.

It was the usual regatta party, a cookout buffet and buckets of beer. Frisbee games on the lawn as the sun went down.

My neck strained, my eyes seeking him everywhere.

"You're here early, Jean. Who're you hunting down?" Suddenly Junior Burke was at my elbow.

"Just Sara and Rosamund." I made myself focus on Junior's thin, ferret face. "I hear your cousin's in town.

"Yeah, yeah. Seems like all the girls have smelled him out. Gil is Dad's latest renovation project." There was a whiff of bitterness in Junior's voice. "And you missed him by five minutes. He and Oliver stopped for burgers, then they took off to pick up their chicks."

"Chicks?" The word kicked me in the stomach. "What chicks?"

Nothing got past Junior. He sensed the press in my question and he let me dangle. Slowly, he drained his bottle of beer.

"Oliver and Julia are pretty serious," he said, wiping his lips with the back of his hand. But I already knew about Oliver and Julia.

"And Gil?" I asked, when it was obvious that Junior was saying nothing more.

"Got it bad for Fritz O'Neill."

I made an effort to appear casual. "Oh, really? Since when?"

Junior made a mock expression of skepticism. "Let me think. Wait, I know! Since the second he looked at her and realized she was the smoking hottest girl here! No offense." He grinned. "You don't look happy. Did I put you in a bad spot? What kind of answer did you want from me, Jean?"

Junior wasn't too happy, either. He'd had a thing for Fritz since Minnows years. Everyone knew that. Still, there was nothing to say, and so I left him, eventually meeting up with the girls. I drifted through the evening in a lurch of vertigo. The hopeful platform of all my summer hopes had collapsed around me. I inhaled its dust. I endured the party for as long as I could, and then, saying good-bye to nobody—not even Bertie, which wasn't very nice, but I couldn't begin to handle Bertie on a night like this—I walked home alone, ate two packages of Pop-Tarts, and slept so late into the next morning that I almost missed my Friday tennis lesson.

"Take it easy on your return, Jean. I don't know who you've got it in for, but it's giving you the yips." Coach Hutch's face was more sun lined than you'd expect from someone under thirty. He was Australian, and I imagined him there on the off-season, roaming the outback under the baking sun.

"What's the yips?"

Coach jogged up to the net, signaling for me to meet him at

the midline. My body was slick with sweat from charging around the outdoor court. "The yips are when doubt starts to guide your game."

"Sorry, Coach." I flushed because I knew he was right. "Tomorrow, I'll leave my yips on my porch."

"Custis, I don't want to ride you too hard. But 'better tomorrow' is what you've said every day all week. What's breaking your concentration, Missy?"

"I don't know. I'm sorry." I wiped my sweating face with the shoulder of my shirt.

Coach had been training me at tennis since I was old enough to call a serve. I braced for his usual ribbing about lady problems or boyfriend problems. Instead he let me go with a tap of his racquet to my visor. "Will I see you tonight?"

"Yes." And then I ducked off before my face could betray me any more.

Tonight was Punch Night. My parents would never let me get out of it.

I hated even to think about it.

There were no showers or locker rooms at the Tennis Casino. Just an outside water fountain. I gulped until it made me nauseous, and I biked home with my racquet jammed under my wet armpit and my stomach in a slosh. Would I ever get my game back? Or would my yips overpower me—one morning I'd wake up too depressed to go to practice?

And was I being a silly, stubborn mule with all this practicing? If Fritz O' Neill entered the Junior Cup this year, she'd take it from me like it was nothing.

The same way she'd taken Gil.

Upstairs in my bathroom, I stood under the water until my toes and fingertips turned hard as raisins. Out of the shower, I dried, changed, and spritzed myself with some Charlie from a bottle I'd found on Daphne's dresser in her bedroom and joined my parents in the dining room for a late lunch.

That afternoon, Mrs. Otis had dragged out a pitcher of her unsweetened spearmint iced tea, along with a platter of crab salad, fruit salad, and tomato sandwiches on thin buttered bread.

On cue, Mom and Dad picked up forks right at the moment I sat down.

"Sorry." I picked up my own fork. "Also, I might be quitting tennis."

"What a thing to say," said Dad cheerfully. "How will you win your rematch if you've quit?"

"Exactly. And your dress arrived," said Mom. "If the alterations are right, you can wear it tonight. Hip-hip-hooray." She smiled at me.

I took a breath. "I might have a headache. I might not go to Punch Night."

"Now, that's simply bad form, Punkin," said Dad. "What will Bertie do? He's expecting to dance the night away with you."

"Daddy's right. And even if you don't go," said Mom, "we still need to know whether the dress fits. If not, I'll have to send it back to Miss Delaney."

I gathered a bite. The mayonnaise-slathered crab looked like a forkful of sneeze. "I'm not very hungry, I don't think."

Dad sighed. "You're not being very fun, Jeanie." He looked to my mother for affirmation.

"I agree. You're excused for a nap," said Mom. "But you can't be surly for tonight. It's not fair for those of us who want to have a good time."

My parents were both committed to fun in all its forms—parties, tea, cocktails, dancing. My gloomy preparty mood broke a big rule for them. I couldn't help it. I slid off my chair, dismissed. At the foot of the stairs, I swiped the long dress box with its corner-tucked peach business card of Miss Delaney's Fine Alterations.

Mom and Dad's predictable insistence on Punch Night also annoyed me. Why couldn't they let me stay behind? And why did they think meals and naps solved everything? No amount of sleep or food would make me stop fixating on Gil Burke, how he'd slipped away before I'd learned how to hold on to him.

I stomped up the stairs and slammed my door. In my room, I dropped onto my bed and stretched out like a starfish. Tucked in on my bookshelf across the room, my Mrs. Beasley doll stared at me with her demonic, bespectacled eyes.

I reached for my copy of *Goodbar* and read for a while, then tossed it to the edge of the bed. I couldn't concentrate. Maybe, for once, my parents were right. A nap might help; my eyes felt so heavy.

When I woke up in the same position I'd flung myself into, it was a beautiful purpling dusk, and the breeze through my window was silk on my skin. Punch Night. How I'd fantasized about going as Gil's date. That bubble had been popped, but I couldn't wriggle out of it—not without a fuss. Last night, Bertie had very deliberately firmed up our plans.

Besides, my parents didn't believe in too sick, too tired, or simply not up to it.

I could already hear them downstairs, clinking through a first round of cocktails.

Punch Night was an annual occasion. Everyone came, everyone ate, and everyone got silly on the club's signature spiced rum punch. Mr. Forsythe, Bertie's dad and the head of the Association, always stood and gave a speech about how well the staff and volunteers had looked after Sunken Haven during the quiet months of winter and spring. Then he reminded people (delicately) to remember to write big checks. Finally, everyone raised glasses to Sunken Haven, the happiest place in the world. Kids danced while the older people smoked and drank and watched contentedly. It was a friendly, easy night—in fact, Daphne was conceived after a Punch Night, my father once exuberantly blurted out at a dinner party, to Mom's horror.

But tonight, I wouldn't be able to hide. Tonight, Gil would be there for sure. With Fritz. Gil and Fritz. Fritz and Gil.

I took care with myself, first removing the dress from its box and slipping it on. I hadn't liked it in Bergdorf's, but Mom had bought it, anyway—and it wasn't nearly as plain as I'd thought. The sash pinched me a waist where nature hadn't. The peach softened the violence of my sunburned nose.

Maybe Gil just needed to be reminded of me?

Maybe when he saw me he'd want me back?

I brushed my cowlicky curls as best I could and barretted them down. Blotted my favorite Estee Lauder matte, "Pink Kiss."

Then I took my jade-and-jet earrings from my travel bag.

I'd reclaimed them out of Daphne's suitcase, tiptoeing into her room while she slept, exactly as I'd warned her I would. That next morning, she hadn't said a word. I'd waited for the fireworks. None came, though I assumed she'd checked. But as she hugged me good-bye, she had pressed her mouth hot against my ear and whispered, "They're not yours, Jean. However badly you want them. What you did was wrong."

When Daphne had worn my Christmas earrings, they'd seemed perfect. But now, when I dangled one against my jawline, testing it, I was struck by how small and skinny it looked, not right for me at all.

Guiltily, I dropped them into a dish on my bureau. There was too much else to think about. I slipped on my flats and popped my lipstick into my monogrammed Bermuda bag, then clapped its wooden handles closed. Last year, Tracy Gibbons-Kent had poked fun of how many of my items—shirts, sweaters, bags, belts—were monogrammed, and she'd jokingly asked if it was my way of safeguarding my things against borrowers. Her tease had privately annoyed me. A monogram gave me a sense of precision, was all.

I looked long and hard at my face in the mirror.

"You look pretty, Jean," I spoke softly to my reflection. It sounded like a lie. "Promise," I whispered. "You'll be okay, whatever happens tonight."

When I met her at the foot of the stairs, Mom's face brightened. "You seem rested. Quitting tennis! Of all the featherbrained things to say in front of Dad! He's waiting for us on the porch. Now let's go enjoy ourselves."

I nodded. I knew not to argue with the fun imperative.

Outside, my parents strolled comfortably in step, carrying gin and tonics in paper cups. I stayed to the side, walking my bike. I needed it to get to Rosamund's after party. Stray children yelped like wild dogs in the beachfront playground across from the church. Sundown was a rainbow sherbet across the sea.

"Truly, we are blessed." Dad always addressed sunsets as if he thought it was his duty to compliment the artwork God had created exclusively for Sunken Haven.

As we approached the clubhouse, I could hear "High Hopes" from Billy Boyle and the Lamplighters, who'd set up as usual on the far side of the wraparound deck. Uniformed caterers—a combination of Sunken Haven kids, who often worked the parties, along with Bay Shore kids—slipped among the guests, serving from trays of crudités or mushroom caps.

Sara and Rosamund had claimed the deck corner with the wicker chairs. As I broke from my parents, skimming ahead and up the steps to join the girls, I saw that Fred Hasty was with them, wearing the club's catering uniform.

Rosamund pouted. "Fred promised he'd be my date, but then he took a shift instead. Now I'm single tonight!" Rosamund looked sweet in a checked sundress, with her pageboy neatly winged on either side from its center part. Poor Sara had tried to dress up, too, but her boxy skirt, golf shirt, and rope necklace made her look like a gym teacher. The necklace might as well have been a whistle or a stopwatch.

Fred shrugged. "I'm saving for a car."

"Then go get me a drink," said Rosamund. "It's the least you can do." But Fred sat and tapped out his cigarettes instead.

"Marcy Pency's going to fire you, Fred," I said.

"Marcy Pency knows she can't rely on Sunkie kids," said Fred. "That why she hires all the Bay Shore kids. We Sunkies just don't have that snap-to-it."

I tried to smile, to keep the banter going, to steady my focus on my friends and not look around for Gil and Fritz. My heart was hammering. I didn't see them.

Maybe Junior had overplayed the Fritz and Gil romance? Maybe it was nonsense. And maybe, maybe Gil was secretly hoping to see me as much as I was wild to see him.

"Jean!" Bertie, snazzy in his club blazer, cut through the

crowd to drop a kiss on my cheek. "You cut out so early last night. You'll have to make up for it tonight." He stepped back and gave a low whistle. "That dress is perfect on you."

"Thanks." Bertie always noticed when I wore something new. I imagined his brain with a labeled accordion file on me, and he never forgot a thing in it. But I was grateful for his compliment tonight, even if it was only because it would boost my confidence when I saw Gil.

And at least Bertie had never tried to make me feel guilty about not being in love with him. Bertie's best quality was that he was tactful. If I saw Gil tonight and we recharged our spark—please, please, please!—then Bertie would know to discretely fade off.

"I checked name cards—we're table seven," said Bertie. "I can put your wrap there now, if you like."

"Thanks." As I handed it over, Bertie strode off with the air of someone on a diplomatic mission.

Was Gil here already? My underarms were hot, and I didn't want to start sweating through my dress. What if, when Gil saw me, he remembered everything about our night in New York and realized what a fool he'd been? Or what if Gil wanted to spend time with Fritz *and* me—and other girls, too? What if he didn't want to be seriously attached to any one of us?

Or what if all he wanted was Fritz?

Every door of the club was thrown open so that guests could slip back and forth from the clubroom to the deck. From inside,

I caught that dry, distinct harrumph of Carpie's laugh. My nerves spiked. Did Carpie's presence mean Gil was here, too? Wouldn't Gil have arrived with his aunt and uncle?

"Jeanie?" Bertie was flapping his hand in front of my face. "Come in with me? I thought we could wait for drinks together."

"All right."

Scooting behind Bertie, I felt the weight of satisfied parental gazes on us. Jeanie and Bertie! The older generation always admired a likely romance. A way to keep Sunkies with Sunkies. We sidled into the crowded clubroom, the smaller of the two large rooms that made up the main floor.

How many times last week had I imagined arriving with Gil for Punch Night? Necks craning, all the girls green with jealousy but Rosamund and Sara both officially admiring.

"Sit here?" Bertie huffed at my side. "I'll shoot to the kitchen's service bar. Maybe somebody there can fix us up drinks quicker."

"Okay." I slid onto a barstool. Alone, I clicked the handles of my bag in time with the Lamplighters, who had launched into "Somewhere Beyond the Sea."

Aside from my tube of lipstick and my Binaca breath spray, my bag was empty. You never needed anything at Sunken Haven. No I.D. because everyone knew who you were. No money because we all signed our account numbers for our bills. No house keys because we never locked up our homes.

"Jeanie!"

My head jerked like a kite in the breeze to see Junior Burke, standing a foot away, with his hands coned as if he'd been shouting at me from a great distance. And there, standing next to him, was Gil.

The week since I'd seen him felt like both a minute and forever. He looked absolutely perfect, in a tailored pale-blue shirt that emphasized his butter-toffee tan. But his smile on me was hesitant.

"Hey, Junior. Hi, there, Gil."

"Why, Jean Custis," said Gil. "I guess I've been looking for you. It's nice to see you again."

Heat flooded the surface of my skin.

"She was hoping to see you, too!" Junior rewarded Gil's back with a too hard thump. "You should have seen the hangdog look on Jean's face last night, when I told her you'd already split."

As awful as Junior's words were, they seemed to ease Gil's mind, as he stepped into the tight space next to me. "Sounds like we've been ships in the night, then," he said. We were close enough that I could sense the lightest warmth of his body.

"I guess so. How's your first week at Sunken Haven?" My heart pounding, pounding.

"It's been fine and dandy. But ever since I got here, I kept thinking, I dunno. That I'd run into you."

I cleared my throat. "I've been around."

He nodded. "But I bet you didn't know that yesterday afternoon, when I was leaving the bay, I did see you? Out on the courts, playing tennis?"

"My game was so off yesterday." I could have melted from

shame, thinking of Gil watching me klutzing around on the court.

"I waved from my bike."

"But I didn't . . . you ought to have come over."

"You looked mighty intent on your game. Aw, I *knew* I shoulda stopped."

"I'm getting a longneck," Junior broke in. He strolled away.

"Don't rush back," Gil murmured, short of Junior's earshot.

I had to laugh. "The noncharms of Junior Burke haven't worked on you, either?"

Gil shrugged. "He's better when he's not showing off," he said, easily. "This party's pretty high class. 'Punch Night' means something else where I'm from."

"I've missed you," I blurted. Then I laughed lightly, as if I might not mean it.

"Me, too." Gil seemed to know that I didn't want to chitchat. "My uncle sure has been talking you up since that night in the city."

"Oh, gosh. What pressure. I hope he hasn't been trying to push me at you." I said it jokingly, but was it true?

Gil's smile was tight-lipped. "Well, I kept thinking, I don't know . . . that we'd run into each other naturally, and then we'd catch up."

He hadn't called, and he wanted to be sure I wasn't hurt that he hadn't called? The knot of my anticipation and last-ditch hope for this night was coming undone, a slipping, slippery sense of loss. My eyes prinked. "I suppose I should be happy for you, that you didn't need to rely only on me to enjoy your—"

I stopped. There she was. Fritz O'Neill. She'd crept up slyly, in a faded red-cotton sundress that was too casual for Punch Night. But Fritz had a style all her own. Her effortless wash-and-go looks made me want to trade my Capezio sandals for her Cherokee wedges, my Piguet watch for her copper bangles and elephant-hair bracelet. Fritz was six months younger than I was, but she'd always made me feel as if she were older. Ever since I'd known her, she'd had that same high-wire sense of fun. Kids believed what she said and followed where she led.

As she moved in on us, I rippled a fingertip hello. I'd never disliked her so violently as in this moment. My Junior Cup defeat was nothing compared to my sinking despair as Gil shifted position, a casual pivot away from me so that he faced Fritz directly.

And in that shift, the universe.

"What's up, Green Bean Jean?" Fritz asked in her raspy voice that made everything sound dirty.

My baby name, a leftover from a few summers ago, when I'd had that green Speedo. Fritz had a teasing streak in her. It wasn't exactly mean, but in the moment I felt childish and silly. Worse than that, I could sense it, a connection between Fritz and Gil, a current between them. It made me feel light-headed, almost physically ill.

"Oh, nothing much." What to say, what else to say . . . tongue-tied, I was relieved to see Junior returning, beer in hand.

Bertie trailed behind with our cocktails.

"Hey-ho, what's this? The Junior Cup rivals, together again?" Junior brightened at the possibility of a conflict. His eyes lingered on Fritz. When we were younger, he'd been relentless, snapping Fritz's swimming goggles or stealing her sand pail, always trying and failing to get a rise out of her. Fritz had a breezy, laid-back personality that put up with a lot—even when another girl might have been outraged. It wasn't her strength, though she played it as one. It was more like Fritz didn't know how to get mad, especially about someone like Junior, with all his spoiled-brat Burke power.

"I saw Jean on the court yesterday," said Bertie. "She's in top form."

"Yeah, I was just saying," added Gil.

"You're competing again this year, right, Fritz?" asked Junior.

"I guess. I haven't practiced much." Fritz stretched her arms to gather her slippery-fine, sun-streaked layers off her neck and into a twist that she jammed in place with a chewed swizzle stick she'd picked up on the bar.

"Give the other girls a chance, right?" Junior raised his beer. "We should hit a few around sometime, Fritzie. Like clinic days. You always used to wallop me. I bet this year you'd eat my dust."

"Dream on, Junior. You'll never catch me eating anything of yours," Fritz drawled, as the guys all laughed, Junior loudest of all.

"You're a natural athlete, Fritz," admitted Bertie, "so it's too bad you're not committed to the discipline of the sport. That's what becomes crucial about tennis. Discipline. It's where Jean will end up roasting you." He was defending me, and I was comforted by his chivalry—yet at the same time, I hated that Bertie thought I needed defending at all.

"Oh, man, you're probably right, Bertie." But when Fritz leveled me with her wickedly beautiful cat's eyes, I felt as if she were mocking Bertie and me both. That she found us clownish and dull, and would be laughing about us with Julia later. The whole night was turning sour, and I wished a trapdoor would open under my feet. I took a sip of punch. I willed the alcohol to fuzz out the intensity of this moment.

I knew what a guy might see in Fritz. More than prettiness or sexiness, she had a flair for the unexpected—from how she moved, to what she said, to how she said it. She couldn't be predicted, and apparently this made her fascinating.

What I couldn't bear was that Gil—*my Gil*—had fallen for it.

Except he'd never been my Gil. And I'd been an idiot to imagine otherwise. I didn't know where to look or who to turn to, but I needed space to breathe.

From the open arch of the ballroom, which had been fashioned into a dining room for tonight, Rosamund and Sara were signaling me. I nodded.

"Yes, let's go," said Bertie, as if we'd made a decision together. "The quicker dinner is over, the quicker we get to the other thing."

The other thing was Rosamund Wembly's party. I knew that Gil and Fritz had heard Bertie. Why not invite them along? Nobody should be excluded from a house party. Then again, why did *I* need to be the one to make Gil's evening perfect, if he was interested in Fritz instead of me?

Gil and Fritz. Swallowing their names together was like taking a teaspoonful of poison.

"What other thing?" Gil asked. "Is there a party after this?" Something in his eyes reminded me of that night, the way he'd been so worried about being denied entry to Hollander's.

"If there's a party, you can count on me to know about it," I said lightly. It wasn't a brag. It was true. But I knew that Gil had heard what I meant.

"It's over at the von Cott place," added Bertie.

"Ah, okay." Gil nodded, pleased.

"Fun," said Fritz. "I'm game."

"Cool." Gil flicked Fritz's upper arm. Just as he'd done with me that night, in the cab. In a conversation full of awful moments, the flick was the worst. It reminded me of something so good, so private, all gone.

"I'll go tell Julia," said Fritz. "She's with Oliver, out on the deck."

"Spectacular!" Bertie winked. "See you in there."

"Good grief, Bertie, why did you lie?" I murmured, as we separated and moved off into the dining room. "There's no party at the von Cotts tonight." Or any night. The von Cotts were away. Nobody was even renting their house this summer.

Bertie pulled out my chair. "It was a joke. Junior says that

Southern-fry cousin of his is a kiss-up who's got his uncle totally fooled."

"Well, who can blame Junior for getting bent out of shape? Gil Burke is soooo much better than Junior Burke," said Sara, plopping onto the seat next to mine. "Oh, crab salad. Yummy."

More crab salad. I pushed my plate away and drained my punch as Sara dug in. The room was a sea of white: white linen-covered tables; thick, white, centerpiece lilies ringed in white plates of gelatinous crab. Across the room, I saw Fritz and Julia sitting with the Tullivers, and I watched Gil settle in at the Burke table at the far end.

Everyone was getting comfy, sipping ice water and buttering rolls. Soon the Burke table disappeared from view behind the seated crowd, until all I could see was the top of Weeze Burke's marigold-blond bouffant.

Had I done my best with Gil? Maybe if I went over and explained that Bertie had been kidding? I could hear my own voice, soft in his ear. "Gil, that was only Bertie's joke! The real party's at Rosamund's house, on the bay. Right after Punch Night. Come by!"

The pain of my disappointment was working through me like venom. Punch Night was as agonizing as I'd predicted, but in miserably different ways than I'd envisioned.

Gil hadn't been standoffish. He'd been friendly and sweet.

But the unspoken pull that Gil and Fritz had on each other had shut me out.

And now I was standing alone, trapped inside the burning-down walls of my hopes.

"Penny for your thoughts." Bertie handed me a freshened drink before he reseated himself at my side. When had he left? How quickly had I finished my last punch? I took the cup. Tried to click in, though I felt partly anesthetized. Gossiped with Sara. Chatted with Bertie, who always glowed under extra interest from me. Finished half my plate of roast beef and baked potato. Clapped along with everyone else when the waiters blowtorched the baked Alaska. Allowed Bertie to trot me over a third drink.

Then I stood, a bit unsteady. It was now or never. I'd invite Gil to the party, and then maybe he'd ask me to dance? Yes! It would be the most natural thing!

And perhaps in that easy moment of reclaimed closeness, Gil would finally realize how much he'd missed me.

There were only coffee servers breezing around the room, delivering teas and Nescafé. I had an easy path, but I moved with care. Gil was still seated, his head bent, listening respectfully to his Aunt Weeze.

Slowly, I wound around the tables, pausing to say hellos.

And then—Fritz. She swooped across the room, light as a toy glider, beating me to Gil in the last moment.

It was deliberate. She'd seen me. She was cut-and-plunge intercepting.

No, no, no!

I had to stop. I watched, sick to my stomach, helpless to do anything. Now Fritz was leaning into Gil's ear. And now he was standing.

And now they'd slipped out the side door to dance on the deck.

I could feel the silly, confused half-smile on my face as I turned around and stumbled back to our table. There was nowhere else to go.

"Here you are, Beautiful." Bertie's body was in a full sail of attention. "Care to dance?"

"I'd love to."

I allowed Bertie to take my hand and lead me outside. I made myself not look over my shoulder, not once, to where I knew Gil and Fritz were taking up space in a far, dark corner. I felt as if I'd been riding too long on a roller coaster. I bumped and twirled with Bertie, and then with my father and then Coach Hutch and then Bertie again.

"Do you have a headache, Jean?" he asked, peering at me. "I can take you home, if you like."

"Not at all." I smiled at him, then said in his ear, "but let's leave for Rosamund's now."

He nodded, ever ready to be my coconspirator. A few minutes later, we'd pushed off, our flashlights rolling in our bike baskets. Our lights beamed and swerved as we pedaled along the walk.

Memories were sticking at me like needles. The hot press of Gil's lips against mine. He'd kissed me with such purpose that night. As if choosing me. As if claiming me for more important activities. Things that, so far, I'd only done with Bertie.

Sweet old Bertie. Even now, he was being so chivalrous, biking ahead to give me more light, guiding my path through the breeze-dampened darkness. By tenth grade, Bertie and I had gotten pretty close to having sex, but we'd never tried it. Bertie always acted as if he didn't mind. He talked as if we'd made a mutual decision to wait. I knew Bertie would do it in a heartbeat if I wanted. But now, when I thought about my hookups with Bertie compared with that one kiss from Gil, I knew sex could be two entirely different acts.

Even if Gil never kissed me again, he'd ruined Bertie for me.

Would Gil ever kiss me again? At the club, when I'd mentioned that I was always first to know the parties, I could sense his attention. He wasn't all laid-back Southern charm. Gil liked to be in the right clothes, the right places. There were specific things about me—Sunkie things—he wanted to understand. Fritz was so aggressive and unladylike. Well, she might appeal to some animal nature in him, but she'd never satisfy all his cravings about his uncle's world.

My fingers gripped the handlebars. I could almost hear my heart pounding with the outrage of it all. Tonight, my good manners had landed me in second place.

And that was so unfair. So wrong.

My head swam with unhappiness, too many cocktails, all the things I wanted to scream.

Bayview was one of the smaller homes, a knotty-pine fisherman cottage, built in the earliest years of Sunken Haven. Inside, kids already had the drinking games going, but Rosamund and some of our set stayed outside on the porch.

We settled in. Glancing around at everyone, I felt restless and at odds. The flickering citronella candles made Sara look strange, and I started laughing, and then I couldn't stop.

"What? What's got into you?" Sara asked.

"It's just, you . . . you look like a little sailor pumpkin," I told her. "Like, your collar, and then your face is round, like—"

"Okay, I get it, Jean. I'm hilarious."

Now Sara looked like a grumpy pumpkin. "Grumpy pumpkin," I said, to hear the two words together. Knowing that I was annoying her seemed to make it funnier. "Pumpkin head."

"You know what? I don't need this." Sara stood up and slipped inside. After a moment, Rosamund followed.

"For God's sake, pull yourself together, Jean," said Bertie quietly. "People might think you've been smoking grass."

"Smoking grass? Bertie, are you trying to sound *cool*? Because I don't think you have a permit for that." I dissolved into giggles again, but it wasn't funny—and I knew it wasn't. I couldn't seem to break myself out of it.

"Jean, it takes us all by surprise when you get silly," said Bertie. "It's not like you—usually—to show such bad form."

"You're a fine one to talk about bad form, when you told Gil Burke that the party was at the von Cott house!"

"Please. He's the newbie. That's called tradition, to rib the new guy."

"He's not the usual kind of new guy. He's new to the Burkes, he's new to our whole crowd. You can joke a bit, but you don't want him to feel unwelcome."

"The way you were looking at him tonight, I'm sure he felt plenty welcome." Bertie stood. "I'll go get drinks."

Bertie rarely jabbed. I went quiet. Bertie and I had known each other so long, we even sounded like an old married couple. I didn't want to continue the argument.

Now I was alone on the porch. I leaned back against the railing and closed my eyes. My head hurt, my thoughts felt soupy and confused. I wished I'd invited Gil to this party when I had the chance. Even if he'd brought Fritz, at least they'd be here, instead of thrown on each other in an empty house, doing God knows what. Meantime, I was stuck in this night, hurt and wounding everyone in my orbit.

Bike bells jingled. I peered through the shadows to see Oliver Olmstead and Julia Tulliver brake out front. There was no sign of Gil and Fritz behind them.

"Jean, nice to see you here." Julia held my gaze as she climbed the steps.

"Where's Fritz?" I asked, as Bertie, returning with our drinks, resettled himself more closely next to me, then made a late-night decision to yoke his arm around my shoulders.

"Bertie banished her and Gil to the von Cott house. Remember? So they went off and did something else." Julia dropped into a chair. She popped the can of root beer that she'd brought along.

"Bertie and I were just talking about his bad joke."

"Hey, I was only playing," said Bertie. "Sunken Haven isn't some vast metropolis. It's not hard to find out where the real parties are."

"You look upset, Jean. Do you have something against Gil and Fritz?" Julia dealt me a smug look. "As a couple, I mean?"

"Me?" I psshed. "I don't even know Gil Burke."

"He told us that he went out with you once, in New York."

At my side, I felt Bertie go tense.

"Carp *asked* me to show him around—goodness, it was nothing!" There was a squeak in my voice that mortified me. But it felt like they were shining a watchman's flashlight right into my hidden secret.

"Didn't mean to activate the volcano." Julia smirked.

"It was nothing," I repeated softly.

My head was really pounding now. Too much punch, too much disappointment. I took a sip of my drink and craned my neck, peering into the cottage kitchen, scouting for a place to relocate, away from Julia.

When Rosamund saw me staring through the window, she rolled her eyes and said something to Sara, who nodded.

"That date was nothing," I said again, even though nobody

was talking about it anymore. "Gil liked that I got him into Hollander's. I mean, it's a bore to me. I get in there all the time. Maybe it was cool for Gil. But it meant nothing to me."

"Oookay," said Julia. "It was nothing. Got it."

"Jean, I think we ought to push off," said Bertie, standing and pulling me up with him.

Later, as I was delivered to my door, I let Bertie kiss me on the mouth. Then I got a bit more into it, though it seemed wrong. I was kissing Bertie and thinking of Gil. "Tomorrow, I think you need to apologize to Sara," Bertie said when we'd paused. "She looked hurt."

"She'll be fine."

"You might not think the same way once you've slept it off."

After he left me, I ran up to my room. As bad as my headache was thumping, I knew it would hurt even worse in the morning. I used my top quilt to wrap myself up like a cocoon, willing sleep, and the end of this awful night.

Tomorrow, I'd make it up to everyone. Tomorrow, I'd force myself to stop mooning over Gil Burke. But tonight I'd let myself drown in it. Tonight I was overloaded, bleary, drunk—and a bit astonished, as I sank into murky sleep—by my capacity to feel so much pain.

FRITZ

"Got your eye on anyone here?"

We'd hit it off like *bang*—firecrackers. Anyone working the lunch shift at the yacht club could have seen that.

But then Gil hadn't asked me to go with him "officially" as his date to Punch Night—in spite of Julia's clunky hints the night before.

"He's playing it careful," I said, as we got ready. We were over at Whisper—Julia's mom had all the nicer shampoos and make-up, plus a stronger hair drier. "Last night was fun, but he didn't kiss me good night, even with you and Oliver swapping spit five feet away. And he's mentioned Jean Custis a couple of times. Maybe he's got the hots for her?"

"Ha. There's no way." Julia was adamant.

"You never know," I said. "She's got that whole fresh-pressed thing."

Julia scoffed. "Who ever liked a girl because she was tidy? If Gil wants to keep his options open, fine. But I can't see him with Jean Custis. I could see him with Daphne, maybe. But not Jean. She's so plain vanilla."

"Jean always makes me want to check my fingernails."

"Her manners melt quick as the Wicked Witch of the West once she has a couple of drinks," said Julia. "Then she's sloppy."

"You just described half of Sunken Haven."

Later, seeing Jean and Gil together at the bar, their sparkly togetherness kind of threw me. Jean's face was flushed and she looked so soft and happy, like a princess on her day off. Gil was harder to read. Was he respectful because the Burke and Custis families were close? HANDLE WITH CARE was practically stamped on Jean's forehead.

Gil never wanted to mess up anything here. I got that. As many summers as I'd been coming to Sunken Haven, I was always aware of when I might appear wrong—my red prairie dress tonight being the latest example. I tried to convince myself that I looked like a "free spirit" in it, but after the first once-over from Sara Train, I knew I should have borrowed Julia's wrap dress when she'd offered.

Luckily, Bertie Forsythe's prank moved the night in the right direction.

As we made our way over, I'd been sweating it, imagining the rest of the evening at the stuffy von Cotts' mansion, where Jean would swan around, giving Gil an earful of stories about how her family and the von Cotts had been best friends since Mayflower days.

But as soon as we got to the big, dark, empty house, I knew we'd been tricked.

"There's no party here," I said, half annoyed and half relieved.

"Whoa." Julia and Oliver, also on bikes, had skidded up right behind us. In their flashlights' beams, the place lurched like a haunted house. I shivered; Gil drew closer and snapped his sports jacket over my shoulders.

"Jesus, and it's bug city tonight." Julia dug in her basket and then began to squirt from a bottle of OFF! "Die, skeeters! Who said the party was here, again?"

"Bertie Forsythe told me," said Gil. "He looked me right in my eye and told me it was here."

"Ah, don't get sensitive about it. Bertie Forsythe's full of crap, and this is his idea of a joke," said Oliver. "I'm pretty sure the real party's at the Wembly place. I heard about it at the beach earlier."

But Gil didn't know how to take it other than personally. It was different for Julia and Oliver—they were Sunkies themselves. The prank hit them at a softer angle.

"The guys are always pranking each other. But we could skip everything and walk over by the dunes," I said to Gil quietly, so the others couldn't hear.

"Yeah, okay. I'd like that."

I raised my voice. "You two go on ahead without us."

"Wait," said Julia. "Seriously? You're not coming?"

"Nah," said Gil. "I don't feel like more parties."

"Me, either."

I'd been annoyed about Bertie's trick, but the feeling was already fading. The real night was Gil and me. In spite of the blazer, I shivered again, and Gil moved in closer. He began to rub my arm. But I was shivering with excitement, not cold.

Gil Burke. The dunes. That worked.

"See ya, kiddoes." Julia gave me a tiny "told you so" smile. "You can't stop smiling around that Burke boy," she'd told me. "Pretty giddy for a girl who said she wasn't ready to fall in love this summer. Now it's all Scott *Who*lihan?"

But Gil was so different from Scott. So much older seeming, with his law firm internship and his college courses, his studio sublet in New York City. The only cool thing Scott ever did was go to Tampa for football camp. Gil versus Scott? Those two names shouldn't even hang out in the same sentence.

We redirected bikes and left the house behind. At the juncture, where Oliver and Julia veered toward the bay, I signaled the turn for the beach.

There, we dropped our bikes in the grass, kicked off our shoes, and raced each other to the ocean. We walked along the edge of the surf, checking out the perfect half-moon and the sky with its crazy blaze of stars.

"I love this smell," I said. "It's sweet with a kick. Kind of like spicy grapes."

"You can smell sage and bayberry all along South Beach," said Gil.

"Bayberry! Listen to you." How did he know that? "You'll be an honorary Sunkie by Labor Day."

"Unless I'm kicked off the island for my crappy band and beer T-shirts. Here every shirt's got a collar and a club emblem on it."

"I like your crappy T-shirts," I said. "You're probably the only person ever to show up at the yacht club in a shirt that says 'Keep on Truckin'." And I want to borrow that orange Frank Zappa one you had on Tuesday. Where I'm from, you look kind of refreshingly normal."

"Well, thanks. But I might look less normal as the days go on. Aunt Weeze's real stiff and proper about my clothes." Gil took my hand; my heart leaped. "She leaves these stacks on my bed, with notes about how Junior's got doubles of these sailing shorts, or how Uncle Carp never wears this sports coat."

"Because finally she's got a boy she can dress up like a Ken doll. It's got to be pretty depressing for Weeze, to see you standing next to Junior."

"To be honest, I think it upsets her," said Gil. "I'm not the one Weeze aims to shine."

"But you're her kin—you're her nephew."

"Yup." Gil kept his gaze out on the ocean, and I felt a scratch of doubt that I'd done the reverse of what I'd intended, by reassuring him.

"Though it's got to be tough," I said, "since she never knew you as a kid. Just—bam, here you are, all grown up and dropped in the house. You've got the same last name, but you're a stranger. I'm sure Weeze wants to treat you like family, but maybe she doesn't know how yet."

Now Gil nodded in real agreement. "I never had a name to live up to before. But being a Burke—that really means something here." He laughed, a little self-consciously. "Listen to me, I sound like I think I'm the next king of France. And speaking of names, what's the deal with 'Fritz'?"

"My dad had really hoped for a boy," I explained. "In fact, he was so sure I was gonna come out a boy, he told everyone. When I was born, he stuck to his guns and named me Fritz."

"I like it. It's sporty."

"He pushed me when I was little. Karate class, racquetball, Little League. But it worked out all right. Especially since my kid brother, Kevin, ended up being not much in the sports department. Someone had to bring home the medals."

"Like the Junior Cup Tennis trophy?"

I paused. "Jean Custis tell you about that?"

"All I know is that it sounds like her family screws the pressure down pretty tight."

We walked a bit longer, comfortable, letting the tide lap over our bare feet. I wasn't sure what to say about Jean. Her eyes on me tonight had been a little wild, even frightened. Like Gil was up for grabs — and we both were grabbing.

"A lot of the adults rooted for Jean, because her family's been winning that cup since Old Testament days," I said quietly. "Traditions are so important to these people. Last summer, on the ferry back to Bay Shore, I sat with it between my knees, and I couldn't even look some of those old Sunkies in the eye. I felt like I'd robbed a bank."

"Jean doesn't seem like someone who'd be fun to crush in sports."

"I know," I agreed. "She's very ladylike." I knew better than to speak against Jean. It always came off crummy to snipe about a girl behind her back. If I talked against her, I'd come off small, like a hick. And I didn't want to sound jealous, especially when she'd looked so classy in that peach silk dress with her matching initialed bag. I'd never owned anything silk.

But Gil had gone quiet. Was he thinking about Jean and their night in New York? He'd told me and Julia all about it, how they'd hit some trendy bar and ate these amazing burgers. Burgers in a bar didn't seem like any big deal until you set it against the backdrop of New York City, which somehow made the whole thing like a movie.

We got to a sandy embankment, where we stopped. Gil shook out his blazer and dropped it as our landing zone. We settled in, shoulder tip to shoulder tip, knees just touching. Gil stretched, letting his arm fall loose around my waist. When he turned to look at me, I kept staring out at the sea.

The silence was smooth. I waited for his voice to skate across it.

"Okay, Fritz O'Neill," said Gil after a couple of minutes. "Here's a night full of stars, and only you and me on this beach, and everything real nice—so I'm just gonna ask, but I think I need to know. You got a boyfriend back home?"

Scott Houlihan's name was a faint pain through my body. Hardly there at all. "Not likely," I said, with all the dismissive boredom I could muster.

Gil laughed. "You face tells the end of that story. I reckon I won't ask more."

"Well, and what about you?" I knocked my leg against his, and then let it stay there, quietly buzzing. "You got any girlfriend pining for you back in New York, or in Elmore?"

"Me? Nah. Not there, not here. Unless you want to count this hot and heavy thing I've got going with my Intro to Law books."

My vision had adjusted to the darkness. "Got your eye on anyone here?" I asked him, keeping my eyes fixed on the ocean.

"Maybe," he said. "Yeah, you could say that. You could say I got my eye on someone here."

Anyone could tell Gil was a sociable type, giving it his best shot this summer, to impress his aunt and uncle, hoping they saw him as a solid striver who was worth their investment. A girl like Jean Custis was a natural fit for a guy who wanted to get ahead with the Burkes. But I also knew, and I knew it down deep, that Jean was wrong for Gil Burke. He'd never be free with her. With

Jean, he'd always be on his toes, playing the part, working to impress.

"I'm going to kiss you," I told him.

"Yeah?" That smile. "I'm gonna let you."

I moved closer. My fingertips barely landing, butterfly-light, along the edge of his chin. Then I gave myself a moment, memorizing the dark brush of his lowered lashes and the outline of his cheekbone, before I leaned in and let my lips come to rest a moment on his.

At my touch, Gil reached for me, pressed in, his arm encircling my middle, his hand twisting in my hair, his lips parting. The two of us together, invincible, and nobody strong enough to pull us apart. I didn't know everything about Gil Burke, but I knew right then we were as magnetic as the tide.

Gil and me. Me and Gil. That was all.

JEAN

That's me — the sophisticate, the daredevil.

The problem with feelings and hangovers was that they didn't mix well. This morning was no exception. The pumping of my bruised heart only amplified the throbbing of my aching head. I couldn't remember the last time I'd felt so alive with pain.

I squared my sunglasses, swallowed the bile in my throat, and staggered the rest of the path to the gazebo.

Mom and Dad, also looking a bit queasy by the morning light, were fussing with their breakfasts. "Jean, your food went cold while you slept," said Mom, "but you're going to have to eat it anyway or you'll hurt poor Mrs. Otis's feelings. She was up before any of us, making our breakfasts."

I lifted my fork. Ever since Mrs. Otis had come marching in to pull up my bedroom shades twenty minutes ago, I'd been jolted into such specifically awful memories of Punch Night. Gil's gentlemanly, remote kindness. Fritz's scratchy laugh. The two of them slipping through the side exit to dance in their private corner of paradise. While I stood alone, stupidly, in the middle of the club dining room, trying not to cry.

I'd lost him. He'd slipped away before I'd even had a chance.

My parents usually ate breakfast at the gazebo, as long as Dad didn't taste too much quartz dust in the cross breeze. It was the prettiest corner of our property, with rose mallow climbing the trellis walls, and a sweeping view of the ocean below. But I couldn't find any joy in it today.

My eggs were runny side up. I gagged down a mouthful and smiled.

"Mmmm," I said to Mom, who woozily served one back as she passed me the juice.

"Was Rosamund's after party fun?" The words had no sooner formed on Dad's lips than he jumped up and bolted. Hands clamped to his mouth, he sprinted the path to the back door, presumably heading for the powder room toilet bowl.

Mom and I kept eating as if we hadn't noticed. In the Custis house, everyone was too good a sport to point out something as messy as a hangover.

I reached for the Arts section. Mom scoured the front-page headlines.

"Quite honestly, there's only so much a person should have to read about Beirut," she murmured, a note of blame in her voice.

Last night kept hemorrhaging through me. Gil and Fritz. Sticky-sweet punch. Those mean and stupid things I'd said to Sara. Sara, who was my friend, who deserved better from me.

Regrets, regrets . . . I closed my eyes and let egg slime slip down my throat.

Opened them to see Dad slide neatly back into place.

When Mrs. Otis reappeared with the aspirin bottle for Mom, I intercepted it and shook out a handful for myself. "I'd better get ready for tennis."

Mom took the bottle from me. "Goodness, everything was so fun last night, and then the next morning we all need so much medicine. Life's little ironies. . . . If you're done with Arts, I'll have it."

Leaving the house on unsteady legs, I got all the way to the end of the drive before I gave in to it. I let my bike fall and I doubled over, gripping my knees as my insides cramped and heaved, and all my breakfast came up in a torrent of egg yolk and orange juice, into Mom's pachysandra.

Now my breath was disgusting. I'd have to clean myself up at the casino.

I arrived to find Coach Hutch out on the courts. As I scurried to the women's restroom, the twang of his Australian accent carried through the open window.

After rinsing my mouth, I gave myself a stern look in the

mirror. A wan, sad, frizzy-haired girl frowned back at me. Was it only last night I'd told the mirror that I looked pretty?

I was a joke. I was a pathetic joke.

I felt too sick to get through a tennis lesson. Not today. Outside, I wheeled my bike around the other side of the building, out of Coach's sight, and pushed off toward the bay.

It was a gorgeous morning. Blue sky and blue water and a warm bay breeze. Cherry-red, apple-green, and lemon-yellow bathing suits flapped on porch railings. My headache fuzzed my vision, and I nearly fell over twice as I rattled around the corner onto the narrow slatted boards of Bay Walk, where I saw Sara and Rosamund sunning themselves bottoms up, on deck chairs on the Wembleys' double-story porch.

Sara must have stayed over at Rosamund's. It meant they were extra angry with me. They clung to each other whenever they felt I'd wronged them.

But I had wronged them. Why had I said such hurtful things? This apology wouldn't be easy.

I braked a few cottages away, got off my bike, and leaned it against a tree. Plastic cups were scattered in the Wembleys' bottle-brush hedges; up the steps, I caught that skunky bite of stale beer in the air, more proof of last night's party.

"Hi, girls." I waved, buoyant and awkward. "That's a nifty new swimsuit, Sara."

Their heads lifted. "It's Rosamund's," said Sara, and she put her head down again.

But Rosamund was scowling at me. "You have some nerve, Jean. Showing up here, with your phony compliments."

"What do you mean?"

"You haven't forgotten already!"

No, I hadn't forgotten. It's always been my curse to remember everything, no matter how much I've had to drink. I stayed quiet.

"For example. Do you remember," Rosamund prompted, "that you called Sara a pumpkin?"

"I was only kidding."

Sara's head jerked up again. "You were *drunk*. And when you get drunk, or angry, or any combination of both, you put your foot in your mouth."

"Well, excuse me. I thought I was being funny." My fingers found the deck railing. I steadied myself.

"It's *always* that you think you're being something else," said Rosamund.

"Look, I didn't mean it. I'm sorry."

"You botched it worse than sorry," said Sara. "Maybe you could go be somewhere else today? I don't want to pretend everything's superduper with you again."

I knew Sara loved this a little bit. Usually I had all of Rosamund's loyalty, but the minute I didn't, Sara lost no time twisting the knife.

"Okay." My face burned. I had nothing else to offer them. "I really didn't mean it. For what it's worth."

The answer was silence. I stumbled down the steps and back

to my bike, and I rode all the way past the fisherman cottages, right to the very end of Bay Walk, where the reed grass grew so fast and thick along the freshwater that as a little girl, I had nightmares of swimming into it and being swallowed whole.

Around the bend by the boathouse were the shallows where the Junior Minnows took swimming lessons. I'd learned to swim here myself, in this silvery-blue inlet. My memory could still loop back to my girl body, a flipping dolphin in my "green bean" Speedo, my toes wriggling for the silky mud bottom.

Make-up Minnows was under way. Years ago, Julia Tulliver's mother had mentioned that the weekend Make-up Minnows program had been set up to foist off children into a morning class while their parents nursed their hangovers. But when I reported this comment to my mother—I was forever being dropped off at Make-up Minnows—it created a bit of a firestorm.

Always mellow Oliver Olmstead was watching over everyone from the lifeguard chair, while Tiger and Gil stood waist-deep in the water, shepherding the kids. Their voices were low as they urged the squealing Minnows to trust them, let go, breathe.

I parked and walked to the water's edge. I kept still and silent until Gil noticed me. He seemed surprised, but not unhappy, as he turned and said something to Tiger, who nodded.

As he came sloshing in, I wanted to run. What did I really need to say to Gil Burke, anyway? This was another one of my usual bad impulses.

"Jean, what's going on? Everything okay?"

"Not really." Hearing his voice, tears welled in my eyes and then, worse, began to spill down my cheeks.

"Hey—hey! What's wrong?"

"I feel like an idiot."

"You? Never. Talk to me."

"I can't say."

"Sure you can. That's why you're here, right?" His voice was so gentle. All that Southern comfort. "You want to tell me something, and I want to hear it."

"Honestly? Fine. Here it is. I'm an idiot, and it's all because of you." I wiped my eyes with my arm, humiliated by my own raw confession. "Because ever since you got here, I've felt wrecked. I've been in a sort of agony about not seeing you, and last night I said crummy things to my friends, and it was only because I was . . . I was sad. Because . . . because . . ."

Oh, good grief. Where was my dignity? This was such a stupid idea. My words were sputtering out and I needed to blow my nose.

But when I looked up at him, Gil's expression was as calm as the blue sky above us. "Jeez, Jean, now *I* feel bad. It shouldn't have got this mucked up between us."

"Back in New York, I thought we had some kind of—I don't know. Click. When we were dancing at Hollander's. Walking home. In front of my apartment. Didn't we? Or was it all in my head?"

"No, it was real, we were—look, I sort of might have reckoned *you'd* gone off *me.* You never went out of your way to find me here, and of course you've got all your Sunkie pals."

"Really?" Was that the truth?

"Yeah, for sure. I didn't want to breathe down your neck. But let's not talk about fault and blame—when it's so easy to start over."

"Start what over? Aren't you keen on Fritz O'Neill now? I should tell you *nobody* in our set likes Fritz, and it might become—" I made myself say it—"*harder* for you to make the friends that you want, if you've got Fritz hanging around you."

Gil lifted his hat, bent to dunk it in the water, then replaced it on his head. The look in his eyes was no longer so soft. "Fritz's real," he offered. "She's her own person."

"Well—so am I!" I tried to picture my sister in this moment. I imagined the set of Daphne's hard little chin, her haughty gaze whenever she sensed she was being wronged. Daphne always decided her own terms. "We should be friends, at least," I said firmly. "I'm not sure what's happened between us. But we weren't meant to be less than friends."

"Of course we're friends! I'd hate for anyone to think we weren't," said Gil quickly. There was a note of unease in his voice.

"You mean you'd hate to upset Carpie and Weeze." I knew it was true, and I knew he was embarrassed for it to be true.

"Aw, Jean. Sure, but also you. You've been nothing but cool to me. Look, I gotta get back to the Minnows, and then I'm working dinner shift at the yacht club tonight. But I'd really like to see you again."

Would he? If he really meant it, he'd pick a time. I waited a moment. "So maybe after you're finished work at the club?"

"After my shift?" He looked surprised. "That's kinda late."

"How late would be okay to come see you?"

"Reckon it doesn't hafta be tonight. I'm here all summer." He laughed, but when I kept staring at him, hoping, he went on. "Well, look. I guess you could drop by Snappy Boy later on tonight. So long as we were real quiet, and didn't wake up the house."

"Yes! I could get away—and you could slip me inside . . ." My head was a jam of thrilled confusion as I tried to envision myself tiptoeing around Snappy Boy.

Gil looked perplexed by the plan. My suggestion had been too bold. "If it doesn't put ya in a pickle," he said, slowly.

I smiled. "No pickle at all. Really. I'd love to."

"Eleven, then?" He stepped back, his brows buckled. But he wasn't saying no. My daring intrigued him. Suddenly I was that carefree New York City girl again.

"Perfect. Rosamund and Sara and I sneak out to see each other late night all the time," I lied. "It'd be such a goof—a neighborly drop-in!"

That seemed to do the trick. Gil allowed himself a small smile. "If you say so. I'm on the third floor, the window above the dormer farthest from the path. Toss a pebble, and I'll let you in quicker 'n a speeding ticket. Okay, I better go check in with the rug rats. Catch ya on the flip."

"See you later. On the flip." Even repeating his words had me shaky with anticipation.

Gil turned, but not before he'd leveled me with a last look, that same admiring look he'd given when we slipped through the door at Hollander's.

Yes, that was me—the sophisticate *and* the daredevil. I could be that girl for him.

And now the rest of the day was only a string of hours until night.

I went back to the casino, said sorry to Coach for my lateness, and played better tennis than I had all summer. At the candy store, I picked up two cartons of Breyers, chocolate and strawberry, for Sara and Rosamund. The girls weren't at Bayview, so I left the ice cream in the kitchen freezer with a note. They'd come around eventually; they always did.

Home for lunch, I kept my parents mildly entertained with lighthearted, Daphne-style stories about all the fun I'd had last night at the club. Secretly, I was ticking off each hour. Nap, tea, book, tennis. Was it always so boring here? How had I ever whiled away the hours on Sunken Haven all these years, before I'd met Gil Burke?

After dinner, the rhythms of the house drove me crazy. Why did my parents insist on drinking brandies in the living room? Why did Mrs. Otis, tucked in bed, never turn off her bedroom light? From where I was pretending to read *Goodbar* on the loveseat,

I could see across the lawn to the lit window of Mrs. Otis's room, a separate lean-to that had once been a potting shed. Where she might be awake all night with her Bible or a romance novel.

Time was officially crawling.

"Good night, I'm turning in," I said on the dot of nine.

"Sweet dreams, darling," Mom said, lovingly, to her glass of brandy.

Upstairs, I changed and changed again. Suddenly my white-and-red striped boater shirt looked too conspicuous for traveling by night. I swapped it for my navy shirtdress with the cord sash that Mom had bought for me in Paris.

Last, I prepared my knapsack with a bottle of Beefeater gin—I'd have to water it down when I replaced it later tonight—two limes, a paring knife, a Baggie of ice, a bottle of tonic water, and paper cups.

Was this crazy? Maybe, but no time for the yips. Back in my room, I returned to reading my book in the windowseat, and I listened to the muffled sounds of my parents finishing up second nightcaps and then, *finally*, thudding off to sleep.

The minute hand inched its journey around my watch dial. My heart beat on a hummingbird's wings. The rooms of the house seemed to settle in for the evening. A cough, a door shut, a lamp clicked off.

Another ten minutes, and at a quarter to eleven, I was out the back door like a spirit, my knapsack of goodies slung over my shoulder.

On my bike and *whoosh,* wheels hissing.

Sunkies didn't grow up fearing the dark. We enjoyed our black nights, with their sounds of cicadas and barn owls. My flashlight unspooled a rope of light to guide me as I shot down from our private lane off Ocean Walk, straight past the church, and past the casino's outdoor courts. I leaned into the fork, onto Ridge Way, around one bend and then the next. Downshifting. I lifted forward and pushed up over the handlebars as the incline grew steeper.

As familiar as I was with every path and turn on Sunken Haven, my nerves had me in a jumble. Twice I was sure I'd missed the turn. Had this mile marker always been right here? Was that a shrub or a raccoon?

The driveway to the Burke property was marked only by a chunk of Cumberland rock, painted white, with the number 58. The low swoop of a night heron rattled me as I bumped over the bridge, as did the mournful *tink* of the knife blade against the gin bottle in my backpack.

What if the Burkes caught me out? What would I say? I'd had some mischievous moments with Sara and Rosamund and Bertie—but lone acts of rebellion weren't my usual sort of thing at all.

I didn't notice until pain bit my lungs how long I'd been holding my breath.

Snappy Boy rose up like a fortress. What if Weeze and Carp were outside? Or what if Junior was awake, watching me right now with that telescope he used to brag could let him see all the way out to Jones Beach?

Off my bike, I wheeled around the back wall of the Burkes' massive three-story cedar shake house. I picked up a flat pebble and tossed it at the square window above the second dormer, where it hit the shutter.

Gil's face appeared immediately—he'd never doubted me.

He pointed for me to meet him at the kitchen door, and I nodded.

The darkness was intensified by the buzz of katydids, along with the occasional sleepy croak of a toad in the cordgrass. Snappy Boy's quiet was absolute. No ghostly flicker of a bedroom television. No hush of talking through the walls. The Burkes didn't have dogs or live-in help, but I imagined all sorts of unsettling scenes involving me, caught on their property, attempting to explain what I was doing here.

I pushed off those thoughts. I had pressed Gil for this meeting. I'd been brazen about it. And now that I was here, I could feel how much I craved another chance with him. I wanted to sit on the edge of Gil's bed, pick up his hairbrush, peek inside his bedside table drawer or his shaving case. I wanted to touch the things that he touched. I wanted to prop a pillow behind my head and treat myself to his morning view out the window. I wanted to let the space that was Gil's space hold me, too.

And of course I wanted even more than that.

Gil opened the screen door with a finger to his lips. In deep shadow, in his sweatpants and a T-shirt, his body was less intimidating than by day, all sun-bronzed in his swim trunks. He reminded me of how he'd looked on our first night, when we'd stood in the darkness of Hollander's, and his arm had wound me close and our hearts had pressed together.

"Everyone's sleeping," he whispered. "Cross your fingers we can keep it that way." But as he led me through the house, he didn't seem fazed, which calmed me a little.

Weeze Burke had always been more interested in her bridge game and backhand than interior decorating, and while she and Carpie had made some additions to Snappy Boy, building a patio and a sunroom, I couldn't remember the last time anything had changed inside. The furnishings reminded me of the Burkes themselves—heavy, solid, with an old-fashioned frill. We passed closed doors and kept moving, up the staircase, around two corners and to the end of a short hall, then up a steeper flight of steps.

We held our breath against every creak in the floorboards. We smiled at each other in the shadows. At the end of the hall, Gil opened the door, then moved past me, deep into the room, to snap on his bedside table lamp.

"This is me."

The glow of the lamp was forgiving, and the room itself was scrupulously neat, but the cramped space and mismatched furniture could not hide how dismal it really was, and I wondered if Gil knew this had been Junior's old nanny's room. It seemed mean that the Burkes had stuck him here. As if he were more of a servant than family.

I imagined Fritz sitting on the bed. Fritz, with her bracelets jangling, her sly gypsy moves—*except I was the sly one tonight, wasn't I?*

Gil adjusted the crooked lampshade. "Russian spy returns to inspect living quarters," he said. But there was hesitation in his face.

"Now that I'm here, you have no idea what to do with me, right?" I teased.

He took a small step back. "We can play cards—that's what my friends and I are usually up to, after hours."

"You're worried about the Burkes finding us out, aren't you?"

"Naw. I mean, I don't think so."

But he was. I could see it in his eyes. Maybe even to the point where he regretted allowing me to be here. Decisive, I reminded myself. The way Daphne had announced one night at dinner that she was spending her whole summer in Spain.

"Look. I brought us a party." I set my knapsack on the hooked rug, then sat next to it and unzipped it.

"Oh, yeah? What's in there?"

"Consider it a housewarming gift."

Gil pulled his hands through his hair and grinned. "You got some stones, Custis. Prancing in here at midnight with your Beefeater."

"Please. So easy." Though I was breathless as I presented the knife, the ice, the tonic, and tossed a lime for his catch. "It's all very civilized, see?"

Gil, watching me, finally seemed to resolve to the risk. He

matched my position, dropping to sit cross-legged opposite me, then reached over to select an album from a stack at the bottom of his bookshelf.

"Too bad there's no stereo in my room," he said sheepishly, "and Junior only wants to play Frampton. But we'll use Tom Waits as our tabletop. Just don't spill." He spun the album, then handed it to me.

"'The Heart of Saturday Night,'" I read as I placed it between us. "Well, now that's us, I suppose. You'd mentioned him before, at Hollander's." I set the "table" with the paper cups, then carefully poured the gin and the tonic.

"Yeah, yeah. Wish I could play him for you." Gil cupped the lime in one hand as he cut it into wedges, wiping off the pulp on his sweatpants. "Waits, he's the real deal. You know he'll always be a loner, telling it like it is, but from a distance. He's got this kickass raspy voice, too—damn, I wish you could hear some—"

"Oh, it doesn't matter!" I cut in. Fritz had a raspy voice. I didn't need Gil thinking of her in any way tonight.

"Arright, cheers," he said, accepting his drink and raising it. "To the predictably unpredictable Miss Custis." He leaned over and tapped the paper cup against mine.

"Cheers." I did it. I'd really done it. If only my parents could see me like this, so assured and sophisticated! But they never would, because I would always be my best and boldest, my Daphne-est self, when they weren't around.

We downed our drinks like shots. I fixed two more. The gin

rolled along with me like a happy friend. I'd stop at the end of this second drink, though. I really didn't want to say silly things, too many things, things I'd regret.

"This afternoon, when you suggested it, I gotta say, I was jittery," Gil said. "I'm always sweating the rules here—fact is, even my manners get on Uncle Carp's nerves. The other day, he told me to quit it with the 'no, sirs' and to stop asking permission to leave the table or look in the icebox. But I'm that unsure."

I laughed. "You'd do well to stay by me," I told him. "Carpie's a big old pussy cat. You just need to know where to scratch him." I could feel Gil's envy of this idea, of my genuine ease with the Burkes.

"I'm by you now," Gil murmured.

"And I was in heaven all afternoon, knowing I'd get to see you later."

Our eyes held. "Jean, listen," Gil spoke softly into the moment. "What you said, earlier. That nothing should stop us from being friends? I thought about it all day, and want you to know—I one hundred percent agree with you. But the thing is . . ." He ran his tongue over his upper lip, as if trying the flavor of how to speak his next piece. I was already tensed for it. "I don't know if you know, but Fritz O' Neill and I are seeing each other now, if you catch my drift. I reckon I oughta tell you that right off."

I knew it already, of course. But it didn't stop my heart from dropping in a free fall. "I understand," I said, but I didn't. Why? Why Fritz and not me?

Somewhere outside, an owl hooted, breaking the moment.

We laughed.

Gil stretched his arm to give me the lightest chuck under my chin. I smiled. Sipped my drink and said nothing.

Fritz mattered, of course she did. But she didn't matter every single moment. Not this moment. Fritz had moved fast, but it wasn't over. The last set might have gone to Fritz, but there was still time to save the match.

Gil had finished his drink, too. The cups were pretty small. When he topped us up, I didn't say no. "My tolerance is already higher since I got to Sunken Haven," he said. "You Sunkies get soused. Uncle Carp and Aunt Weeze and Junior looked wiped out this morning at breakfast. But they were planning to get right back to it by lunch."

"Being buzzed all day is like a hobby here," I said. Fresh drink in hand, I unbent to stand, and to prove that I was mostly sober, I walked a straightish line to the bookshelf. "Gosh, look at all of those boring history-of-law books. And are you really planning to read these old magazines?" I riffled through the stack, mostly Carpie and Weeze's old *New Yorker*s and *Saturday Evening Post*s.

"They're a good education. I feel like I've got a whole lifetime of civilization to catch up with."

"Well, I don't know how you do it. All work and no play."

Above his desk, shoved among the shabby spines of the complete works of the Bronte sisters, was a photo album, the plasticky binder kind that was sold in drugstores. I glanced over at him. "Do you mind?"

"Go ahead."

I'd think about it later, that momentary sharpening in Gil's face. At the time, I'd assumed it was only about my prying; my desire to ooh and ahh over Gil's baby pictures. I prided myself on being observant, but sometimes I didn't see the importance in the things that I noticed. And when my mind returned to consider all that happened this night, I'd rewind right to here. I'd stare into the quicksilver memory of Gil's expression as intently as if it had been a crystal ball.

The drinks had rubbed and softened my edges. Gil watched as I pulled the album from the shelf, then slid and stretched out on his narrow bed. Had anything happened between Gil and Fritz here? On this mattress, hard and musty as stale bread?

Don't think about them. You're the one who's here now.

Gil stood and took his drink to his desk. He began to push through his papers and straighten his notebooks. I knew he felt strange about all this, me lying on his bed, flipping through his album.

I felt strange, too. But not so strange that I could give it up.

So I stayed where I was, peering at every page of curl-edged Kodak prints pressed to sticky paper and protected by clear plastic covers. I skimmed faces. Many of the pictures were of Gil and his mom, and a pair of grandparents. No father anywhere. Not that I was going to touch that—Gil's last name was a good indicator that his mother had been single when she'd had him. Surely that was why they'd never been invited here, with all of the embarrassment Carpie's sister and her out-of-wedlock child must have caused him.

The stepfather entered the pictures when Gil was a baby, along with a small, ugly house and a muddy patch of yard, and then, in quick succession, two more kids.

So poor. I didn't think I knew anyone who was poor like this.

"Such sweet little boys," I said. "What are their names?"

"That's my half-brother Trevor." Gil pointed. "He's seventeen; my stepdad let him join the navy. And that squirt is Tommy. Fourteen now, starting high school. He's the one who'll take over my stepdad's business."

The kids looked fine, but the stepfather looked hard. He matched the squat, ugly house and the skinny dog and rusted car.

I knew Carpie's parents had died years ago, and it seemed almost cruel of Carpie to let his little sister live like this, so far away and on the edge.

"Come over here," I said. "Come tell me more about your family."

"Aw, you don't want to know more about my family."

"You're so super-wrong. I do." My voice slurred. Almost three gin and tonics in less than ten minutes. I could feel my wheels starting to come off, as Mrs. Otis would say.

Gil finished his drink in a gulp, then pushed in beside me on the bed. Our shoulders grazed. Our elbows and forearms. He flipped the pages backward to start the book over. "Okay, here's me as an infant." He pointed. "Me as a toddler. Here's me on my fifth birthday, when my mom and stepdad gave me a Radio Flyer."

"That's you leaping through a sprinkler." I turned a page. Our ankles touched. Hip bones. A lot of parts of us were touching now. "And you in a turtleneck and double-breasted blazer that make you look like a like a . . . like a . . . television preacher! A child talk-show host!" I could feel my words slipping out carelessly. Had I insulted him, the way I'd hurt Sara the other night? I took a breath.

Gil didn't seem upset. "Everyone thought I looked real handsome in that." But he reached for my drink and took it over.

"Your stepdad seems . . . no nonsense," I said.

"Hank swims in Lewis Smith Lake every morning. He swears by it," said Gil. "And everyone likes when Hank gets his exercise and tires himself out, else he comes after us." Gil made a swinging fist motion; even as a joke, it seemed frightening.

I closed the album. "Your family looks very 'salt of the earth.'"

"One way of putting it." Gil shrugged.

"I'm glad Carp's got an interest in you," I said, carefully settling on the most honest thing I could think to say. "He's a powerful person, and you're his kin, and you know the saying—blood is thicker than water."

"One of the first truths my stepdad ever taught me." Gil kept his words empty of emotion, but he shoved the album hard out of sight, under the bed. "I never counted on that lesson working to my advantage till this summer. Now I reckon—who needs a hardware store, when I could live in a house like this, with my beach on one side and a boat docked on the other? Not even the mayor of my town lives like Carpie Burke—or your folks, for that matter. I won't lie, I'm hungry for it."

"And you deserve it. Carpie wants you here. Finally, the Burkes have something better to show off than Junior. I know it must be overwhelming sometimes, but . . . I'm always here to help, you know. Any way you want." My buzz was speaking for me again. Too much, too fast. I was spinning clumsily through this complicated moment.

Gil smiled. He was staring at me, and I could see some of that hunger.

I pressed my legs harder against his.

He didn't move. He didn't react at all. But he wasn't pushing me away, either. Maybe he was waiting for me. I wouldn't let my chance pass me by this time. I linked my arms decisively around his neck. Pulling him toward me, against his slight resistance.

"Please? One kiss? You've kissed me before."

"Jean, I wonder if maybe you've had a lot to drink?"

"So have you. More than me. Don't you like me?"

"You know I like you."

"It's just—we had such a fun night last week," I whispered. "Was that night a mistake?"

"No," he said, after a moment. "No, I guess not."

"Okay. So let's make another not-mistake." I sat up and snapped off the lamp, giggling, though I couldn't tell if what I'd said and done was funny or not. But when I lay back down, the dark felt soothing. Easier.

"That night in New York." Gil's voice was a hush through the darkness. "It held a magic for me. Like you'd lifted me up so high and given me this big view. You made me feel part of the *real* New York City. I wasn't stuck on the ground, on the sidelines, an Alabama boy, eating alone in a diner or punching in my overtime at the firm. That night, it was my turn. And there you were, Uncle Carp's own goddaughter. But I gotta be honest, it also felt like pressure. All night I felt like I was in another sphere, handling crystal. I really don't want to mess up with my uncle and Aunt Weeze."

"Oh, stop it. I'm not crystal. I'm not going to break."

I heard him drain my drink, then felt the creak of the bed as he leaned over to set the cup on the floor. "And the truth is, I was relieved that I didn't see you right away, when I first got to Sunken Haven."

I kept my voice looser than my feelings. "Because if you had?"

Gil didn't answer. Maybe he didn't want to admit it was less pressure on him to date Fritz O'Neill. But I didn't think I could bear to hear him say it. I'd worked so hard not to mention her, not to pollute the night with her presence. I leaned forward and touched his mouth with mine, my lips soft against his. I'd never in my entire life wanted to kiss anyone as much as I wanted to kiss Gil Burke.

"We had a magic night," I said. "I wouldn't mind another one."

In his moment of uncertainty, I pushed up Gil's T-shirt while, with the other hand, I deftly loosed my dress sash. Slipping open its buttons, my cotton bra the only barricade against his bare chest. He was breathing hard, then harder, and then all at once a spring seemed to release inside him, his own decision made, as he kissed me back, pressed against me, over me. His hand sliding up my leg, testing the limits of my intentions.

It wasn't as if I hadn't imagined this exact moment a thousand times. It wasn't as if I couldn't feel that Gil was hard, or that the change in his breath wasn't telling me to keep going.

And I knew I would keep going. I slipped my finger beneath his waistband, pushing down. Watching his eyes open, register my action in a glance of surprise.

I was careful with the heft of him—his *thing*, we all said at Dalton, as in "I felt his *thing* when we danced close" or "he wanted me to touch his *thing*"—but this was more than a thing, it was real and warm and belonged specifically to Gil, and tonight, to me, too.

Over the years, I'd given Bertie more hand jobs than we could count. The first one was in seventh grade. We both were so young that while it had been fun at the time, we'd felt shy about it afterward—to the point where we didn't speak for months.

Getting hot and heavy with Bertie these days was never really about daring. It was boozy, almost funny behavior that I remembered in friendship and left Bertie to think about any way he wanted—as long as he didn't bring it up with me.

That's not what I wanted this night to be. With Gil, my feelings were potent. I wanted to keep going. I wanted to go all the way.

"Jean," he whispered roughly, breaking off just once to look at me. In the darkness, his eyes were heavy lidded as he searched my face for secrets. "I guess I'm confused about this. Are you sure you want this? What exactly do you want?"

What did I want? I wanted Gil to belong to me more than he did to Fritz. I wanted this night to blossom naturally from all the potential of our night in New York. I wanted to be exactly that girl he'd imagined—the sophisticated Upper East Side Princess, sexy and independent, plunging headlong into this moment exactly the way I'd pushed through the door at Hollander's. That distant, enchanted night.

I wanted Gil to be my first so that Bertie never could be. And I wanted Gil to understand what Fritz could never be for him, if he wanted to make the right impression at Sunken Haven. That I could give him every bit of what Fritz could—plus even more. I could be his alliance here. I could be his "big view," his future.

Would that be so awful to admit?

None of my thoughts were calm or rational, or even particularly sane, but they were the right answer. "I only want tonight," I told him. "That's all. Just tonight, all of it, all the way."

"Okay." Then his eyes closed, as if he were accepting and denying the moment all together at once. "Sure. Yes."

I hadn't been totally honest.

But I'd never wanted anyone as badly as I wanted Gil.

PART TWO

FRITZ

"It kind of knocks me out how you care this much."

"Red alert! People are coming!" I sat up.

"Noooo!" Gil tugged me back down next to him.

"Yes!"

We'd been mellowing out underneath the clubhouse. It was only a stone's throw from the main beach path, and in full plain sight of anyone who might have snooped through the slats.

Nobody did.

But if there was one thing we'd learned over these past couple of weeks—we liked time to ourselves. Whether stealing kisses in the library out of sight of frumpy Mrs. Davis, dozing over her knitting at the circulation desk, or sharing lunch in the church with its sleepy smell of furniture polish, our happiness felt private.

We'd sit, feet up in the pew, wolfing down tomato sandwiches that we'd slapped together after working a lunch shift together at the club, and I'd think: There's no place I'd rather be than right here, and no moment more golden than with him. The best part was I knew Gil felt the same.

And so we scouted for the secret places of Sunken Haven. The shortcuts and the hidden spots where the adults wouldn't think to go.

Because there were plenty of chaperones around. Gil had me watching out for that. I'd never really noticed before.

"So many damn eyes on us," he'd say. "All these gossips, you couldn't buy an hour on your lonesome if you tried."

It must have been the structure and checkpoints of my life on army bases that had made me so oblivious. I'd never paid mind to all these Sunken Haven eyes before. I'd never felt spied on by adults—only protected. Of course, Gil was fresh blood at Sunken Haven. He was being extra watched. He told me that in the three weeks he'd been here, he'd been asked about his future more than in his whole, entire life in Elmore.

"Everyone's curious about you," I said. "Carpie never mentioned hide nor hair of a sister and a nephew—and now here you are, crushing poor Junior in every category. I'm not surprised people have a hankering for more."

But Gil didn't like the attention, and as a result, my own eyes and ears were peeled, too.

In this case, though, my red alert turned out to be some of

the younger kids stomping down the stiles that led to the beach. I pressed my hand to Gil's mouth as he tease-bit my fingers. We watched the parade of scabby legs, close enough to pinch. Gil pulled down my hand and nipped the outline of my chin.

I stifled my laughter as they tramped past us.

"Trade you for grape-flavored?"

"Stick bugs are predators!"

"Woof woof woof listen to me! I sound like a real dog!"

"Shut up, they eat grass."

"Where should we go that's private?" I asked. "It's getting hot."

"We could drop by Bertie Forsythe's barbecue. It starts at eleven."

"That's not private. Let's hang out at your house."

Gil looked uneasy. "Eh. Junior."

"We can always handle Junior," I said. "Plus I know Weeze is playing doubles. And Carp's only ever at the club."

"I hate how Junior looks at you. Like he's mentally beating off to you."

"You're not used to him. I am. I can't stay long. I've got my waitress uniform in my bag, so I'll leave from there to work my shift. Come on, I want to watch Wimbledon."

"The thing is . . ." In the shadows, it was hard to read Gil's face, but I could sense his discomfort. "Weeze gets so uptight when I bring guests over."

I sat back on my elbows. "Really? Why?"

"I don't know, but . . . she gives me a hard time about girls. She doesn't like me getting serious."

"Oh."

"I mean, it's nothing personal. It's not you. Weeze wouldn't cotton to *any* girl coming around."

Gil wasn't a good liar—just the fact that he'd had to emphasize "any girl" confirmed what I basically knew: snooty Weeze Burke *did* have a problem with me, personally. Of course Weeze would have preferred Gil to go steady with a Sunkie girl. But now other doubts needled me. How much did Weeze dislike me, exactly? Did she speak out against me? Was I unofficially banned from their house?

I reached out and pinched Gil's nose. I didn't want to seem insecure about it. "Nobody's home to disapprove. And it's our best option for TV and free drinks."

"I'd need to ask Junior not to tell. I don't like owing him."

"I'll tell him. Junior wouldn't rat us out." Kids never narced on other kids to adults here, not even bad eggs like Junior. Gil still looked reluctant, and we finally agreed to spend an hour at the house if there was no Carp and Weeze, and to detour over to the Morgue if the Burkes were hanging around.

We scrabbled out from the pilings and picked up our bikes. The late-morning air felt clean after we'd been hunkered down in a crawl space where the club's beach chairs and extra sun umbrellas were stored.

Gil rocketed off like he always did, eating up the distance like he was being chased. He shortcut the path through the Forsythes' garden to hook up with Ridge Way. Daring me to cut, too, and to stay on whip-smooth pace with him. He was fast but so was I, even if I barely kept him in eyeshot.

Fifteen minutes later, after the final uphill turn-in, sweat was running off me in rivers.

"Slow down!" I shouted to the back of his straw hat.

In love with the speed, Gil pretended like he didn't hear me. Or maybe he really didn't, he was so intent on rushing into any opportunity to feel free.

You couldn't even see Snappy Boy till you wheeled up the private entrance, which rolled over a wooden bridge that crossed their pond, then widened out to a wild lawn of knee-high salt hay.

Until this summer, I'd never been once to the Burke house. I still felt like an intruder as I crossed the path to where Snappy Boy stood on the highest point of the ridge, overlooking the sea. It was an ideal party house, except Weeze and Carp only held small, exclusive adult parties. The Burkes weren't one of the families known for fun. The thing they'd been best known for, until the good luck of Gil, had been the bad luck of Junior.

In the few weeks since he'd been here, Gil had put Sunken Haven in a stir. He was so different. He didn't have any of those usual smirking prep-school airs. Girls wanted him and guys wanted to be him. Even Junior liked to claim him, doing all he could—in public, at least—to make everyone think that he and Gil had a special, cousinly bond.

But whatever pride the Burkes might have enjoyed through Gil, he was also here on trial. "I've never known Carp to put Junior to the test like he does with you," I'd mentioned to Gil once. "He'd never make Junior take off a day to caddy for him over at Rockaway, or tell him to wash down his boat, or ask him to tend bar for free for one of their Association dinner parties."

"Junior's got a legitimate claim on Carp," Gil answered. "But right now, I'm nobody."

"Yeah, but I bet Carp already favors you over Junior."

"No he doesn't. And he never will." Gil's words were flat and hard and sure. "But if I can get Carp to trust me, that would make a difference."

Going in through the front door, I heard the tennis match, turned up loud. Junior was lounged in the den, a cig and a Rolling Rock in one hand, two empties on the coffee table in front of him.

"Fritz!" He raised his beer.

"Heya, Junior." I paused in the den's open archway. "I'm supposed to be starting my shift at the club, so you didn't see me here, got it?"

"Sure, no sweat."

I turned to Gil and winked. *See?* "Come back with a lemonade?" Gil nodded and headed to the kitchen.

Junior's eyes were now perving all over me like a tuna net to drag me down. "So Fritzie, are you a tenny-bopper for Borg like all the other chicks?"

"Borg's all right." I crossed my arms over my chest. "Who's winning?"

"Come closer and see for yourself." Junior patted the place next to him. "And maybe we can talk about anything else that pops up."

I stayed where I was and made my face a mask. I wouldn't react to his dumb joke. Ever since Minnows days, Junior had picked me out as the girl to say the dirtiest things to—and I let him because he was a Burke, and the Burkes had power.

But now I had another Burke, a better Burke, and it probably tortured Junior. Who knows, maybe it was partly why I liked coming over to Snappy Boy. Maybe making out with Gil in Junior's own house was my way of getting back at the kid, after all those years he'd harassed and pestered me.

"You look sore, Fritz. I was only playing." Junior heaved his whole body forward with the effort of stubbing out his smoke in the ashtray. "I won't bite. Sit down over here if you want."

I gave Junior a smile, and I stayed put as I faked watching the tennis even though I could hardly see the set.

As soon as it went to commercial, I found Gil in the kitchen. "You were never going to rescue me, were you?"

"Nope." He handed me my lemonade.

"He's in a good mood."

"It's Bicentennial parties all weekend and Goldwater's backing Ford for President. The whole Burke family's in a good mood."

"The *whole* family?" I teased. Gil was a Southern Democrat, with pretty strong opinions about Vietnam and Watergate and Jimmy Carter, but at his Republican uncle's house, Gil held his political views close. More than once, I'd seen him glaze over and clam up when the topic of the elections came up at the club. But he'd never step out of line and risk rousing Carpie over politics.

Gil'd always take me through the conversations later, his fingers tight-laced through mine, whispering fiercely as we strode along the dunes. He'd explain how Carter was a real stand-up guy, not "soft" or "fuzzy" like how the Sunkie Republicans slammed him. Then he'd tick through his own plans about how he wanted to become a lawyer for his town, and how he'd represent the shop owners and schoolteachers of Elmore who couldn't afford a strong legal voice.

I melted, listening to him. Gil never seemed so soulful as when he spoke about his plans, and he was just as good at listening to mine—even if my future changed by the day, from marine biologist to news journalist—anything, basically, where I got to travel.

But in the Burke house, Gil obeyed Burke law.

Now I followed Gil up the front staircase, where we locked ourselves in the second-floor rec room. Gil's attic bedroom wasn't an option. We'd tried it, but between the single bed and lacy curtains, it was too old ladyish. Which seemed unfair, since Junior's bedroom was huge, tricked out with a foosball table, a beer-stocked mini fridge, and framed blowup photos of every regatta he'd ever won.

Lip-locked, we fell into a pileup on the saggy sailcloth couch. We were so new to each other that every moment felt like a first. I buried my nose in Gil's shirt, inhaled his beach-salted skin.

"Today's report is that you smell like sunshine," I told him. "I'm also getting a whiff of Coppertone, some mustiness from our crawl space, fabric softener . . ."

"You'd make a good bloodhound." Gil lifted my chin to kiss me.

"I can't help it. You smell terrific."

"*You* smell terrific. What was it again, Lip Smackers and Wella Balsam?"

"Nice data. You'll make a killer lawyer one day, Mr. Burke."

Gil's kisses were expert. One of the many jolting things I'd learned from that blue-plastic photo album—Gil looked like he was eighteen by the time he was in seventh grade. And he'd probably acted like it, too. Sometimes high school guys felt like terriers, all sniff and wag and pant until you had no choice but to push them off. But Gil didn't show me any of that desperation.

Maybe that's why we'd ended up going so far . . .

I folded my arms around his shoulders. Pulled him over me, to feel all his weight. Our mouths met and stayed, and with each kiss came that draggy-melty sensation that there were only the two of us in the world, and that we were the sweetest gifts we could give each other.

From downstairs, Junior yelled curses at the television.

We ignored him.

Junior yelped. Swore, called someone a twat.

On that word, our eyes popped open. We stopped and came apart. Smiling but annoyed. Gil butted the crown of his head into my shoulder in mock frustration. "Cousin Junior, what a charmer."

"Believe me, he wants us to hear him."

"I should probably cut him a break. I'd sure be pissed if my cousin was up here necking with you." He reached over me to pick up my lemonade glass. "He'll head out to the boathouse once the tennis is over." He kept the full press of his weight on me as he drank and replaced the glass. "No matter how close we get," he said softly, looking down at me, "I always want to be closer."

My nerves drew up from my center like a gathering of magnetic filaments to meet his next kiss. Deep in my bones, I knew that I wanted Gil to be my first. I'd probably known from Punch Night, when we'd sat out on that damp beach till midnight. But these past days, opening one by one into our bright, hot, blooming summer, had me at a fever pitch.

Downstairs, Junior bellowed.

I fell back. "He's such a bonehead. You *know* he's doing it on purpose."

"Betcha Nastase's losing. Only Junior would back Nasty." Now Gil clicked the remote control that turned on the Burkes' newest gadget, a Sony TV, no bigger than a toaster oven and battery-rechargeable.

The camera was all over Borg. First in a close-up on his foxy, serious face. Then a cutaway to his slow-motion victory slam over the grass. Then back to Borg, shaking hands and double-kissing officials.

"Wow! He did it!" I sat up.

"And he's only twenty." Gil whistled low as he leaned in to watch, too. "Youngest Wimbledon champ ever. Pretty hot upset—reminds me of Tommy Train cleaning everyone's clocks in the junior volleyball tournament."

"What the—you're comparing Tommy Train's volleyball serve to *Wimbledon*? Ha! Gil Burke, you are turning into a total Sunkie!"

Gil laughed like he was in on the joke, but his eyes were puzzled. "How do you mean?" he asked, after a pause.

"I mean how this place is so soft. Come on, you've seen football in Alabama. I bet even your neighborhood dodge ball game plays harder than Tommy Train. But here at Sunken Haven—he's an animal! Whoa, Tommy's put down his rum punch—watch out for his offensive spike!" We were both laughing now, so I wasn't prepared for the directness of Gil's next question.

"You're not gonna play the Junior Cup rematch this summer, then, are you? Against Jean Custis? Too easy, right?"

"Oh. I don't know."

"I mean, since you got the trophy last year." Gil reached out and curled a twist of my hair around his finger. "Maybe she needs a turn. Make her feel good."

"Listen to you. You're still kinda sweet on Jean, aren't you?"

"Nah. I shouldn't have said that. Play to win. Do what you want. Obviously." Gil's fingers grazed my shoulder blade, and then his hand pressed, warm, down my spine, which had gone rigid at the mention of Jean.

"You still think about that one dumb date, huh."

"It wasn't dumb."

"But do you think about her? I mean, since you had that great time in New York and you kissed her and everything." *Shut up, Fritz.* From time to time I'd bring up Jean to see how he'd react. I hated that I did it. Hated how I poked around it, letting my mistrust nag at me, when Gil never gave me any reason to doubt him.

"You know why I kissed her. I've said why. I kissed her because it was that kinda night."

"*What* kind of night? A night of true confessions and darkest secrets?"

"Fritz, I feel like we've already been over what kind of night it was." Gil seemed to be tugging for the right way to put it. "Jean's a friend. And sure, we had a pretty good vibe in New York. But this was before I even met you."

"The other day I caught her staring at me at the candy store. If looks could kill, I'd be dead on the floor. I'm sure Jean'd take you back anytime."

Gil stretched. Scratched at his stomach lazily. "Why does it feel like you're fishing for compliments here? You know how crazy I am for you. But I'm not gonna say I don't think Jean's sweet or nice or a good time—because she is."

In all my years at Sunken Haven, I'd hardly ever thought about Jean Custis. It was Daphne who was the golden girl—the one I'd have worried Gil might fall for. But this summer, Jean was out from under Daphne's shadow. I'd find myself noticing things about her—her smooth, long neck and straight shoulders, her dewy eyes, those crisp, tailored dresses.

"Jean's great," I said now. "Especially how she thinks it's 1932 instead of 1976." I sounded catty and I hated it. *Drop it, Fritz.* "I love how she says words like *nifty* and *fellow* like she got pulled out of a time capsule."

Gil's fingers found and dug at my ribs, tickling me. "You know, where I'm from, that's called trash talk. And we'd call someone doing it mean as a one-eyed badger."

"Oh, Gil, you nifty fellow, stop tickling me or I'll pee!"

He stopped. We lay side by side, our breath heavy with laughter. Privately, I vowed never to mention Jean Custis again. It brought out something low and a little bit pitiful in me. On the television, Nastase's face was slack with defeat. Why did the camera always linger on the loser?

I clicked the set mute and kissed Gil, and he kissed me back, and then in the next second we were wild all over again, our mouths melding and our bodies pressed up hot and aching for each other.

Gil knew I was his girl. I loved him, but maybe even more important, I understood him. With me, Gil could confess not just politics and ambitions, but the small stuff, too. Like how hick he felt when Junior made fun of his accent in front of Carp and Weeze, imitating how Gil said "caint" or "turrble" or "*in*surance." He told me how his stepdad was the worst kind of redneck who used to rough him up, and how he'd never imagined he'd get this shot at bettering himself, he was so used to his stepdad's voice in his ear. Gil knew Carpie was hard on him, too—but the idea that Carpie truly cared made all the difference, in Gil's mind.

I might have had a loving family instead of a jerk stepfather, but I knew how much it meant to be self-made. With Gil, I could explain how my dad enlisted for Korea right out of high school, then met my mom in a Laundromat when he was stationed at Camp Bullis and she was barely out of her teens. They'd built a solid life together, buying a dining room set on layaway and every year saving up enough for a family vacation, and they wanted even more for Kevin and me—college, for one. My mom was proud of my being here at Sunken Haven, and my friendship with a high-class girl like Julia Tulliver, because it meant I'd been brought up right. It meant I knew how to hold a fork and shake hands. Not even Julia could fully understand these things. Gil did.

"You want to meet me after my lunch shift?" I asked, after we'd let go of each other. "I'll be off by three."

Gil paused a long pause. "Tiger wants to hit Floyd's Clam Shack and then shoot hoops."

"Your loss."

Celebrations were revving up on TV. "Damn. Bjorn Borg's

only a year older than me," Gil said. "Now he'll be rich and famous forever." The jealousy in Gil's voice took me by surprise.

"You're doing okay. The Burkes have adopted you for the bargain basement price of your soul."

Gil went quiet.

From downstairs, we heard the front door open.

"I'm hoooome," sang Weeze.

"Time to hit the road," I muttered, as I reached under my shirt and rehooked my bra from where Gil had just as deftly unhooked it. "Tomorrow's the Fourth of July," I reminded him. "A big night."

A perfect night for *that*. For *us*.

"It's gonna be rowdy." This was Gil's semicoded way of saying "we still don't have a place of our own."

We both wanted our first time to be special. Nothing was going to happen here in the Burkes' rec room. Or out on the briny, bug-biting dunes, or up in the Morgue, with its boiling heat and plywood walls.

"Last week was fun, searching. Like that B and B in Robbins Rest."

Gil nodded. "That place looked good. Not too rundown. What was it called?"

"George's," I said. I finished tucking myself into my waitress clothes. "We could look again this afternoon. Put down a deposit."

Gil sat up. Cracked his knuckles. "It doesn't have to be tomorrow, Fritzie. Right? I'm okay with it not being tomorrow."

"Tomorrow's the Bicentennial. It's sort of a big-deal day already. Don't you think?" I glanced down, tying the strings of my waitressing apron. I was shy to meet Gil's eye. The words were hard to find. "I don't mean to sound overly practical. But the Bicentennial's the one night nobody'll notice if we stay out till Monday morning."

When I looked up, Gil was staring at me. He nodded yes, but I sensed he wasn't all the way there yet. "All I mean is that if it doesn't work out for tomorrow . . . July Fourth is just another Sunday."

"You don't feel like I'm pressuring you, do you?" I spoke in a tough-guy voice.

"No, but . . . I know it's a heavy thing for girls," he answered, serious.

"It's heavy for you, too, right?"

"Sure me, too. But it also feels like my responsibility. To get us right."

It was a new thought. Would this be Gil's first time, too? I'd never asked, and he'd never offered me any specifics.

Or maybe it was the opposite situation, and Gil had been with lots of girls, and he knew exactly how unspecial sex could be, so he wanted it to be perfect?

Funny thing about Gil—I could easily imagine the truth both ways.

"Four o'clock," he said, suddenly. "Okay? We'll go on a ride. Outside Sunken Haven. Head back to Robbins Rest, make a reservation, deposit, whatever you do."

"Yes!" I moved toward him, hooped my arms around him. "Yes times a hundred."

"You're such an amazing girl, Fritz," he whispered. "I don't want to screw us up. Especially something like this."

I let my chin drop back to steady him in my gaze. "It kind of knocks me out how you care this much."

Gil's slow, answering smile charged me to my highest voltage. "Meet me at the gate. We'll go check out George's again. I've got a good feeling."

One last head-spinning kiss. Then I snuck out, down the stairs, rippling a wave good-bye but not stopping for Junior, and steering well clear of the kitchen, where Weeze was fixing up her usual, a pitcher of martinis. Slipping out the door and vamoosing before she caught sight of me. Last time I was here, she'd made a point of asking me to remember to call her Mrs. Burke, even though the entire island referred to her as Weeze.

And even when I apologized, she still looked peeved.

I cringed to recall it. Sure, Weeze didn't like outsiders. Everyone knew that. She'd be pleased as punch if Gil ever dropped me for Jean. It was dumb to dwell on what I couldn't change. But lord love a duck, when had I ever sneaked out of a Sunken Haven home in broad daylight? How had it come to this?

I straddled my bike and took one last look around me, the long grass bending in the wind, the salty taste of Gil's kiss on my lips, the burn of the sun reminding me of our own heat. I wouldn't let that snob Weeze Burke wreck my day. Her view was overrated, and her nephew belonged to me.

JEAN

"You know how life's got these gray areas . . ."

It was a secret between us. Then it was a lot of secrets between us.

The first secret of that night was my virginity.

I knew it had shocked him.

"There's blood," Gil had whispered to me.

He'd held his fingers up to the window. Moonlight had spilled a heavy glow through the dormer window onto the bed sheet.

I'd seen the blood, too. My head had been reeling on that hard single mattress. I knew the blood had come from me. I hadn't known what to say, so I hadn't said anything. The New York sophisticate had flown. It hadn't occurred to me that Gil would get to find out it was my first time. I hadn't thought about *evidence*.

I'd been so caught up in being the girl who'd brought the bottle of Beefeater's.

But I'd also sneaked in the purity, and the complications along with it.

I hadn't even fully processed what I'd just done. I'd been fixated on the sting between my legs. I hadn't touched the condom, and Gil hadn't let me near it after he was done, though I'd seen him use his hand to keep it in place as he'd pulled out. Everything inside me felt slippery and peeled, and I couldn't settle my thoughts into any one complete reaction.

"I better go," was the next thing I'd ended up saying.

Gil had sat up, modestly bunching the sheet as he bent to scoop his sweatpants off the floor and wriggle into them as quick as he could. He picked up my clothes and passed them to my outstretched arms. "Let me walk you to your bike."

Outside, he'd hugged me for a long time. I'd let myself bask in the full-body heat of him. But his hug also meant the end of everything. The end of us. Garbled as my head felt, I was not too drunk to understand. He'd kissed me on my cheek and forehead, not my lips. He'd had me and now was refusing me, all in the same night.

When he'd stepped back, I could tell how strange he felt about it.

"We're still friends, right?" I'd asked, clumsily.

"Aw, Jean. You know we're friends. Better than friends."

But I'd returned to Lazy Days in a fog of gin and regret.

The next morning, I had been so nervous about running into Gil that I'd made my parents late for church. We'd slipped in during the first reading and taken the last pew, closest to the exit. I'd been terrified of the prechurch chitchat, of pretending with any of the Burkes that everything was normal.

Throughout the service, I'd stared at the back of Gil's head, my heart thudding, wondering what was going through his mind. Was he even thinking about me at all?

I'd bolted home afterward, sneaking away from my parents before I had to endure the postservice social. I'd been so sure I'd run into Gil at Tiger's grill-out birthday party later that afternoon, I had called Bertie to change plans, and we'd biked all the way over to Ocean Park to see *Taxi Driver* instead.

Bertie was always happy with any plan I made with him—even if it meant skipping a big party.

"Are you okay, Jean?" he'd asked, over pizza, after. "You've been so quiet."

"I'm A-ok. I'm great."

But I hadn't been okay. My emotions had ricocheted between furious and depressed. Thinking about Gil and Fritz together at Tiger's had made me want to slug someone. It wasn't Bertie's fault, I'd reminded myself.

Home again, behind the gate, I let Bertie take me to the dunes to make out. It was as if I wanted to test how unexciting it was with Bertie, after being with Gil.

I also felt guilty, of course. I'd betrayed Bertie. I'd gone and had sex with Gil on a — what? Drunken whim? Desperate last resort? Gossamer hope that Gil would think that our time together was irresistible, and show up here on my doorstep, pledging his undying love for me?

I might not be a virgin anymore, but I was still a childish daydreamer.

That night, I lay sleepless all night in an agony of self-questioning.

Did Gil hate what we'd done? What was our status now?

I had to know.

And so the next morning, after breakfast, I biked to the bay, where Gil was teaching Minnows. Sitting with my book, I kept myself at a distance on the sandbanks, near the boathouse. Not bothering him. Unless my very presence was a bother?

Gil didn't seem preoccupied by me. He smiled and waved.

"Hey, Jean. How's it going?"

Still friends. Just as he'd promised. But then he kept himself busy. He turned a shoulder away from me while he was in the water. He never caught my eye, not once, maintaining a purposeful stride to and from the boathouse supply shed that stored the boogie boards and arm floaties.

After class, I kept an eye on him as he struck up an intense conversation with Tiger, centering himself tight in Tiger's focus so that they could leave together. Something about the way he kept his back to me seemed purposeful.

I went home sick with frustration, with feelings I couldn't explain to anyone, or even to myself.

The next day, I showed up at the bank again, and Gil was plain startled. He avoided looking at me until the end of class. Then he put up a hand and snapped me a wave that was almost like a salute as he and Tiger ambled off, talking sports.

I knew Gil figured I was making a scene. But I thought about him so much, could it be that he really never thought about me? What had he imagined I was going to do, drift away from him? I couldn't.

Even if I must have seemed a bit unbalanced, hunting him down.

Less than three weeks ago, things had been so easy between us. But now Gil was quicksand, and any time I spent near him only got me in worse and deeper trouble.

When I showed up at Minnows on Wednesday, Gil waited until the end of class, and then he made a beeline for me. There'd been a set to his body, a force to the way he planted his feet in front of me, like a soldier reporting for duty.

"How's it going, Jean? I kept thinking you'd come over and talk. So I've let you be. But maybe you don't want to be the one to come over." He paused. "So here I am. Did you want to say something to me?"

"No, not really," I lied. And then I couldn't speak.

But I wasn't tough. I barely knew how to act tough.

Of course he knew I wanted to talk.

"It's just," I began again. "This thing." I swallowed. My nerves felt like steel bands around my throat. "This thing that we did. It feels like a big thing."

"Yeah, I know," he said, softly. "It's been on my mind."

"Listen, I don't regret it."

"God. I mean, good, I mean, Jean, Jesus, I had no idea—I didn't know you were a—"

"No, no." I waved his words away. "I didn't want you to know. I didn't think it was worth mentioning that I'd never—anyway, you're off the hook." My laugh was tinny. "I'm sorry to keep showing up here. But I don't know how to feel okay about what we did, because I don't. Feel okay, that is," I finished miserably, picking at the edge of the denim skirt I'd finally chosen after half an hour of debating what to wear for him.

"Can I tell you something?" His eyes crinkled with his smile. "I don't feel so great about it, either." Then he laughed. "Boy, it feels good to say that out loud. Hey, you wanna go somewhere?" He reached for my hands and pulled me up off the sand. "Someplace we can hang out? I think we can—I think we *should*—deal with this better than how we've done. Sound like a plan?"

"Yes. Oh my gosh, yes!" I could feel relief expanding through my whole body. Friends. Better than friends. "What about the von Cott house? It's closed this summer, but I have a key."

"Ha, of course you do. And I've been wanting to scope out that place since the fake party." He winked at my obvious embarrassment.

"I've got some lunch, if you're hungry." I'd packed it almost to dare myself. It was the same bag I'd used to bring the gin and tonics the other night. Now it held a couple of innocent sandwiches and a thermos of limeade.

But if Gil thought I'd been presumptuous, he didn't let on.

"Perfect" was all he said. Taking my knapsack and swinging it over his shoulder. A gentlemanly gesture that filled me with gratitude. He *was* kind. He *did* care. Or at least he wanted me to think that he did.

Lunch became another secret between us.

No gin. Nothing sexy—so far. Just lunch together on Wednesday.

Then Thursday, and then next Monday, Wednesday, and again on Friday.

If anyone had been watching us, they wouldn't have seen so much as a stolen kiss. As for why Gil kept agreeing to meet or to make a plan—was it his guilty conscience? Did he think I'd run and tell everyone about what we'd done together, and how he'd been a cad about it, if he didn't keep me happy?

No, I concluded. It wasn't all guilt. It wasn't only to soothe my feelings. It was because the spark between Gil and me hadn't died. If the whole summer was like this, that would be enough. Me, waiting on Looking Glass Lane, bringing my book and knapsack to the bench beneath a sugar maple. Gil, strolling over after Minnows to pick me up. Looking Glass Lane was unused and far away enough that we never ran the risk of being seen together. Even if a tiny part of me wouldn't have minded the gossip, the issue of Gil's trust was by far the more important.

At the von Cotts', we shared another picnic on their deck roof while catching up on general news: movies and music and regattas and tennis.

As usual, we didn't discuss Fritz.

As usual, we didn't speak of our night together.

If these were Gil's rules, I was ready to play by them. Seeing him every day was enough reward. And Gil himself seemed comfortable enough with the arrangement that today, watching him drink from the Thermos I'd brought, his eyes closed and his hair starting to curl out a little wild, like a young lion, I let my mind wander. Maybe these lunches were Gil's shifting toward a realization that while Fritz might remind him of some hometown fun, I was ultimately his real and better choice?

I didn't let myself get too carried away with it, but it was hard not to hope.

These past days, no matter what had been in my schedule, tennis and tea, beach parties or backgammon, I could always count on a secret little marker of joy for the next time I got to see Gil. Even in those painful moments when I'd spy him going around with Fritz—the two of them playing beach volleyball or riding bikes or strolling a path or sharing an ice cream—as awful as those run-ins were, I could hold my head high, because I knew that sometimes he was my Gil, too.

"So, Monday, then?" he asked, as we gathered the plates, the Thermos and napkins. "If we all survive this weekend and aren't still barfing up red, white, and blue."

"I'm already looking forward to it."

And I was. Monday was a twinkling diamond in the plain band of my weekend. It didn't matter that I'd be spending most of it with Bertie, if I secretly belonged to Gil.

"Something's going on with you, Jean. You've been like the cat that ate the canary," Rosamund mentioned, the next day. We were all at Bertie's, in the shade of the verandah, testing Mr. and Mrs. Forsythe's new low-slung Indonesian teakwood patio furniture that everyone thought looked strange but was carefully complimenting anyway. Morning tennis was over, and there was nothing to do but sit with the girls and breathe through the blue haze of charred ribs.

"Yes, Rosamund's right. You're being strange." Sara's eyes were still red from last night's conversation with Tiger, who'd finally had to sit her down and let her know that no matter how furiously she flirted with him, she had absolutely no chance. "Strangely happy," she concluded.

"What's there for me to be unhappy about?"

"I guess that's true. You really are the luckiest of us. Bertie's such a love," said Sara dolefully, as we watched the guys fooling around at the grill, basting and flipping. "Can't you see him as a dad? He'll be so sweet with your kids."

"I really wish you wouldn't talk like that, Sara." I sighed and stretched and shifted in my chair so that I didn't have to see Bertie. "You make me feel like we're all thirty. We're not old and bald just yet!"

"Heigh-ho, Young Miss—I heard that!" Mr. Forsythe looked up from where he was reading, on the other end of the porch, rattling his paper as he mock shook his fist. Mr. Forsythe was mostly bald, and at the moment, he looked so much like Bertie, it felt like a knife in my heart.

"There's morning showers predicted for tomorrow," said Sara. "And then it dries out."

"'Into each life, some rain must fall,'" I quoted.

Rosamund scrunched her nose. "See, that's exactly what I'm talking about. You're not yourself, Jean."

"As long as I'm all right," I said lightly. "Am I all right, Rosamund?"

Rosamund shrugged. She didn't like my question; she thought I wasn't taking her seriously—and I wasn't.

Because there was nothing wrong with me. Maybe I couldn't tell her my best secret, but whatever else the others thought of me, I was more myself than I'd ever been.

FRITZ

"Nothing gold can stay."

"Ah, you're the best. Goddess of the breakfast run." Julia leaned up in her bed and squinted out the window. "It looks so dark out. Is it raining on our Bicentennial?"

"Just drops. Here ya go. Extra ketchup, no pepper." I reached into the paper bag and tossed her a foil-wrapped egg and cheese on a roll, our latest breakfast obsession, compliments of the deli section of the grocery store.

Then I got back in my own bed. We chowed blissfully. "There's so much sand in my bed, it's like I'm sleeping in a sugar donut." Julia brushed out a few crumbs, then wiped her fingers with a paper napkin. "But I'm not gonna shower till after we swim."

"Me, either. I could eat, like, six more of these." I popped the last eggy-cheesy bite in my mouth. "Is Oliver setting up at the beach this morning?"

"Yeah. Gil, too, I'm sure. All the able-bodied dudes report for duty."

"I love the Fourth. The food, fireworks."

"You're definitely getting some fireworks tonight!" Julia gave me a smirk as she balled and tossed the foil wrapper, missing the trash basket by a laughable distance, then swung out of bed and pulled on her bathing suit. "I'll dump all our junk into one beach bag, okay?"

"Yeah, great." I got up, too, to help her grab for stuff—lemon-juice spritzer for lightening our hair, cocoa butter, a few of the loose A&W's we kept stored on the bookshelf. "Hey, Jules. Answer me this. When you see Tiger, are you okay with it?"

"With what?"

"You know. That you did it. With him, I mean."

"Do I regret that I had sex with Tiger?" She stuck a comb and a pack of fruit-stripe gum in the bag's side pocket. "No. The opposite, probably."

"You never wish your first time could have been with Oliver instead?"

"Not really. Last summer, I was so into Tiger, don't you remember?"

"So you did it because you wanted *Tiger*? Or because you were ready?"

Julia had to think a minute on that. "Both, I guess. No

regrets." Now she lifted an eyebrow and made her hand into a microphone. "Fritz O' Neill, will you tell our studio audience and all the folks watching at home, are you and Gil Burke thinking seriously about *going all the way*?"

It was my turn to quirk my eyebrows. I couldn't do the classy one-brow lift like Julia. "Wanna know a secret?"

"Spill it."

"Hang on." I went and listened at the door to make sure none of the girls were lingering in the hallway. "I think tonight, this might be Gil's first time, too."

"Gil the Thrill? No, no way!" Julia clapped a hand over her mouth as her eyes rounded in disbelief. "Uh-uh. He's so old! How do you know?"

"I don't. But he says things. He wants everything to be perfect. And yesterday afternoon, we biked out to this bed and breakfast place in Robbins Rest . . ."

"Fritz, the minute this goes down, I want every single detail."

"I don't know—it feels so weird to talk about. Even with you."

"You can't get all secretive. Not with me, when I'd tell you anything about me and Tiger—or me and Oliver—if you wanted."

"Okay, okay." I couldn't deny that going all the way with Gil was all I was thinking about. It was also a relief to tell Julia, and to get her approval—not that I thought for a second she wouldn't give it.

"Let's swing by Thriffaney's before the movie," she said, on our way out. "I need rickrack for my minidress."

"No sweat."

Thriffaney's was a tiny secondhand shop near the harbor, just by the six-foot chain-link fence topped by two feet of barbed wire that separated Sunken Haven from Ocean Bay.

As we propped our bikes against the fence, I saw Floyd's Clam Shack on the other side. It wasn't even ten o'clock and there was a brunch crowd. People were braving the spitting rain to dine on plastic patio furniture. Even though I'd just eaten, my mouth watered for a Floyd's lobster roll. I hadn't had one since last summer. These days, lunch was usually an after-shift grilled cheese at the club. Gil and Tiger sometimes enjoyed a chow-down at Floyd's together after Minnows class, but I'd never been invited. Gil had made it pretty clear it was a guy thing.

Mrs. Walt had started Thriffaney's after Mr. Walt died, and it was open whenever she was in the mood—and always on Sundays, because she never went to church. I'd heard she was still annoyed with God for stealing her husband. The cottage was a dumping ground of secondhand stuff, with profits going to Sunken Haven's treasury. One dollar got you christening blankets stained with baby spit-up, or an entire shelf of chipped plates. The only new items Thriffaney's sold were sewing supplies and matches.

Mrs. Walt was in her usual spot, smoking and playing solitaire behind the register. "There's no money in the strongbox. Unless you have exact change, you'll need to use your house account," she said, without looking up from her cards. Mrs. Walt hated that I used cash, and she always made sure I knew it.

"Not a problem, Mrs. Walt," said Julia sweetly.

I went straight for the display case. Sometimes there were fun costume pieces here, castoffs from Sunkie moms cleaning out their jewelry boxes. The other day I'd bought a puka-shell bracelet to take back for my mom, and that's when I'd seen those earrings.

"They're not here," I said.

"You looking for the emeralds?" Mrs. Walt shuffled her cards and cut the deck. "They got snapped up. They were too valuable. 'Nothing gold can stay,'" she added, in a quavering recital voice.

"But they weren't *real*," I said. "They weren't emeralds."

Mrs. Walt looked up to make sure I saw her disapproving face. "They're as real as you want them to be."

"Or as real as fake things can be," I said softly, as Julia trotted over with her tape of rickrack, which she signed to her parents' account.

"Is this for your mom?" Mrs. Walt asked her.

"No, it's a project for me. I'm jazzing up an old dress."

"Lovely. You inherited her knack for . . ." Mrs. Walt suddenly looked unsure of herself. "You must have caught the bug from watching her." Her teeth raked at her bottom lip, as she returned to her cards.

We banged outside. Thunder was rumbling in from the ocean. A patter of rain on the porch roof almost instantly joined it. Real rain, this time.

"Did you hear that? I *did* inherit it," said Julia. "The reason I like to sew is because Mom does."

"Of course you did. Come on."

But Julia stood there, staring into the rain, piecing a twist through her hair.

"Don't let batty old Mrs. Walt get to you."

"I'm not."

"Let's sit," I suggested. "We'll wait it out."

Julia nodded.

All at once, rain was dumping down in buckets. We could hear the whoops from Floyd's as dockside customers ran into the restaurant for cover. We plopped on the top step of Thriffaney's porch. "I grew up watching Mom sew," said Julia, "learning patterns and stitches from her."

"Mrs. Walt's a loon."

"I could practically see the flashing neon sign in her head: 'Julia's adopted! Julia's adopted!' It always reminds me about what happened with me and Jean. I mean, I'm past it," she added quickly. "Or maybe, mostly past it. But then it hits . . ."

"*Jean*? What does Jean Custis have to do with you being adopted?"

"You know that stupid story."

"No, I don't know that stupid story. I never heard it. Tell me."

Julia dropped her chin in her hands and looked across. I followed her gaze to a view of rain and chain link. From this angle, we could have been in a prison yard. Sunken Haven was the only village on Fire Island that had built a Keep Out wall. Today it looked especially harsh.

"Okay," she started, shaking her head like she was clearing the cobwebs. "So remember how I told you, the summer before you first started coming here, that Jean and I had been good pals?"

"Kinda," I said. "But then you had a fight or something?"

"It wasn't really a fight."

"Jean stopped being friends because she found out you were adopted?"

"No, *I* stopped being friends with *her*, because she went and *told* everyone I was adopted. Mom and Dad hadn't said anything to anyone, and you can guess why. *Adopted* at Sunken Haven isn't the same as *adopted* on an army base. There's tons of adopted kids in the army. But hardly any here. That we know of, anyway."

I nodded. Sunken Haven was all about celebrating your excellent bloodlines. Adopted kids could sort of interfere with that enjoyment. "But what's Jean got to do with any of it?"

"She was spending the night, and we were up late. I told her I'd been adopted back when Dad was stationed in Germany. I didn't say it as a secret. But she knew it was private. And then the next day, Jean blabbed it to *everyone*.

"By lunch all the Minnows knew, and they were teasing me, talking in pretend German, asking if my 'real' parents were Nazis. I got upset, naturally, and I went crying to my mom, and she was so mad. There are people here, like the Burkes, who took it so far as to tell Mom they felt like she'd lied, trying to 'pass me off' as theirs." It was rare for me to see Julia lose her composure, but I could sense the memory ran deep in her.

"Sunkies are snobs about the dumbest stuff," I said quietly. "It shouldn't have any shock value left, but it always surprises me what they care about."

"Me, too."

"Come on, let's go. I'm sure everyone's at the casino by now. And by the way, thanks for that story, because I didn't even *need* another reason not to like Jean Custis!" I made a face, and was glad for Julia's answering laugh as we grabbed our bikes and dashed out into the downpour.

"Yeah, I know how much you love her. That story was just a freebie. But what I always say about Jean, she's her own worst enemy," said Julia. "She steps right into it, and then she can't get rid of the smell, you know?"

Gusts of rain had made puddles around the tennis courts, sending wavelets in both directions as our bikes cut down Ridge, making us squeal as water splashed our shins. Sunken Haven was never prepared for bad weather. Every thunderstorm flooded out the stiles and caused a boatload of damage that volunteer crews went out and rebuilt like happy beavers.

As we turned in to the casino, bikes were doubling back from Ocean Walk, while a few kids, still in their Sunday best, were heading over from church. Inside, the door and windows were taped up with red, white, and blue crepe paper, in preparation for the informal dinner tonight.

"They're making us watch some dopey chick thing!" Oliver called.

"Marcy said it was *Love Story,*" Julia called back. "A classic."

"Classic means speeches and somebody bites it at the end," said Oliver. Some other guys were also grumbling about why did it always have to be a tampon movie, but mostly everyone was ducking inside to watch it.

Gil wheeled up soaked. "Happy July Fourth, baby."

Today was the day. Tonight was the night. The perfection of this moment, as he kissed me, was all about the promise of more.

"Barbecue starts after the movie," he whispered. "Maybe hang out in the afternoon, and take off around sundown?"

"Cool."

"Let me go help Coach Hutch store his equipment."

I looked over to Coach, who was skidding along the wet courts, dealing with ball hoppers and carts. Nobody else was bothering to help. "Meetcha inside."

"Right on."

In the casino's main room, lights had been dimmed and the *Love Story* soundtrack roared murkily from the speakers. Julia and Oliver already had tucked themselves up into a private back corner.

As I scouted for a place, I saw Jean, Sara, and Rosamund a few rows up—ugh, no, thanks. Not there. Junior Burke and his regatta crew were all sprawled along the back seats—not there, either. Some of Gil's buddies, including Tiger, were scattered in twos and threes—nope; and some of the Ocean Beach girls, Marissa and Kath and Donna—nope, nope, nope.

I stood trapped in the middle of the aisle like a worried giraffe. Just then, Jean Custis turned all the way around in her seat and launched me with her thousand-mile stare.

Whoa.

It was like a flashback to last summer. Jean across the court. Her face burnt with sun and strain. Her hounding, opponent's eyes. Was her expression also strangely, smugly knowing? Like maybe she even knew what Gil and I were planning for tonight?

No. That was ridiculous.

But it put some starch in my spine that Jean believed she could look at me that way. As if she had the right. She certainly had the nerve.

Well, I had some nerve of my own. I took her challenge, forcing myself to hold her stare across the room until she caved first, ducking her head and whispering something to Rosamund, who flipped around to look at me, before she whispered something back to Jean. Lordy, it was so eighth-grade cafeteria here.

When Gil reappeared, shaking off water like a dog, I felt rescued. He hardly gave a thought to choosing where we should sit—which was plop in front of Julia and Oliver and on a back-diagonal from Jean and her girls. Once he picked it, the choice seemed exactly right, and I couldn't believe I'd put myself through all the stupid doubt.

"What'd I miss?" Gil hissed. He folded his fingers through mine as he checked in with the screen. "Hey, is this an ice-hockey flick? *Ice Hockey: A Love Story*?"

"No dice. Doomed love between a nerd and a jock who happens to play ice hockey."

"Aw, a nerd and a jock." Gil nudged against me. "Like me and you."

I stifled a laugh, then got comfy to watch the film, even though I'd seen it half a dozen times already.

When I knocked my knee against his, Gil leaned over and quick-kissed me in that joke way, palming my head, with a stamp of his lips over each of my closed eyelids. Like he was performing some kind of miracle for the blind. It wasn't till after I'd resettled that I saw Jean turn away.

Wow times two. She'd been watching us.

But now she must have sensed I had my eye on her.

My heart was pounding, but she didn't turn around.

At the movie's ending hospital scene, my idea popped me off my folding chair. I'd give Jean Custis something to watch, if she wanted to stare. "Come find me, after," I whispered to Gil, before I crept off to the back of the room, where Junior was still slouched, his legs stretched and his hands cradled behind his head.

"Hey," I whispered.

"O'Neill." His bored expression didn't fool me. I knew how much Junior was loving my coming over to speak with him. "What gives?"

"I know how this flick ends. Want to hit a few around?"

"Why not?" In the next second, he was out of his seat and leading the way.

My first summers here, Coach Hutch had teamed me up against Junior, who'd always been torn between enjoying time with me and resenting that I could crush him. But now Junior was psyched that I'd picked him all on my own. On our way out, he grabbed a fresh can of balls from the supply shelf.

Then we slipped though the archway that led to the casino's indoor court. Junior and I weren't in regulation whites, and we hadn't signed up for a time. But that didn't matter—nobody was around to stop us. As I took a ball and squeezed another into my back pocket, my muscle memory primed me for my serve.

My serve was one of my strengths. I set my weight heavy on my back foot and let the random racquet I'd picked up off the shelf fall loose over my shoulder. It was a longer fallback than Coach liked. My toss was higher than most, too. But I knew my spans, my lengths and widths, and when I slammed the ball in a roar across the court, Junior had to lunge to neutralize my topspin.

Lessons are one thing. But nobody can instruct that killer groove of tennis, the gut and soul of how to chase that ball all over the court, how to let your body free itself to take its chances.

And that's the piece I knew best.

Junior and I were all warmed up and at it hard, by the time the movie ended. Yawning kids, drawn by the sound of the game, drifted in and stayed. A few dropped into the small section of bleachers. Eventually Jean came in. I caught her eye in my periphery. She was sandwiched between Rosamund and Sara, all of them in courtside chairs, everyone looking faintly bored, like they had better things to do. But wild horses wouldn't have dragged them away. Sunken Haven was tennis crazy, and I was looking good.

Next inside was Gil. I had to hold my focus, playing a classic Chris Evert two-handed backhand with more power than I'd had last summer. Probably I'd gotten stronger from carrying all those heavy yacht-club waitressing trays. I felt fierce, charging that ball, making Junior work for it by slamming it or popping it so it died right over the net.

Jean hadn't seen me on the courts yet this year. I'd taken to playing night games with Oliver, over on the Olmsteads' private court, while Julia watched. Oliver was a solid player. He was the one who'd told me that he'd heard people speculating, since last year's victory, that I'd publicly dropped the game cold. I'd never even attended a single clinic, group lesson, or weekend mixed doubles.

But the truth was this: I wasn't planning to sign up to compete for the cup until the last minute. And I was doing it because I wanted to give Jean ants in her pants. I'd been practicing enough with Oliver; come next month, I'd smack her backward. And after a stare-down like she'd just given me, I didn't see the harm in letting Jean Custis—and everyone else—know that I was still number one.

Junior always slammed his returns. I was faster and more nimble. Over and over, I drove him to the net. Our volleys heated up. When I won the next point, I knew I had the room hooked. I won a game, Junior took the next, and then I squeaked the third in a nail-biting double advantage. When I took the set, the bleachers were a crash of applause.

Junior grinned and bowed, a signal that he was done. He was okay with stopping in the white-hot bang of the middle, if it meant he could save face. As I twirled my racquet and swept off court, Gil was right there, lunging for my waist and lifting me into a spin. He was still rain damp and I was slick with sweat, and we came together like we'd choreographed it.

"Stone fox!" he whispered, then he kissed me long and hard on the lips. "I've never even seen you play, do you realize? You are some absolute magic, baby."

I didn't even bother to look at Jean. Not till after we'd all spilled out the doors. The rain had stopped and an afternoon breeze was sucking up the muggy air with a promise of sun blazing behind the clouds.

When I did glance over at her, my insides twisted. Jean's face was still, like a statue. Only her eyes betrayed her fury. Maybe it was partly because of the tennis. Maybe it was partly because of Gil. But I knew that all of her despised me.

I saw it and there was no unseeing it.

JEAN

"If you were mine, I'd never let you go!"

I pretended I wanted a shower, but what I really needed was a little time. Just to collect myself.

To anyone watching me, I must have seemed just fine. I sat as still as a doll in my white folding chair. Where I watched Fritz play a more powerful, agile, and surefooted set of tennis than I could ever hope to land. She hadn't even practiced since she'd been here. She knew I knew that. She played to spite me. Even if there was no way I could prove that, I was sure it was true.

I heard the crowd go wild. I watched Junior look across the net at her as if he wanted to lick her up like an ice-cream cone. And then, worst of all, I watched Gil cross the court and lift her and kiss her with a passion that was completely different from the way he'd ever touched me. I'd been like a glass figurine to him. A china girl. Fritz was something else. I watched him hold her in his arms. I watched him say something in her ear.

They fit together like a pair of athletes, but with the grace of dancers. Gelsey and Misha, my mother would have called them. For a moment, I fell into a kind of horrified, baffled love with both of them. His tanned hand pressed to her flat, freckled back. His passionate, movie-star kiss. Her hair spinning out like parade streamers as he spun her. His secret in her ear.

We all were watching them, frozen in the moment. We were all licking them up. But when the moment passed, all I wanted to do was to escape. I made some excuses to the others and told them I'd catch up with them later, on the beach.

Coming into the house, I saw my mother on the phone, in the position she took by our living room window when she'd caught sight of Baryshnikov—her feet planted, one hand on her hip, her smile unhinging her face, her fixed stare slightly popeyed with delight.

"Well, for Pete's sake, I didn't think anyone was noticing," she was saying, but she sounded very pleased that someone had noticed—whatever it was. "Oh, of course. I'd be happy to. It's really nothing, I learned it at Friday Evenings, this little dance class Mother—Daphne's grandmother—forced me to attend." Flirty, I realized. Mom's voice was flirty.

"Who is that?"

Mom put a hand on the receiver. "The Burke boy."

My heart gave a little shudder. "The Burke boy" was Gil. Funny how Gil had so quickly replaced Junior as the Burke boy. Funny—yet unsurprising.

Why was he calling me?

Mom wasn't relinquishing the phone in a hurry. She laughed at something else Gil said. Waited. Said, "Oh, stop!" and laughed again. And then, finally, she remembered herself. "Now, I don't want to keep you another moment from Daphne, because she's just walked in. See you later! Bye-bye!"

"You mean Jean," I whispered. My mother blinked. "You said Daphne. Twice."

"I did? Oh! Sorry, darling." She passed me the receiver, with the gleam still lighting her face. "Something about that boy must remind me of your sister."

This was already an embarrassing call, and I hadn't spoken a word to him yet. I put the phone to my ear. "Hello?"

"Your mom says she'll teach me to foxtrot next time there's a dinner dance at the club. She's great."

"She's something." I watched her skim out the doors into the garden for lunch with Dad. "Happy Fourth." I took a breath. "I saw you, earlier." Kissing your girlfriend, in front of me.

"Yeah, I saw you leave, and I'm real glad I caught you." Gil's words were rapid. "I don't mean to come at you, but I've got some free time before we all hit the beach. Could we meet in half an hour or so? Same place? Just us, and not long?"

I was silent. No, I wanted to say. What I wanted was our

Monday, and I didn't want it rushed. Something was off with Gil's tone and his request, something misshapen, and I didn't know how to push it back into form.

"I mean, I know it's a crazy day, if you've already got plans—"

"Half an hour is fine."

"Cool, see you then."

"Yes." I hung up and stared unhappily at the phone.

Why did he need to see me so urgently?

I found Mrs. Otis, asked her to pack a quick lunch for two, then ran upstairs, showered, and rummaged like a thief through my closet until I chose a teal, arrowhead-pattern sundress that Bertie said brought out my eyes. I was walking briskly down Looking Glass Lane with minutes to spare.

"Hey, there! Thanks for coming on short notice!" Gil stood up from the bench.

"I was just glad to get the phone out of Mom's hands."

Gil laughed. He looked awfully relaxed. I tried to relax, too. Maybe he'd needed to see me simply because he'd wanted to see me! Did everything have to be so complicated? Maybe he'd felt as terrible as I did that he'd kissed Fritz in public, and he wanted to make sure everything was all right between us.

Looking Glass Lane was the one path on Sunken Haven where the trees sprang tall, their cathedral canopies shutting out so much sunshine it felt like twilight all day long. The von Cott house was visible over the footbridge.

"Did you know that pond below is freshwater?" My nerves

made me chatty, as I ran my fingers over the bumpy wooden rail, still damp from the morning downpour. "People always assume it's salt, but it's not. It's made by rain. Freshwater trees and plants aren't the same as what can grow in a salt marsh, that's why all the vegetation along here is different."

Gil stopped to heave the burden of my knapsack from my shoulder over to his. Then he smiled at me, that hero's smile that thrilled me to my toes. "You sound like a troop leader for the Girl Scouts."

"I like these trees," I said. "I like all the history of Sunken Haven."

"I've been meaning to ask," Gil said as we continued walking. "Do you know the real ghost story? The legend of Hairy Hand? Tiger and Junior were being pricks the other day, not telling me. They said I gotta be here ten summers to hear it."

"I know it from my grandfather, who swore his version is the most authentic." I was happy to show off a story I didn't remember *not* knowing. "It used to scare me to death as a child."

Gil snorted. "Try me."

"Okay, so about a hundred years ago, after a storm took their boats off course, a traveling circus found lodging right here on Sunken Haven. An ape and his trainer were put up for the night, and everyone went to see a 'moving picture show' on another part of the island. The ape was chained up in a house, but he got scared in the storm, and he knocked over a nearby oil lamp.

"When everyone returned, there was nothing left of the house but smoke and charred wood and—" My voice sounded strange in my ears, chattering on and on like a squirrel in the woods. None of the words I was saying had anything to do with what I really wanted to talk about. I cleared my throat. "—the ape's hand, still chained, smoldering in its water dish. Some say on a dark October night, you can hear it scuttling along Looking Glass Lane. Searching for its body."

Gil burst out laughing. "That's it?"

"It's scarier when you're an eight-year-old."

Even if Gil didn't like the story, he enjoyed knowing it. Sunkie lore was another way he enjoyed belonging to Sunken Haven. And as rigid as Carpie and Weeze could be with him, it was obvious that Gil also enjoyed being a Burke. No doubt he had to downplay it with Fritz, who lived on the outskirts and was ignorant of the codes, in spite of all her years as a guest. The Tullivers were a perfectly acceptable Sunken Haven family, but they certainly didn't wield any power here.

Years ago, Mrs. Otis had worked for the von Cotts. She was still paid to mind their home; to dust and polish, to water the hanging planters, to check that recluse spiders hadn't built nests under the porch. I'd come along with her as a little girl, back when she babysat me, so I knew her habit of entering through the storm doors and unhooking the kitchen key from the nail at the top of the cellar steps.

Gil kept close at my heels, as always. "Let's hit the library, just quick."

"Of course."

I led him, sliding open the pocket door. We passed into a hush of walnut-paneled bookcases, studded club chairs, and a mantelpiece that was taller than my head. With anxious fingers, I pulled some new curiosities from Mrs. von Cott's writing desk as Gil slid into a chair at the games table.

"Hey, I saw you on the court yesterday," he said, as I began handing over trinkets: Japanese fighter figures, a carved wooden fan, a lacquered box of dried corals and sea glass and seashells.

"Then you know Coach Hutch is still riding my backhand."

"You held your own." Gil picked up a Samurai figurine and ran its needle-fine sword along his jawline. "These things could be in a museum."

"Would you like to see the guest books?"

"Yeah, show me."

I flew to where they were stacked on the bottom of a far bookshelf. Which one of us was procrastinating? I watched as Gil leafed through pages as brittle as dried leaves. He studied the yellowed photographs of ladies with parasols and men in boater hats, glue-framed above faded violet-inked notes of thanks for weekends of tennis and sailing and sundowners.

Next I passed him Mr. von Cott's pack of Edwardian playing cards featuring half-dressed ladies with rosy nipples and dimpled rear ends. I'd been planning to save the cards for a future lunch.

Today, I had to show Gil every trick I had.

He flipped through the cards and set them aside.

Inwardly, I wilted. So far my dress, the guest books, the naked ladies, none of it made a difference. I could catch Gil's attention, but with Fritz blocking us, there was no moving forward. And this meeting, I knew to my core, was about Fritz.

"Okay," he said. He was going to do it now; he was going to say the thing I didn't want to hear.

"I brought us a bite," I said quickly. "Homemade."

"You did?"

"We can eat on the roof, how about?"

"Okay, sure."

We wound our way up the stairs, and as usual Gil stuck his head into the guestrooms, decorated in soft pastels of celery, peach, and cantaloupe. His fingertips touched the silk wallpaper the same way I'd seen him brush the forehead of a frustrated Minnow.

At the end of the third-floor hall, Gil jumped and caught the string on the ceiling hatch that took us up to the rooftop deck. He climbed the folding ladder first, so that he could hoist me up and out to the view of the harbor.

We put up the umbrella, and then I unpacked a Thermos of iced tea, tomato sandwiches, macaroni salad, two perfect pears, and two slices of shortcake.

"You were right about Chad Tingley getting suspended from tennis for the rest of the year," said Gil. "I never realized what a big deal line calls are."

"Cheating is awfully frowned upon," I said. "Not one single infraction—lateness or swearing or uniform violation—comes close to cheating. Sportsmanship is so important, because it's about character."

I served the cake and poured out the last of the tea. "My compliments to the chef," said Gil. "That lunch took some doing."

"Oh, none at all."

"Not you. Mrs. Otis." He popped a bite of cake into his mouth.

My face reddened. Here I'd just talked about character, and he'd caught me trying to pass off that I'd made this lunch when I hadn't. "How can you be so sure it wasn't me?"

"Just the way it was packed so neat. My mom cleans houses and babysits other people's kids, and there's just a worried way you do things for rich folks."

I reddened. "I was in a rush to meet you on such short notice. Anyway, Mrs. Otis was happy to do it."

"You sure you know how happy she is?" Finished with his slice, Gil cut a bite of cake off my plate. "Coupla summers ago, I worked Red Cap service at Amtrak," he said. "Three months of hauling luggage for quarter tips. Hardest thing I ever did. A hundred times harder than prelaw."

"Carp wants better for your future than ticket taker!" My voice was raised. "Plus I've never forgotten to tip Amtrak," I added. "It would be a terrible thing, not to be tipped." The longer Gil was quiet, the more mortified I felt. "You think I've said these princessy things," I blurted.

"Aw, don't sweat it." Gil leaned forward. "That first night, I remember watching you trying to fit in with those Upper East Side people. Anyone could see how having that crowd in your home made you feel prickly. Not like Daphne, who floated through. It was so easy for her. But it was harder for you. That's how you stood out from everyone, in my eyes. In a funny way, I guess it relaxed me a little."

I flushed hot. Gil meant it as a compliment, but it was embarrassing to take it as one. I'd always thought Gil had seen me so differently, as a New York swan—as a Daphne. Had he only been teasing me about that? Had he fallen for me because he thought I seemed like a misfit in my own home?

"What I mean to say, Jean, and why I wanted to meet up today, is to thank you. As different as we are, I reckon I might have seen something of myself in you."

"But you fit in so well here," I said. "I mean, not that I don't. But you're a natural. Everyone adores you. It's like you've been coming here all your life."

"Nah, I'm an impostor." Gil looked thoughtful. "Red Cap manners *are* different from the manners of some guy you might meet at a boarding-school dance. Even if they look exactly the same."

"I think *all* the parts of you are wonderful." I leaned forward, reaching my hand out to squeeze the tips of Gil's fingers. I felt such a strong urge to touch him, to show him that I was right here, in touching distance. "Everyone does," I added quickly.

"Everyone talks about you all the time. You heard my mother on the phone—and she hardly notices *any* of the teenagers around here. It's a joke how quick the Burkes would trade Junior for you tomorrow, if they could. Oh my gosh, Gil, if you were mine, I'd never ever let you go!" I'd said too much.

My words were like claws, digging into him with my yearning.

But then Gil stood and pulled me up, folding me into a hug that rescued me from more blundering. With my ear pressed to his chest, I could hear his heartbeat.

Gil had never hugged me, not once, since that night.

"It's hot as soup on this roof. Let's pack up," he said. "We can go downstairs and wind a tune."

"Yes." I closed my eyes. I didn't want to pack up. I wanted our afternoon to last forever. If there was a reason Gil had telephoned and had needed to meet me specifically today, he still hadn't said anything. Maybe because everything was all right? And he'd only missed me?

Downstairs was one last room where Gil liked to stop—Mrs. von Cott's dressing room, because of her windup Victrola and records. Gil had never seen a Victrola before, and it fascinated him—both as a gadget and as a piece of history.

"Don't put on a war record this time," I told him, as he absorbed himself, flipping through the paper sleeves. He seemed so calm. Was I out of hot water? Had Gil only wished for a nice lunch and my company today?

He slipped on a disc, setting the needle to the tinny crackle.

But as soon as it started playing, I shook my head. "This song feels sad."

"Don't be sad, Jean." His words sounded ominous.

"Are you all right?" I asked him. *Are we all right?*

"Dance with me?" Gil sounded formal. Our eyes held.

I took a breath and stepped into his arms. First, our hug—and now it was so achingly strange to dance with Gil again, all these weeks after Hollander's. It was as if he'd made a pact with himself not to touch me—a pact that now, for some reason, he was deliberately breaking.

Because he's ending it . . .

"Goodness, if you want, I can teach you to foxtrot. You don't need my mother for that!" I adjusted our positions. "It's a basic box step rhythm; slow slow, quick quick . . ."

"Aw, I'm a clodhopper, I'm two left feet."

"You're not." I smiled my best Dalton uptilt.

I was waiting for it. I was preparing for whatever he was about to say. But I felt so fragile, like I might shatter from it, too.

"What?" I made myself ask. "What's wrong?"

Gil's whole body was poised for the plunge. "I'm sure you can tell how much I've enjoyed spending time with you, Jean." His voice was so gentle. "If I'd grown up knowing you, if we'd been New York City kids and Sunken Haven kids together . . . if I'd had, say, Junior's life—why, I bet you'd have been exactly the right girl for me."

"What? What do you mean?" My pulse was a blood beat in my head. I had to remember to breathe, not to trip over my feet. "I could still be that girl."

"That night, when you came to see me at Snappy Boy, we got too close too quick. I'm not that kinda guy, and I reckon you're not that kinda girl. I feel lucky that, these past days, I got another chance to learn you slower. You're such an outta-sight person, you know you are." He paused again. "But the main thing is . . . see . . ."

"You can tell me anything . . . ," I prompted, faintly.

Gil's fingers had anchored push points into the small of my back. He was learning the dance steps better with every turn; he didn't want to break the rhythm he'd set. Gil always liked learning something new and different. "The thing is, I'm really with Fritz. We've got a lot in common, Fritz and me. For us, Sunken Haven is kinda like landing in a foreign country, where everyone speaks this private language, while Fritz and I are like a coupla tourists, sharing the phrase book back and forth, you know?"

"That won't be you always. Fritz is like a tourist, but you belong here."

"Well, you might be right. But, for now, I feel a little left of center here, and I'm not ready to pretend to be more—even if it pleases Carp and Weeze to see you on my arm. It'd be like I was using you. And that's not what I want for either of us."

Anger surged in my chest. "I don't feel used by these lunches! Not in the least!"

"I'm glad to hear it." Gil nodded. "It's been a special time for me, too. But we shouldn't keep it up. For one, I don't think Fritz would dig this scene at all—you and me meeting on the sly, hanging on to each other like we are. I never told her about us. I'm guessing you never told anyone, either. But I don't want it to keep going like this all summer. Sure it's innocent now, but there's times I'm sorely tempted by you, Jean. And I don't want you and me to get any more complicated than we are already."

My face felt almost contorted in my effort to seem relaxed. I swallowed past the stick in my throat. "But we *can* keep it simple! What's *ever* happened here? *Nothing.* Sandwiches and conversation. Us being us."

"Right, I know. And I know how we clicked right from that first minute. But I couldn't explain it to Fritz any more than I could explain . . . the other thing we did. I want to be as true to her as I can, you know? And I want to be true to myself."

Didn't Gil see how these hours were my favorite of the whole week? How could he not sense that? But now the record had ended and the needle was hissing and bumping, over and over. Gil broke from me to reset it. As the tune began again, he returned and held me. The warmth of his body against mine made me feel unsteady with desire; I could have clung to him forever. We listened one more time to a long-dead man singing for his Daisy Bell. It wasn't a sad song, but I could feel tears smarting in the corners of my eyes.

"You're not too regretful about that night we spent together, are you? I suppose you feel like it doesn't fit at all with who you are."

"If I did it," said Gil slowly, "then it does fit with who I am."

"But you probably see that whole entire night with me as a mistake," I pressed.

He paused. "No. I don't. But now I think we gotta move on from it."

"I can't."

"C'mon. I really want us to be cool about this."

But how? I felt so intense about it. Cool was Fritz—all Fritz had was her cool.

Maybe that was the whole point. The point I was missing. A guy who was in love with Fritz couldn't be in love with me.

"*But you were mine first!*" I wanted to shout at him. That should count for something! How could Gil be slipping away from me for good? I couldn't bear it. It wasn't in any way fair. Even now, he was releasing me from the hug, chucking me under the chin.

"I mean it one hundred percent, Jean, when I say getting to know you has been one of the best things about my summer."

"Me, too," I managed.

But of course, Gil didn't know me, not really—or he'd know that his decision to break off our afternoons had left me heartbroken.

FRITZ

Gil's kiss on the tennis court had sealed something. Until that moment, we'd been playing tonight kind of shyly, with a whole string of qualifications—like if I wasn't feeling it, or if he wasn't feeling it, or if we got cold feet, or if we wanted to stick around and party with Julia and Oliver. "No pressure," we'd kept saying to each other.

On the court, when Gil had picked me up and kissed me and held me like that, with everyone watching, a surge of electric connection had looped our bodies together, and we both knew.

Yes. Tonight. It was happening. No doubt.

As the day lightened up and dried out, Gil went home to check in with the Burkes, who always had him doing one thing or another for them—and apparently Fourth of July was no exception—while the rest of us headed to South Beach for the barbecue and an afternoon of diving in and out of the ocean, either with surfboards or for a simple swim. The sun was out and the ocean was perfect. When Gil finally came back, he was with Chip Knightley. They'd both picked up their guitars, and so we all got to mellow out to their Gordon Lightfoot and Grateful Dead covers.

"Play a classic, play 'Little Wing,'" someone called, from over where Junior and his crew were sitting.

"Aw, man, that's too hard," said Chip. "What do you think, that I'm going pro?"

But Gil's long fingers were already exploring the silky, bluesy opening chords, and we went silent, letting him work into it, figure it out and deliver it to us in the loose, fun way we'd all come to expect from him. I watched his expression, deliberately calm, knowing what the others didn't, that underneath his ease, Gil was dead serious and obsessively focused. I'd watched him teach swim class, rig a sail, and manage a crushing lunch shift at the yacht club in basically the same way. Making it look easy was all part of the work.

The afternoon sun sank into its ripe pinks and reds. The crowd thinned as kids began to move bayside for the fireworks show. I rode with Gil back to Snappy Boy so that he could drop his guitar. I waited outside—for a moment, watching the door, my body went taut with apprehension. Were Carp and Weeze in the house? Would they give him permission to go?

When Gil appeared again, his windbreaker on, his smile untroubled, relief flowed through me. Why'd I been so worried?

I was paranoid, that was all.

We booked, speeding through the gate, and we left Sunken Haven behind.

Seaview, Saltaire, Robbins Rest.

George, the guy who ran the place we'd found the other day, was a cool, low-key hippie type, the kind of dude that Sunken Haven parents and all Fort Polk parents were united against because he was easygoing about being gay.

Tonight, George and his boyfriend, Eric, who looked like a Swedish action hero but was actually a math teacher from Michigan, were out on the porch enjoying a couple of Strohs.

"Hey! I hoped I'd see you two cats again." George tossed me a beer. "How's things on the Haven?"

"Totally perfect and boring," I answered. "Same as always."

"Eric and I've got a running bet that there's snipers behind that locked fence of yours. Armed and ready to pick off queers."

"You're not too wrong," I said. "Sunken Haven's kinda like East Berlin, but with more tennis."

Which made George and Eric laugh, and earned us another beer toss, this one for Gil. I knew Gil felt disloyal when I joked about Sunken Haven, so I was glad that tonight he was laughing, too. Maybe Gil was feeling relaxed not to be playing the part of Weeze and Carpie Burke's perfect nephew.

We took the porch stairs and settled in. I hoped I seemed like a girl who talked to gay guys all the time—George didn't need to know he was the first person I'd ever met who was openly queer. But the army didn't let in any gay people, not even for the civilian-type jobs, so they were rare as hen's teeth on base. And if you did have the bad luck to be homosexual, you hid it as much as you could—or else. My friend Stephanie's kid brother, Davey, got smacked around school all day long for having a lispy voice. And my biology teacher, Mr. Sambuca, had not benefitted from rumors. Even freshmen picked on him.

George had been righteous to Gil and me from the very first time we'd stopped by and met him the other week. I'd had an instant, comforting feeling he knew exactly what we were planning, and that he didn't care at all. He didn't even make us put down a deposit on the room, just told us it would be here if we wanted it. So in return, I tried to act cool right back, not to seem shocked when he casually mentioned his "boyfriend," and to treat him and Eric both like I thought they were totally ordinary, which so far seemed to be the case.

"George and I were wondering if you two know a girl named Phoenix?" Eric asked us now. "She works at the Tilt-and-Whirl, over at Atlantique?"

I shook my head and popped my beer tab. "Never been. That's the badlands for Sunkies."

"Atlantique's not far. There's a big party there tonight. A whole bunch of young people."

"Are you going?" Gil asked.

"Nah, we're heading out to see some friends," George answered. "That bar's not the right scene for us old fogies. But last time we stopped in for lunch—they do great loaded potato skins—we met Phoenix, and she told us she used to spend summers in Sunken Haven."

"If there's one thing I can promise," I answered, "it's that nobody from Sunken Haven is named Phoenix."

"You sure? She's a pistol. Bright red hair, Clark Kent glasses, big smile?"

I shook my head. "I think I'd remember anyone who looked like that."

"It'd be fun to hit Atlantique," said Gil. "I've never been. It already feels good to be somewhere else." We exchanged a smile, clinked cans.

"We call crossing that ferry coming to America," said Eric. "It's a real, true freedom, to be on Fire Island." He winked. "Some parts of it, anyhow."

"Toast to that, too," I said, and then we did a four-way clink.

When George and Eric eventually decided to take off for their friends', Gil and I stood up and went with them, so they could direct us to Atlantique. I was curious about this girl Phoenix, and Gil wanted to get a deeper look at how non-Sunkies were celebrating the day.

The energy on the packed boardwalk was contagious. It felt like most of New York had decided to jump on ferries and party on Fire Island for the Bicentennial madness. Nobody was playing it down, either; every single person we saw had gone all out in glitter and Danskins and body paint. There were twisting conga lines of kids dressed in red, white, and blue, there were daredevils doing stunts on stilts and daredevils doing stunts on roller skates. There were party people in full Uncle Sam suits and toppers and pasted-on beards, and there were faces made up like Indians or Old Glory. There were slinky girls in flag-themed short-shorts and tube tops, and there were drag queens everywhere.

Soon we split from Eric and George, but the Tilt-and-Whirl would have been hard to miss. Its windows were lit up by red and green Christmas-tree lights that blinked on and off in a trance of madness.

Through the open door, noise poured out, down the gravel walk.

"You sure?" Gil asked.

"Yeah," I said. "I want to be around it." It kind of thrilled me, being so far away from the pinched sameness of Jean and her friends, and the feeling that I had to be their designated token rebel because I wore cut-off jeans.

Here was something new and different, and I wanted in.

For a couple of minutes, we hung around in the doorway and peered in on a sea of mostly guys; tanned guys, dark guys, light guys, skinny snake-hipped guys, sleepy-eyed, shaggy Jesus guys in slippery silk shirts, guys in T-shirts and sarongs, with prettier hair than mine. There were enough girls that I wasn't totally conspicuous, but I was feeling my femaleness, my straightness, and maybe even a clinging whiff of Sunken Haven-ness.

"Arright," said Gil. "Like my mama says, 'Move, don't ooze.'"

We moved, bumping and jostling against bodies, heading for the packed bar, where three bartenders—two guys and a girl—were working. The girl's back was to us. She was stacking beer mugs from dishwashing trays. Her muscles were flexed to capacity as she shelved the mugs, filled the ice tub, then topped off the mixer bottles. She had sweat marks on her shirt, and her bright red hair was cropped to her ears.

"Bet that's Phoenix," I said.

And yet there was something about the way she stood, the angle of her head, the shape of her ears—did I know her? I signaled to Gil to push in closer. We waited till there was a tiny opening, and then we forced and wedged into a spot at the wraparound corner of the bar.

"Hey!" I called. "Hey! 'Scuse me? Phoenix?" I was basically yelling into the small of her back. "I'm a friend of George Caruthers!"

"Got it, I hear fine—stop shouting!" The girl turned, her eyes amused, slapping her bar rag over her shoulder. It took me a second to realize.

It took her less time.

"O'Neill?"

"Tracy?"

"No way!"

"Oh, my God!"

Laughing, she ducked under the pocket of the bar, popped up by my side, and gave me a giant, gripping hug.

"What are you *doing* here?"

"Same question back atcha!" With a glance behind me at Gil.

"I'm asking first—wow, you look . . . you went red!"

Tracy tugged the bright, piecey ends at her chin. "I'm experimenting. I guess I'm in what you call an experimental phase." She said it in a jokey way, and we laughed, but it wasn't all a joke. We kept staring at each other. Happiness was bursting through me to see her face again.

For as long as I'd known her, Tracy had always copied her mother's look, which was not the typical garden-party, crisp pink-and-green style that a lot of Sunkie moms liked, but more like soft, flowing wildflower-print dresses paired with tortoiseshell hair combs and spaghetti-strap sandals.

This Tracy was nothing like her mom. With her scarlet hair and heavy glasses, she was barely even recognizable.

"I never thought I'd ever see *anyone* from Sunken Haven here. Jeez, Tracy."

"I'm Phoenix now," she said, her voice shy, with a lift of her chin. "I mean, you can call me Tracy if you want," she said. "But it's my old name."

"Phoenix," I said, testing it out. It reminded me of those last days before I'd left Fort Polk, when as a hippie joke I'd been calling my parents Jim and Nancy. How it had reangled my perspective on them, making them seem both familiar and strange.

"This is Gil," I said, as he leaned forward.

"Hi." She gave him the up and down. "You're related to Carpie Burke?"

"Nephew," he said.

"I see that." Phoenix smiled.

"And you pierced your ears." She wore a stud earring in one ear and a long feather in the other. "Finally!"

Last summer, there'd been a whole big thing, because Tracy's mom, who herself only wore clip-ons, had forbidden piercing. "Punching holes in your ears is cheap," she declared. We'd all sided with Tracy, and had felt sorry for her—even Sara Train had been allowed to get pierced ears at age sixteen.

"Did it myself," she said, touching the feather. "Ice and a needle. One of my many decisions about what I'd do for myself this summer."

"But you need to come back," I said. "It's not the same without you."

Something in Phoenix's face lost its jokiness. "Yeah, I got tired of being the life of the party," she said. "But why are *you* here? Or should I ask, why are you *here*?"

"We're celebrating freedom. Bicentennial and otherwise," said Gil. "I heard this place had some killer potato skins?" He turned to me. "I was too deep in the guitar, earlier. I kinda forgot to eat."

Phoenix nodded. "I'll ask Sean to cover for me."

Fifteen minutes later, we were at a far table, happily eating cheddar-bacon–topped skins, which lived up to George's recommendation and then some.

As I added a blob of sour cream to the bubbling, browned, melted cheese, I looked across the table, my eyes reclaiming

Phoenix's face—her deep listener's eyes behind her glasses, her upturned mouth that made her look like she was two seconds from either telling or hearing a punch line.

"I heard stories about you this summer," I said.

Phoenix smirked. "And I bet those stories got halfway around the world before they came close to telling the truth."

"The one I heard most is you came out to Sunken Haven and almost drowned in a hot tub," I said. "Then you went to rehab. Another story, you were exiled to your grandmother's house on the Cape. Last thing I heard you were at Smith College, taking summer classes."

"Wow," said Phoenix. "That's a lot."

"So . . . any truth to any of it?" asked Gil carefully.

She gave him the hint of a nod. "Some," she admitted. "I broke up with my . . . with my . . . special friend . . . this past March. And I got depressed. And I sort of tried to drown myself on purpose."

Phoenix hadn't said girlfriend. So it was slightly different than George. But in a way, it was even more rattling, because I'd known that girl Tracy, who'd talked crushes and boyfriends, who'd once spent a whole afternoon with Julia and me deciding the five hottest guy bods in Hollywood—when underneath, all the time, she'd been thinking about her "special friend."

"Sounds like a rough spring," said Gil, filling up my silence. "I'm sorry."

"Thanks." They were sizing each other up. "I don't know

that I meant to do it. I was so bombed," she said, softly. "But trying to kill yourself has the unfortunate side effect of really scaring people. Mom and Dad packed me off to rehab in two snaps. Even though, for the record, I wouldn't say I had an alcohol problem. I had a heartbreak problem, and a breakup problem. I had a being in love with the wrong person problem." She smiled unhappily.

"Were your folks at least kind of understanding about that?" I asked.

"They were okay to talk about my drinking." Phoenix took off her glasses to deal with a couple of smudges on the lenses, using the corner of her T-shirt. "For my parents, having a drinking problem isn't as shameful. I mean, let's face it, half of Sunken Haven needs to dry out."

Isn't as shameful as a girl being in love with a girl. I still couldn't figure out the right thing to say. So I said nothing.

"So after I finished with the clinic, I did go to the Cape for a while," Phoenix continued. "I lived with Gran in May and June. And then I came here."

"Would you *ever* go back to Sunken Haven?" asked Gil.

"No," she answered, her voice firm. "They don't want me there. They don't want anyone who's different, right?" She looked right at me.

"I guess." Was I in shock, missing the Tracy that she used to be? Or was I having a hard time separating her from my own sugarcoated summer memories, now that I had to think of Phoenix in all that secret pain and confusion?

"Because you're different, too, Fritz," she added. "In all the best ways, of course. And this summer you've even got a Burke drooling all over you." This made Gil laugh, a touch self-consciously. "But Sunken Haven is a closed place. You're tolerated, but you'll never be one of them. Just like me. And tolerated isn't good enough for me." She finished her beer and clonked the mug on the table. "Scratch the surface of tolerated and you'll find plenty of uglier feelings underneath."

"You think you should be *here*, then?" I asked. The bar had become more crowded with boisterous drag queens, dressed in caftans and stilettos, all made up in Cleopatra eyes and red lips.

"Hell, yeah. Fritz, this is celebration, what's happening here." She paused to look around. "I heard something pretty heavy went down today. A few weeks ago, some queen wasn't allowed into a bar over in the Pines, so this afternoon, he and like a hundred of his buddies took a ferry over and basically stormed the Pines—like an invading army."

"But don't you miss your family?" I blurted. I didn't know why I kept harping on it—it seemed like the choices that Phoenix had made were so hard and lonely. Had she really, truly needed to make them?

Her face fell. "Yeah, of course. I miss Mom and Dad and Tiger. Sometimes I feel like I'm in witness protection. I write them letters about how I'm auditing classes at Smith. I send the letters to Gran, who drives over from the Cape and posts them from Northampton." She exhaled. "But those are the lies I've got to tell so I can breathe, you know?"

"And you're not lying to your gran," I reminded.

"Hey, cheers to Gran!" Gil raised his mug and slopped in some beer for Phoenix for the toast, but I knew he was trying as hard as I was to hold on to his low-key Southern cool, to put the pieces of Phoenix's world together into an understandable whole.

I stared around. Strange as it was, my need to bolt was leaving me. Maybe I didn't exactly get drag queens, but I did get army kids. We came into base schools from all sorts of situations. The people at this bar, maybe they weren't like army kids in their style, but they were army in their lonerness, in the ways they always had to push into a new frontier and never look back.

Phoenix had turned her full attention to Gil. "So you're like a new-discovered nephew? The ultimate toy surprise inside Carpie Burke's box of Cheerios?"

"Yeah, I'm the secret decoder ring," drawled Gil, smiling, playing along. I watched him the way I always did when he got circled with these types of Burke questions. I saw the notch flex in his jaw, watched him slowly crack a couple of fingers. He masked his tension so smoothly, you could hardly tell.

Phoenix nodded her approval at me. "What a fun summer romance. I hope you get to keep him after Labor Day."

I kept my smile tight as poker cards, though I squirmed in my chair. People always joked about summer romances because they didn't last. Summer romances were made out of ice cream and cotton candy, intensely sweet before they melted into nothing. But I'd never thought of Gil as a summer thing.

Gil was my real love, my real first.

After we said our good-byes—with lots of promises not to blow Phoenix's cover—we walked along the boardwalk in silence, weaving past noisy partiers, our fingers linked. The things I wanted to say to Phoenix were still stuck inside me—*You're wrong,* I'd wanted to tell her. *Your difference is way unluckier than mine. You have to hide and push back and crumple up everything that your heart wants. But Gil and I are outsiders together, we have each other, we don't care that we don't belong.*

"Whatcha thinking?" Gil asked.

"I'm thinking I'm glad we went outside tonight. It was complicated, but it's good to return to the real world past that fence, right?"

"Amen," Gil answered solemnly. Which made us laugh, which led to a kiss, and a pinwheel of excitement began to spark and spin inside me.

When we reached George's, we tiptoed upstairs. The bedroom was the same as when we saw it yesterday—only with a couple of folded bath towels on the edge. It seemed so grown up, having those towels. Like a real hotel. We both got quiet. The only thing left to do was the thing that mattered most. I sat on the bed, which gave up a squeak so loud that I jumped. That made Gil burst out laughing. Which led to more kissing.

Gil snapped off the bedside lamp and pulled down the paper-thin blinds on our one-story view of the boardwalk, in an attempt to block the streetlamp and the noisy foot traffic.

"Kind of feels like the whole world's in on this night with us." He eased into place next to me. "With all these sparklers and noise blowers and kazoos."

"High on life," I said.

We leaned against the creaky wicker headboard and we passed the beer back and forth as we kissed and joked and then touched. Careful, quiet, slow.

Every time we'd gotten together, as hot as our chemistry always was, we hadn't been able to deliver each other any other finish than frustration. Tonight, amazingly, our bodies could meet and stay together.

Back in Fort Polk, Stephanie Ewart had given me an earful about the physical pain of her first time. On the other hand, Julia had said that with Tiger, it was hardly anything.

In the end, when I felt his weight, felt him in me, melded into this brand-new balance of our bodies connecting in ways that felt incredibly different from anything we'd done before, and yet also felt so natural, it wasn't exactly painful. But it wasn't "hardly anything," either.

Outside, fireworks showered brightly around us. Explosions hummed at our skin and bones as we touched and tasted each other. The fireworks' reflections drenched our bodies in sapphire, ruby, and emerald.

"You," he said softly, and it was the best word he could have said.

It happened. It was almost too much to think about all at once. For a while, I didn't know if I was lying there in peace or in shock. A little of both, probably. But I knew I was different now. I might still look like a girl to some people, but I wasn't. I was a woman. This summer, I'd learned things, real things, private things, about love and seduction and romance, that I hadn't known before.

"Hey." My own voice sounded sleepy and far away in the darkness. "I've been wondering about something. I've almost asked you about it a couple of times before." A few stray fireworks boomed, warming us with a glow of light through the room. I could feel Gil listening intensely. "It's like, in my mind, there's been this mystery to you—that you really are kind of that decoder-ring prize."

"Oh, yeah? Decode me, then." But I could feel in his inhale, in the shift of his body, the way he suddenly pulled me deeper to fit the crook of space between us, that maybe he knew what I was going to ask.

"Is Carp your dad?"

He pulled me a tiny bit closer. Was quiet a while before he spoke. "It was hard on Weeze to learn about me. And Junior . . . he still doesn't know." Gil's voice was slow and deliberate, owning the secret now that it was out. "But I grew up knowing. Carp sent my mom money, sometimes. I met him twice, when he was traveling through Atlanta. Mom took me to see him. He told Weeze last year—I'd always been a good student, but I was starting to win school prizes, made the regional debate team, things like that. I guess I was always hoping my work would pay off. That he'd claim me."

"Wow," I said. I let go of a breath. "That's . . . a lot."

"I'm his nephew, officially," he said. "That's what they'll give me, right now. I respect that."

"Do you feel weird that I know?"

"I guess so, but I'm relieved," he said. "The fact that you can see this side of me so clear—I reckon that's a big reason I love you, Fritz."

"I love you, too." I waited a moment, letting myself hear those words. I hadn't said them to him much; every time I did, it made me feel funny, a joy and a pang, like releasing a favorite balloon. "Was that your first time, too?"

In the silence, I wondered if Gil was deciding to tell me the truth.

"No," he whispered.

Why had I thought he'd answer different?

Because I'd hoped for . . . what?

JEAN

My last apology, done.

It should be me, whispered my most childish voice. The bratty-little-sister voice who screeched at Daphne, who stomped up stairs and slammed doors.

But it was never going to be me.

After I said good-bye to Gil, I left the von Cott house and began to walk. I knew every trail and footpath of Sunken Haven. I could walk for hours up and down this island and know exactly where I was at any moment without giving it a thought. And so I let myself drift, numb, zombielike, down the stiles to the beach, and I tried to accept that Gil was floating away from me, tried to feel this new loss and emptiness of Without. We had been strangers, and then we had been so much better than strangers, so close—I'd wanted to be closer to Gil than to anyone, really—and now he wanted me to be a stranger again.

Find something else to think about. Figure out someone better to be.

Fritz and Gil were devastating together. One look at them this morning had made my own time with Gil, as much as I treasured it, feel almost unbearably naïve. Their intimacy had been a fist that gripped my heart, but I could have justified and rationalized and somehow withstood even that—it was Gil who'd squeezed out whatever last bit of hope I'd been holding.

"I really want us to be cool about this," he'd said.

And of course he'd been perfectly cool about it. His eyes on me were as calm as pond water. Leaving me to tremble at their chill, to push myself through the rough currents of my own emotions. I'd left in a hurry. I didn't want him to see me cry. I'd cried enough in front of Gil Burke.

Afterward, I just couldn't go to the beach and join the celebrations. I kept myself to quiet, unused trails. I walked for miles, aimless and aching, and when my feet were tired and my skin burnt and my mouth dry, I went back to Lazy Days and crawled upstairs to bed, pulling the covers over me as if I could create another layer of time, a dark cave where nobody could hurt me, where nobody would point a finger at me and call me the loser, the Other Custis Sister.

My sleep was so deep that nobody—not Mrs. Otis, calling to me that Rosamund was on the telephone and please pick up; not Bertie, stopping by and trudging up to my room to shake my shoulder and implore that I come out for the bay fireworks — none of it could rouse me.

I ended up missing all of the Fourth of July parties. Considering my luck with parties this summer, it was probably not such a bad thing.

The next morning, I was the only Custis at the breakfast table who was hangover-free. I made French toast. Humming a tuneless song, I whisked eggs and milk and added in the extra cinnamon with a pinch of nutmeg. Just how I liked it.

Part of my better mood, I realized, was that no awful memory from last night had washed up, like a dark, confusing tangle of seaweed, into my waking. Outside of disappointing Bertie, I didn't have to justify anything terrible that I'd done — how I'd messed up, or that I'd confessed too much, or hurt other people's feelings, or damaged anything that I'd now need to mend in my sloppy remorse.

"You look chipper," Dad said tiredly, when I set his breakfast in front of him. A Custis always got points for looking chipper.

"Thanks."

I could look chipper and then, one day, it might come true.

After breakfast, I took a deep breath and made myself call. He answered on the first ring, as if he'd been waiting.

"It's Jean," I said. "I feel terrible about last night, for being a party poop. I had such a headache."

"That's all right." Bertie sounded so lonely and relieved that my heart spiked with tenderness. "You didn't seem well. Though I thought maybe you were . . . sad about something."

"No, no. Only ill." If he knew I was lying, he wouldn't say. I hated to hurt Bertie, and I'd done it so much this summer. "I wasn't myself," I said firmly. "But I'm better now."

"I'm glad. Should I pick you up tonight, say, seven? Chip's hosting Games Night."

"Or maybe something more quiet," I suggested.

"Sure, Jean. Whatever you like."

After we'd hung up, I sat by the phone for a while. My last apology, done. For the rest of this summer, I would give nobody cause to be upset with me again. Yes, I could do that. I could change.

Lighthearted in my resolve, I biked straight to the Coop. Back when I was in Minnows, I'd spent some of my best hours here. In this morning of new awakenings, it seemed obvious that I should sign up as a volunteer. Here was something I'd wanted to do all summer, I told myself.

On our first night out, at Hollander's, I'd pretended to Gil that I couldn't possibly have fit more than tennis into my day. That had been a lie, and I'd stuck to it. But I was always painfully aware of how much free time I had, and how I wasted it thinking about him. Pining for him. Pursuing him.

If I had a truly busy schedule, the way a lot of kids here did, then I couldn't waft through any more empty afternoons. I couldn't wonder what Gil and Fritz were up to, or hope Gil might be free to see me. Besides, I liked art. Painting shells, fashioning sand landscapes and dream catchers and sponge collages, building wind chimes and birdhouses — those Coop afternoons made up a solid chunk of my happy girlhood remembrances.

A couple of generations ago, the Coop had been a real chicken coop, back when it was easier to harvest eggs on the island than to import them. I'd only ever known it as the arts building. Its paste and paper smells reminded me of less difficult years.

Best of all, nobody stopped by here.

Even when I was at tennis practice, chasing the ball around the court and getting chewed out by Coach Hutch, I'd always had an eye straying for Gil's bike speeding along Ridge Way.

Gil would never come to the Coop. No older kids did — the only other teenager here was Donna Brisby, a Bay Shore Community College girl who ran Sunken Haven's arts program. I'd be safe here. Safe from uncomfortable Gil sightings, and safe from yawning afternoons with Rosamund and Sara.

Donna told me straight off that she was overworked. "Monday watercolors? That's today. That one can be all yours," she said. "And then there's Sunday tie-dye, which is super-popular. But basically, if you pick the projects, then you make the rules. The hardware store on Ocean Beach has art supplies. The front office will reimburse you, if you hold onto your receipts."

"Sounds easy enough."

"Start right now if you want. Maybe you can set up a still life? I stink at watercolors, but I'm here if you need anything."

Then she left me.

I walked around, opening the drawers, which were still cluttered with all the same sorts of scraps in the very same places I remembered. One drawer for magazines and construction paper — now I remembered how I used to cut out mermaid paper dolls that I gave fantastical names to, like Aubureen and Odyssia. Another drawer for fabric and yarn. Another drawer for scissors, another drawer for shells and rocks and coral.

Slowly, using jars of leafy twigs and a giant starfish, I assembled a still life, and arranged it at the end of one of the long, gunmetal art tables. Next I took a box of watercolors, a brush, a cup of water, and a sheet of heavy, pressed paper. I sat down and got started on my sketch.

As girls arrived, they began pushing in, either to paint or to watch me paint. It wasn't long before I was fielding all of their chattering questions as if I were a professional artist — advising them on how to apply watercolors to create flowers and beaches, sunsets and boats.

Eventually, the table was filled with jabbering artists, all trying their best for me. In one morning, they recharged me to a self that I'd almost forgotten. I was euphoric. They made me feel happier about art than I had felt all summer about tennis.

Maybe I knew how to break this curse, after all? Though I knew it would take more than one morning.

Because when I closed my eyes, I could still hear his voice: *I really want us to be cool about this.* And I could still see the two of them together. His hand on her back. The lift of her sneakers to meet his kiss. His words for her ear alone.

And I saw myself standing far outside their love, watching it as you would a curl of smoke rise from a chimney across a frozen field. Colder in my own body just for knowing that the heat existed elsewhere.

I painted my still life and I tried not to hate them.

FRITZ

I'd never thought how harsh and quick change could happen.

We woke up in each other's arms. Sunrise had turned everything raw.

"We better get going." When Gil stretched, the thin bedframe rattled with a threat of collapse. "I've got my Monday Minnows class to teach."

"I've got lunch shift at the club."

He leaned on his elbow. Staring down at me. His finger traced the outline of my face. "This beautiful morning. You in it. How does a guy get so lucky?"

But the morning sun had made us shy. We rolled up in George's scratchy bath towels, stole down the hall, and showered together with the shade pulled, sharing a curl of soap and a washcloth.

Downstairs, we found George and Eric in the kitchen. Eric, his blond stubble and messy morning hair making him look extra cute, was reading the paper while George stood in a T-shirt and swim trunks before the stovetop, using his spatula to gather a hill of scrambled eggs into form.

"So it turns out I did know Phoenix," I said, taking a plate George indicated to help myself.

"Oh, yeah? What's her story?" asked Eric.

"Not so much of a story," I said. "It's more like she's trying out a new identity."

"No harm in that," said Gil, already at the table. When I looked over at him, he gave me that smile.

You know me, his smile said. *You know all my identities. And I know you right back.*

I smiled. I knew. And I felt so wildly, perfectly aware of him—an arm's length across from me, the morning sun finding the highlights in his hair, the amber glint in his eyes. I wanted to take the moment and hold it forever. Gil was the one thing I could never get enough of.

"Okay," he said, catching my eye as he crunched a last stick of bacon, then took a final gulp from his coffee mug. "We're late. Like, really late!"

When we stood up, I could feel an ache in my throat for the end of our little getaway, as I impulsively stepped forward and gave George a hug. "Thanks," I said quietly. "For everything."

"You come back anytime," he said. "Depend on me."

And then we were rushing out the door, jumping back on our bikes. Zipping through the towns fragrant with the morning smell of beach salt and cedar.

We flew inside the Sunken Haven gate and bolted it behind us.

We raced each other around the bay, where the Minnows class had already started. When we got there, Gil braked, full-stopped, jumped off his bike and let it fall, and came over to kiss me hard and quick on the mouth. "See you later. I'll come by."

"Okay." And as I wheeled out, I couldn't resist one last glance behind me.

Amazing how we belonged to each other in a way that we never had before. Just when I thought I'd reached this summit with Gil, somehow, it all got better. So I'd never thought—in the space of that time between our good-bye, and when I saw him later that same day, and him looking like the bottom had dropped out of his life—how harsh and quick change could happen.

But that's how it happened.

Three hours later, everything was different.

I sensed him before I looked up from where I was doing tube tubs, rolling a knife, spoon, and fork into a navy napkin, then stacking the roll-up in a large plastic tub. When the tub was full, it would be placed at the patio bussers' stand. My fingers worked steady as a robot's while my thoughts floated, remembering Gil's hands twined through my hair, the press of his lips on my neck . . .

"Hi." I blinked.

"Hey." He was like an apparition, standing right there in the doorway of the yacht club's pantry, where we did all our prep work. But there was no reason he should be at the club. He'd come expressly to find me. His expression made me nervous.

"What's wrong?"

"Weeze knows. She knows I was off island all last night. She knows we were together. She's furious."

"So what?"

"It's one of their things. One of their rules."

"Since when did going out the gate become the biggest crime kids could commit? Since when did I become the worst person you could spend time with?" But my voice was thin and my words didn't count. Being baffled and scared didn't count, either, though I was plenty of both. "I mean, come on. Is it really that bad?"

"I'm not allowed to stay overnight off of Sunken Haven. I didn't think they'd push me too hard. I didn't think Junior would tell."

My stomach lurched. Of course it was jealous Junior, making trouble. "It's my fault," I said stupidly, my brain reeling. "Junior's always been riled, thinking of us together. He can't stand it. I guess none of them can." Which seemed so wrong. Was the Burkes' disapproval mostly about Gil, or about me, or about the two of us? Last night, Phoenix's words had sounded so dark, so dire. But what did Carp and Weeze really think about me under my thin coating of *tolerated*? Was I so awful that they were going to punish us for this?

Gil leaned back against the wall. As if he'd lost that much

strength. "It was really important for me to be with you. You know that."

"Look, I'm not scared of the Burkes." I could hear my voice tremble to say it. "Whatever they think, we don't have — "

"Fritz, they want us to stop seeing each other. At least while we're here, on Sunken Haven."

The rest of my words all flew away from me. We stared at each other. My heart had turned into some strange piece of machinery thumping too fast inside me.

"Seriously?"

"Yeah. This is real."

"But that's crazy. That's so completely crazy."

"You don't have to tell me." I couldn't remember when I'd seen Gil look so unsure. But he'd never trusted the Burkes. He'd always been careful and on guard around them. He'd understood them in a way that I hadn't.

"This day started out so perfect." It was a silly thing to say, but it was all I could think. Was it only this morning that I'd woken up with Gil, knowing I loved him and was loved by him? "I don't believe it's that bad," I decided. "We'll fix this." I moved out from around the table.

"I'm not so sure."

"I am. They're throwing a temper tantrum. People throw temper tantrums and parties all the time in Sunken Haven, that's what it's known for."

Gil laughed, but the sound of his laugh was as weak as my

joke, as he pulled me close. I held his face between my hands and squared him with my smile and told him not to worry, that this was only their bad first reaction, that everything would resettle.

For a moment, holding his gaze, I really did feel like I could challenge the Burkes—their biased resentments, their terms and conditions. I loved Gil the most, and it made me strong. Besides, love always won. Didn't it?

PART THREE

JEAN

I enjoyed their sweet attention . . .

I'd have hidden at the Coop every day if I could, and I began to hold my time closely and carefully, in a way I'd never done before. Guarding myself. I showed up for tennis clinic, of course, and I was out a few times with Bertie, where we planned private excursions to Ocean Beach or found something quiet to do at his house. I went on long afternoon walks. I had dinner with my parents if they were in, and with Mrs. Otis if they were out. Most nights, I ran a bath and read in bed.

Time, calm, and peaceful activities—I knew what I needed to mold myself into a new shape that would get me past the pain of Gil. Removing myself from my friends' gossip and idle distractions was also good for me. But I also knew that my parents saw solitude as an act of rebellion, and I figured at some point they would interfere. My mother asked several times after Rosamund and Sara, and openly fretted when I begged off attending Alice Knightley's birthday party that next weekend, claiming my usual headache.

Sometimes, I wondered why I bothered to stay at Sunken Haven at all. For the first time that I could remember, I daydreamed of returning to the city and finding a summer job someplace where I didn't know anyone, where I was just another girl on the subway, working for her paycheck, and being Jean Custis didn't carry any weight or connection.

Meantime, there was the peace of the Coop, where I could be a different kind of person—authoritative, friendly, loose, helpful, stern. I'd especially relished last Saturday, because Donna Brisby wasn't there and I had full reign.

This Saturday, I arrived early, carrying my project in an enormous plastic bag that had almost tipped me twice on the ride over.

Maisie Walt was already waiting for me on the steps.

"My friendship bracelet's a mess," she said, following me inside and waiting until I'd finished setting up. When I sat down with her, she leaned against me. Her hair smelled like pastry.

"All you have to do here . . . is loop under and over, and then you knot through." I secured and fastened the end of her green-and-navy friendship bracelet, then slipped it over her wrist for both of us to admire. "A tiny repair was all it needed."

Maisie smiled. "We can always tell which ones you do, Jean. You make the bands so flat."

"Aw, thanks. Want to help me finish getting everything ready for the others?"

She gave me a small smile, glad to.

Together we unpacked my bag and piled the table with crochet hooks and rainbow-bright yarn that we would later crochet into piles of granny squares to make into belts and tea cozies and dog blankets. Once the others started trickling in, Maisie slipped to a seat at the end of the table, her shy presence drowned by the others.

At first, I'd been startled by the sheer energy force of these girls. Had I ever been so carefree, so confident? They were always singing and laughing, cracking silly jokes, pranking one another. Their affection for me took me by surprise, too—their bright offerings of friendship bracelets, sticks of gum, Life Savers candies, wilted bouquets of starflowers that I stuck in jelly jars and used as a table centerpiece, then threw out at the end of the day.

Nothing of much consequence was ever said or done at the Coop, but in the two weeks since I had started showing up here, I felt as if I'd reclaimed a secret, lovely room in myself, a room for a girl who hadn't been quite ready to give up making mermaid paper dolls and painting seashells. A room where I preferred corny riddles and earnest compliments a hundred times over trying to be witty and blasé with my own friends.

Crochet squares was a brand-new project—Mrs. Otis had taught me crochet years ago—and once I'd explained it, the table became intense with the sounds of whispering and murmuring as the girls checked on their neighbors' work. I sat at the head and told or listened to stories, all the while chaining corners and undoing their snarled, beginners' efforts.

"Say, did any of you girls hear the story about the hurricane that blew away the yacht club, back when Sunken Haven was first getting started and the club was a private hotel?" I asked now.

"Tell us!" the girls cried.

It gave me a pang, sometimes, to tell the girls the same tales that I'd shared with Gil. But I enjoyed their sweet attention, just the way I enjoyed how they squabbled among themselves for who got to bring me scissors or paper towels. And I loved the shine in Maisie's eyes at the end of that afternoon, when I gave her a few of my own granny squares.

But I never formed a special attachment to any one of the girls. They were all, and none of them, my favorites. Nobody got to win or lose with me.

My Coop, my rules.

"We'll take a break from crochet and get back to it Monday," I instructed at the end of the afternoon. "Tomorrow is Sunday tie-dye, so remember your whites."

A few girls cheered and clapped, as if I'd invented Sunday tie-dye.

By the time I'd finished tidying up, the sun was draining color from the sky. Another day, done. I knew my parents were annoyed that I was not attending Italian Night at the club, but Bertie was coming over to watch television later, and that was about as much excitement as I wanted.

The next morning, I went downstairs deliberately late so that I wouldn't have to go to church, to find Mom waiting for me in one of her twinsets.

"Jean, I really must put my foot down," she began. "You skipped services on the Fourth—which I allowed, because it was a holiday—but you skipped last Sunday, too. God himself does not take off the whole of July. We are *all* going to church this morning, are we understood?" She was spooning coffee into cups of boiling water for herself and Dad. "I'll give you ten minutes to get ready while Dad and I have a second cup."

My heart thudded. Church might mean Gil. I'd been so successful at avoiding him since our last lunch that the very possibility of seeing him this morning came as an icy shock. "Okay."

"Skip as much amusement as you insist, but you can't skip church," Mom said, as if she were cutting off my argument. "You can't keep sneaking to the Coop every single day."

"Mom, I said I'd go. I just need to change clothes."

"Good. Coffee?"

"No, thanks." I found a Pop-Tart in the breadbox.

"Also," said Mom, in a firm, smooth, everything-has-been-decided voice that made me look up. "After service, the Hastys are hosting a brunch for Reverend Franklin. And I want you to come to that, too. With Dad and me. You're feeling awfully 'outside the fold.'"

It was a Sunken Haven custom to host a brunch for the guest

pastor, who we rotated every three weeks. I knew Mom's invitation was more of a command than a request.

"Sure," I said. I followed her out the French doors into the heavy morning heat. "I'm not *against* church or church brunches or anything."

"You've become invisible," said Mom in that same, hard-polished voice. To Dad she said, "Jean will be ready in ten."

I ripped the foil and bit into the Pop-Tart, savoring its candy-sweet strawberry filling.

"Glad to hear," said Dad. "When I was younger, there was something queer about girls who kept themselves away. Girls who retreated from all the fun."

I bristled to see my parents exchange a look of alliance. They'd obviously been talking about me. "I'm not hiding," I insisted. "What do I have to hide from?"

"Good. Nothing." Mom smiled at me over her mug. "It's settled."

And so I finished my Pop-Tart, found a favorite sundress in the back of my closet, and walked with my parents to church. I'd taken some time with my hair, clipping a side barrette in it and using a little mascara and lip gloss—just in case. But I relaxed when I didn't see any of the Burkes.

It was slightly strange to be among my friends again, waving and smiling as if I hadn't been ignoring everyone for days on end. I knew Sara and Rosamund had been irritated with me, even if there was nothing specific they could accuse me of having done.

My parents were right; I had been hiding. But it felt worse to be part of things.

After church—thankfully, among the throngs of Wolfes, Todds, Tingleys, and Knightleys, none of the Burkes had shown up—we all walked over to the Hasty house. Me in the middle. I had a slight sense of being in custody. As if my parents thought I'd make a break for it and race off with a box of watercolors, hightailing it to the Coop.

"Hark! The palace gates," Dad said, with cheerful sarcasm, as we came within view of the scraggly dwarf pines and the wooden sign that read "Catch-All."

Nobody called the house Catch-All. Nobody called it anything except the Hasty house. Then again, the house didn't look healthy enough to have a charming name. The roof was choked in ivy and the lawn was a wilderness of salt-meadow grass and weeds, which gave it the look of a manor under a fairy-tale spell. Most everyone at Sunken Haven knew about the Hastys' finances. Some people said the problem was that Hasty money was so old that none of the new Hastys had learned how to earn more of it.

Mrs. Hasty had prepared a large buffet brunch on the covered porch. My palms began to sweat, seeing how crowded it was already. Would the Burkes skip church but come here?

"When I was a little girl, this house was one of the prettiest on the ridge," said Mom as we picked our way around the prickle bushes and up the tangled path.

"Jiminy Cricket," said Dad. "How did they allow it to go to seed like this?"

"Nobody really *allowed* anything, Dad," I said. "Fred says his family wants to sell. But it's not like they can just put this house on an open real estate market. They have to wait for another family *from here* to buy it. They're stuck."

"Oh my gosh, Fred Hasty shouldn't be airing so much family laundry." Mom shook her head.

"And who could blame anyone here for not wanting to buy it?" asked Dad. "With all the work it needs? You need a bayonet just to find the welcome mat."

"The Hastys got themselves into this predicament," said Mom. "They need to roll up their sleeves."

"Personally, I think it'd give Garth Hasty a real boost to see his house come up to snuff again," said Dad.

"I couldn't agree more," said Mom, clipping off each word.

It was one of those rare times that I wished Daphne were around, so that we could exchange a sisterly eye roll. It was something we both made fun of—how our parents liked to use this sharp, know-it-all tone when they talked about things they didn't understand. For years, I'd heard Dad lecture people on how guitar music was merely a passing fad. And for as long as I could remember, Mom had predicted that all New Yorkers would be in gas masks by next year due to air pollution.

But this morning, their smug little conversation about the Hastys seemed almost diabolical. Did my parents really think that all the Hastys had to do was shake down money from a magical money tree and—problems solved? Did they believe life was that easy? Did they want Daphne and me to imagine the same?

This summer already felt more bewildering than I could ever have explained to my parents, even if I'd wanted to. Maybe that's why I felt so distant from them these days: I knew they didn't have the answers. Sometimes I wondered if that was partly the reason I preferred to spend time at the Coop, where childish conversation came from actual children, and where the only wisdom anyone needed to dispense was about stuff like how to paint a rainbow, or how many granny squares you needed to make a vest.

My eyes scanned again and again for Gil. Nothing. Good.

Pastor Franklin was seated in a throng of moms on the porch swing. On his lap was a plate of toast, eggs, bacon, and fruit salad. Mom scampered off to join. Pastor Franklin might not have been as glamorous as Baryshnikov or Borg, but anyone could see Mom was in the giddy throes of yet another crush.

Sara, Rosamund, Lindsay Hasty, and a few other girls were in the front room, cuddling with the Hastys' setter puppy.

"Well, if it isn't Jean Custis, in the flesh!" Lindsay looked up at me, her eyes narrowed. "We never see you out anymore. How's things at Walton's Mountain School?"

I kneeled to nuzzle the pup. "Peachy, I guess."

Sara made a face. "I'm still trying to get my head around the fact that you *volunteer* to hang around the Coop with my kid sister."

"Libbet's all right," I said. "She likes to help."

"Watch out for little Libbet," said Sara. "She never does anything without a reason behind it."

"A perfect Sunken Haven girl," I quipped.

"Jean, you should come to the volleyball tournament later today," said Sara. "It's on the sports field, so it's near your precious Coop. Everyone'll be there."

"Maybe I will." Knowing I wouldn't.

"Bertie's not bad at volleyball," added Rosamund. "You could show him a little rah-rah cheerleader spirit."

I reddened. "Bertie knows I'm supportive of him."

"And Gil Burke might be there," Sara said. I could feel the others listening. "Did you that know he and Fritz broke up?"

"Oh." I kept my eye steady on Sara, grateful that she couldn't hear the sudden, greedy pump of my heart. "I didn't. Recently?"

"Gosh, it might have been as long as two weeks ago," said Sara. "But they kept it pretty quiet."

"Was there any reason?" The puppy rolled over on its back. I scratched his stomach. Didn't look up. I was in a sudden sweat, cold and trembling for information, as opinions on the breakup rolled in and crashed over me from all sides.

"It was more that the Burkes didn't like her."

"Well, they were way too serious."

"Weeze Burke told my mom at tennis club that they were always shutting themselves up in the TV room."

"And they'd leave the house and be off Sunken Haven all hours."

"My brother heard Carpie Burke say he wouldn't support Gil if he kept seeing her."

"Which is kind of a joke, considering Fritz rejected Junior all those years."

"The Burkes are being cruddy about it. They think if they're getting Gil all the right connections, giving him Carpie and Junior's clothes, then they should get to change up his girlfriend, too."

"I heard if they catch him out with Fritz, he's in deep trouble."

Everyone had something to say about it.

Half an hour later, I'd slipped away, ducking my parents, hurrying home to change out of my church dress, the cotton now damp across the back and under my arms. I took a cold shower, letting the water stream over me in long, freezing jets, and I imagined my blood hardening beneath my numb, goose-pimpled skin. I wished it were that easy—to seal myself off into some kind of icy, emotional vault, so that not even the smallest, most foolish sprig of hope dared to push up from my heart.

Maybe he really doesn't love her anymore.

Of course, I didn't know the whole story, but my rational mind doubted Gil and Fritz were really over. The girls' gossip reminded me of what had happened a couple of years ago, when my parents made Daphne stop seeing Andreas Stephanos, the twenty-six-year-old son of their friend Elio Stephanos, who owned our favorite Greek restaurant. We always went to Elio's on Friday nights. Then Dad found out from Mr. Stephanos that Daphne and Andreas had been out on a couple of dates. Dad was not pleased.

And that was the end of Elio's and the Stephanoses, or so my parents had thought. But all Daphne did was get sly. She'd tell my parents she was at glee-club rehearsal or seeing friends, when she was really meeting Andreas. Our parents weren't much more than stumbling blocks.

Stop thinking about it. It's got nothing to do with you.

For today's tie-dye project, I'd decided on hot pink. By the time I arrived at the Coop, the girls had already gotten started. They were using sticks to stir their knotted clothes in plastic pails of water stained pink with Rit scarlet-red dye.

"I'm here," I called.

Donna was stringing up a clothesline between two trees. She looked relieved to see me and to relinquish the task. A few wet, whorled hot-pink shirts were already pegged.

You don't know the real story.

Girls came and went, dunking their shirts (or scarves or tennis skirts or pairs of socks) for the fashion transformation. No sooner was one batch done than a new group arrived. Nothing beat a Sunday afternoon of tie-dye and Top Hits radio and juice Popsicles.

She was just a passing fling.

"At least we're not doing any more Fourth of July shirts," said Donna at the end of the afternoon, when the last of the stragglers had left. "Are you okay, Jean? You seemed kind of thrown today."

"Me? No, I'm fine." I hauled a bucket of dye to the sink,

dumped it down the drain, and let the faucet run. "You go ahead. I'll finish this myself."

As I armed myself with a bottle of Fantastik and a roll of paper towels, I could hear the room echoing with voices of girls, singing along with the radio and telling dumb jokes. The windows were flooded with a late, soft sun that made the whole room glow like brass.

He hasn't called you, remember. You found out about it from Sara.

I got on my hands and knees to towel up drip pools of dye, and then I mopped the floor.

At the sink, washing out jam jars and spray bottles, her voice startled me.

"Aha! Exactly where your mother said you'd be."

Weeze walked in slowly, looking around, deliberately casual.

"Oh. Hello." What in the world was she doing here?

"Bridge club went late, and there's nothing for dinner. I decided to run in to Ocean Bay, and I remembered your mother said you practically live here. I thought I'd pop in. Pay a call, as they used to say."

Weeze was in one of her bright-flowered sunsuits. Her pink visor had lifted the top of her bouffant like a headdress, making her appear very tall. She looked as out of place as a tiara in a surf shop.

"I guess I do like being here." Adding, so that I didn't sound too reclusive, "If I'm not with my friends, or practicing on the courts with Coach Hutch."

"Oh, yes. That Junior Cup tournament is creeping up, isn't it?" But Weeze wasn't here for small talk. She was paying a call for a reason. Her eyes were bold on me. I turned off the faucet, set a jar in the drying rack, wiped my hands, and waited. "Jean, dear, did you know that Carpie and I are hosting Lobster Party this year?"

"Yes, I did." Lobster Party was always the last Friday night in July. My parents had mentioned it at dinner the other night. Specifically, they'd been talking about how Carpie wanted to be the next head of the Association after Mr. Forsythe stepped down. Hosting Lobster Party was a way of showing the Association your commitment to Sunken Haven.

Other things I knew about Lobster Party were that my parents would never let me wriggle out of it, and that I was going with Bertie as his date.

"It's a special night, as you know. There are people who've been coming to Lobster Night their entire lives. And when you think of how old Mr. Corey is! That's a lot of lobster!" This was as close as Weeze came to making a joke, so I laughed politely.

"When members of the Association are called on to support Sunken Haven, it's Lobster Night that so many of us reminisce about," Weeze continued in a sort of grand, speech-making voice that made me feel embarrassed; it was as if she'd suddenly forgotten that it was only me here. "It's such a special evening, starting with that spectacular view of the bay—first from the library, and then as we proceed down the steps to the harbor and gather together for dinner. Nothing fancy, nothing extravagant. But on that special evening, we become more than the sum of our parts, don't you think? We are one big Sunken Haven family, of shared loyalty and values."

I was nodding, nodding, as my mind worked to solve what this was all about.

"This year, Carp and I invited a few close friends from New York to enjoy Lobster Party with us." Weeze crossed her hands across her heavy, ship's-prow chest. "And Jean, we'd like you to sit with us, too. At the host table. With Gil."

At first, I didn't know what to say. I found a cloth and wiped down a bit of the counter. I didn't want to keep looking at Weeze directly. "Doesn't he have a girlfriend already?" I asked, giving my attention to a blob of dried paint.

"You mean Fritz?" She spoke her name so lightly, so sweetly. "You know, as I heard it, Gil and Fritz decided a little while ago to take things slower. I mean, Fritz is absolutely adorable. Don't get me wrong. But for a night like this, Gil knows he can't appear next to just anyone. You *are* this community, Jean. You know how important it is for people such as Mr. Corey to continue to feel generous and wholehearted toward Sunken Haven. Carpie will be asking for a pledge to refurbish the church. It sustained such a lot of storm damage last winter, from the rafters to the pipe organ. A big night, and the success of the fundraising reflects the success of the host. You'd be a real help to do this for us."

The memory looped through me again: Fritz, in her patched jean shorts and his Frank Zappa T-shirt. That kiss. I'd watched him want her, Fritz O' Neill, who made me feel insecure in ways she never even could have intended—starting with the fact that Julia had replaced me with her, all those summers ago.

"I don't know," I said quietly, as I finally met Weeze's eye. "I think I'd only be in the way of things."

"Don't be silly. In fact, Gil himself suggested you! He just feels shy about it. But if Gil wants to be a real Burke," Weeze continued, in that same large, proclaiming voice, "then he needs to assume the mantle of a real Burke, which includes responsibility to this community."

I'd never heard an adult speak against Fritz before, even indirectly. Of course, Rosamund and Sara and I had always joked about Fritz, nicknaming her Army Girl or Denim Deb or Fritz Oh-No. But it was strange to hear Weeze Burke, a full-blown adult, tell me that Fritz O'Neill wasn't good enough to sit at her table.

"The thing is, Bertie already asked me to Lobster Party," I said. "And I'm not sure that I can hurt Bertie's feelings. Even if it's to help Gil."

But I was already lying. One night. A night with Gil. I could feel the drug of him running in my veins, as my imagination vaulted into visions of this new and improved Lobster Party. I saw Gil, staring across the table at me in the flickering candlelight.

Gil, his teasing, intimate drawl touching on some private joke between us.

Me, standing, accepting his invitation to dance.

Us, dancing the way we had to "Daisy Bell," only this time not in Mrs. von Cott's dressing room. Not in hiding.

Us, the way we were meant to be. The way the Burkes saw us.

"Jean, dear, I don't like to put you in a tight spot." Weeze's voice dragged me back to her. "But maybe you could explain it to Bertie. You know Junior doesn't have a special girl, either. It would be so nice for us all to have a lovely miss at the table. You, particularly. To balance things out."

"Have you told Gil that you were asking me?"

"Why, of course. *We're* asking you. Think of it that way."

My pulse hammered. He wanted me, but he didn't know how to ask, and so he'd sent his aunt. "Maybe I could try to sort out something."

"Well, there's time. You let us know, Sweets. And thank you."

We stood up together, and then she ducked out and was off, trailing her billowing scent of hairspray and strong floral deodorant.

From the sink window, I watched her slide onto her bike and continue on through to the gate.

I finished cleaning. Doing more than I needed. Working until sweat beaded on my forehead.

Back at home, I made a glass of iced tea and used the hose to drench Mom's flower garden and the hanging plants. Then I sprayed down the walkway. I had to keep busy. If it were true, Gil would call. But I wouldn't drift around, waiting. I'd weed the entire garden, I'd take another shower, I'd set the table for Sunday dinner, maybe lend Mom a hand in the kitchen, since Mrs. Otis was off. What I wouldn't do was sit around and wait.

But suppressing all my hope was something else. It was like trying not to inhale its perfume, or maybe its poison. Honestly, I didn't know what to do with Weeze's request.

I didn't know how to wash it away.

I was already half-drowning in it.

When the phone rang, I ran to get it. I knew.

"Hey. Aunt Weeze told me she stopped by to see you." Gil's voice alone brought it back, my desire a hot rush of urgency under my skin.

"She did."

"So you know everything. Look, she came right out and asked who I'd take if I couldn't take Fritz. She doesn't want Fritz, that's the main thing. They've been really uptight about us lately. It's such a lot of garbage."

"I'm so sorry." My voice was disappointment disguised as sympathy. So my hunch had been correct. They weren't broken up.

"Anyway, I feel like you'd understand the situation better than some random girl."

"Okay."

"And Fritz is fine with this, so you know. We're just sticking things out, while we're here. Playing by Aunt Weeze and Uncle Carp's rules and all."

"Yes, of course."

"And you being Uncle Carp's goddaughter. Makes it easier."

To explain it to Fritz, he meant. "Right." I felt confused, slightly shattered. Weeze had added a bite to the invitation, making me feel special, flattering and enticing me. Whereas Gil's request was toothless. All he wanted was for me to be his helpful gal Friday. I took a breath. "Here's the thing. I don't want to upset Bertie."

"Oh, yeah, Jean, sure, I get that. There's a dozen reasons not to do it. So listen, however it ends up, thanks for being a sport."

"Anything for you, Gil." I hung up quickly, embarrassed by my earnestness.

Be smart. You don't want to be a pawn in this night. Go with Bertie.

Mom's attempts to prepare Sunday supper had not created the most confidence-inspiring smells from the kitchen, but it was still a little bit surprising that the lamb turned out that bad, dry as soap, even slathered in mint jelly and surrounded by potatoes and carrots so overboiled that they fell apart on our forks.

Dad heartily complimented everything, meanwhile gulping down extra wine. I played with my fork and moved food around, waiting until Mom had returned with the runny bread pudding to deliver my news.

"Gil Burke invited me to Lobster Party," I said. "Well, technically Weeze Burke did."

"Yes, I know." Mom smiled as she sat. "Your ears must have been burning."

"What?"

Mom clasped her hands and straightened up in her seat like

a kid with a secret too big to keep. "During bridge club this afternoon, I *might* have mentioned to Weeze how you spent all your time at the Coop. Then Weeze *might* have told me that Gil had mentioned you as someone he wanted to sit at the host table, and then . . ." She smiled as she eased back in her chair and picked up her fork. "We decided to let fate take its course."

"It's hardly fate if Weeze stops by the Coop and invites me on your suggestion," I said stiffly.

Mom flicked her fingers. "You can't be upset. She only wants everything to be impeccable for her party."

"But I thought Gil had a steady girl here," said Dad. "Julia's friend, who visits."

"Oh, but you know the Burkes," said Mom. "They want . . . you know. Someone 'appropriate.'" She made quote marks to show that she thought the Burkes were being irrational, though we all understood what the Burkes meant.

"Sounds exactly like them." Dad sniffed. "But didn't Bertie already beat Gil to the punch, Jean? Aren't you going with him?"

"Not officially." I looked from one parent to the other. "So you think it's all right to be Gil's date?"

"Gil Burke is going places," said Dad. "That young man is sharp as a tack."

"It's hard to imagine that Bertie wouldn't be a brick about it, but if it's a question of loyalty, then by all means, Jean, you should sit with the Forsythes," said Mom. "And yet I can't *not* stump one last time for Gil. He's just so impressive. It's as though the Burkes got a second chance at family with their nephew." She passed me my dessert plate. "And Weeze says he always speaks very highly of you. The least you can do is think it over carefully."

"I will." I'd never, ever heard my parents talk about Bertie with anything close to the amount of praise they were heaping upon Gil. We all knew the decision. We'd made it together.

FRITZ

Tonight felt painful, like the end of something . . .

Starting that first week after Fourth of July weekend, we did what the Burkes asked. At first, it seemed like a bad joke.

I could meet up with Gil openly during work shifts at the club, or at the beach with our friends.

"But I'm not just—*poof*—giving you up!" I told him, outraged, when I thought outrage could get me somewhere. "Weeze and Carp don't get to decide how the world is supposed to turn."

"I know," said Gil miserably. "But they did. And I need to take them seriously."

"If this is how it's going to be, then I think we should split. We could make it work. We'll go to Atlantique, and Phoenix can get us jobs. It's high season everywhere on Fire Island, and I bet if

I called George, he'd let us stay with him long-term. We'd work out a deal!" I could feel the airborne possibility of this summer do-over lifting my hopes. "Don't you see? This could be a real opportunity! Who's to stop us from packing up and taking the very next water taxi?"

"Fritz, you know I can't do that."

"Why not?"

Gil's looked unhappy. "Think about what you're asking. I've had this family in my life for one hot minute. They're doing everything in their power to give me a leg up in the world. You want me to just chuck it all, and run away with you?"

"Only temporarily!"

He regarded me tiredly. "You know how bad I feel. It burns me up that they can—and want—to put this on us. But summer will end, Fritz. And I don't want Carp's loyalty to me to end along with it."

"But there's no reason for them to hate me, like I'm some criminal!"

"They don't hate you."

"They wish I'd drop dead! They don't think I'm good enough for you!"

"You know that when it comes to certain things, the Burkes can be about as lost as last year's Easter egg. We gotta keep our wits together. Come on, baby. Are you with me? I need you in this with me." He opened his arms. I fell in, curled up inside the warmth and strength of his hug, and closed my eyes. For a moment

I imagined that his body had created a rocket ship that would blast us both far away from Sunken Haven and all its insanity.

"We need to take care of each other extra," I whispered, "while they're pulling us apart."

"I hear you, Fritzie," he whispered back. "I'm trying."

So we took no big risks. If we wanted to leave Sunken Haven for pizza, or when we went to see *The Omen* to celebrate my seventeenth birthday, we had to join a herd.

We found secret hours, but those hours were rare. We'd wait until late night, meeting up by the dock or setting our alarms for predawn walks on the beach. We snuck away on mini trips during work breaks, using old rowboats or sailboats that belonged to the club. We'd ride bikes to places where nobody else ever went, like Sandpiper Cove or the North Bay bird blind.

When the day of the dreaded Lobster Party finally arrived, we made a plan to meet up at the bird blind. I really hated this place. The only good thing about it was that it was remote enough that none of Carp and Weeze's friends would ever see us. But there was a reason nobody ever came here. The blind was in a stinky marsh, where clouds of gnats mixed with the sulfur in the air. We couldn't even find a place to sit comfortably, considering the ground was nothing but soggy weeds and clumps of poison sumac.

"I got a letter from my mom yesterday," I mentioned, as I spread a towel on the ledge of a flat rock outcropping, and scratched miserably at my gnat-bitten calves. "She wants to host an O'Neill family reunion over Labor Day weekend."

Gil picked up his hat to beat off a dragonfly. "You think your folks'll let me come to that?"

"Are you kidding?" I smiled at him. I'd been crossing my fingers he'd say that. We'd already figured out that Fort Polk was about eight hours by car, from either New York or Alabama. "That'd be so cool. They're gonna love you, even Kevin, once he's finished showing off."

Gil dropped his hat back on his head. "I was also hoping we could do another kind of reunion, a little earlier. How about we head back to Robbins Rest this Wednesday, for our one-month?"

"As in, an anniversary of . . . that?"

"As in, that."

"Wow." I was quiet for a second. That night had been a story of us that existed in a time and space apart from everything that had happened afterward. The way Gil was being watched, we hadn't found a way to have sex again. "You'd really risk it?"

"I've been talking to Tiger, and he says he'll cover for me. You're not the only one who needs a break. It's been one hell of a month."

I nodded. "That'd be so smooth."

"Meantime . . ." Gil slid down from the outcropping to retrieve his backpack. He never kept more than a bottle of bug spray, a pocket flashlight, and a Thermos in there — so I wasn't paying much attention when he pulled out a square blue box with a bow. "Happy belated birthday."

I sat up. "You weren't belated. I thought those albums you gave me last week *were* my birthday present."

"Nope. That was the decoy. Here's the real deal. It took me an extra couple of weeks to pay Mrs. Walt."

I shook my head. "That old lady's got a sweet spot for you. She'd never do a payment plan for just any—oh my gosh." As I popped open the box, my heart tripped a beat. "The earrings! How did you know?"

"Julia told me you were wild for them."

"I figured somebody had bought them."

"Somebody did."

"Gil, I'm . . ." Speechless. The green stones with the jet beaded tassels were old-fashioned but with an edge of punk. I'd never had such a nice gift from any guy. I'd been so bummed out when those earrings had disappeared from Thriffaney's. And here they were, not only reappeared but mine.

He watched as I slid in the earrings' posts and fastened the backs, then shook my head to test their swing.

"I'll sleep in these every night," I told him. "I'll wear them till I'm a hundred years old." They already felt perfect. Not too heavy, and they touched the edge of my jaw exactly right.

"You're a goof." Gil smoothed back my hair with both hands to see the earrings better. He nodded. "I saw a pair of earrings like this on a girl back in New York. She had a lot of style. Like you." He kissed me, and then hoisted himself off the rock and lifted his backpack.

"Wait, you need to go? But we just got here."

"Aunt Weeze invited some of her girlfriends over to the house before cocktails tonight. She wants me to play bartender."

I felt myself clench. "Well, that's a bummer. Will Jean be there?"

"What? No, of course not."

"You *say* no of course not, but I swear your aunt wants to marry you two off."

"I thought we'd been through this. Jean's as much my date as she is Junior's tonight. She's stepping in as a family favor."

"So you keep telling me." Gil would always be a little bit starry-eyed about Jean Custis, her "sweetness" and her "friendship."

I touched my earrings. They were so beautiful. I really didn't want Weeze—and all her tricks—to be a drag on my mood right now. "I guess I'll go pick up Julia. She's on Main Beach."

"I promise we'll get through it. Six hours and it's done."

"I've sat with the Tullivers every year, so nothing's much different for me."

Gil took my hand to help me off the rock. "I know you're putting on a good face, and I know this stinks. I'll make it up to you."

I nodded. "You'd better."

Another kiss good-bye, and then I made my way to the beach. Whenever Gil and I were together, I always felt so springy and buzzed that it was never until afterward, in those letdown hours, that I allowed myself to dwell on all the things that bothered me.

Lobster Party bothered me.

In the army, you always knew who you were because of your dad's rank. The colonels' kids were more important than the majors' kids. The majors' kids were more important than the captains' kids. And so if Lobster Party was like a birthday party for a five-star general, and I was only the sergeant's kid, then I got why I shouldn't be invited. The Burkes wanted Jean Custis, another general's daughter, to sit at their table because she was the right rank.

But now, walking alone to the beach, I fell back on thoughts of how wrong this night felt. I'd only wanted to help Gil. It had been a way to show him my love was more than passionate, that it could spread all the way out to the corners of smart and kind and careful and understanding.

Except there were no ranks on Sunken Haven. It was supposed to be one big happy family. By standing back and letting the Burkes do exactly what they wanted, wasn't I agreeing with them that I wasn't good enough for Gil? And that Jean Custis was?

By late afternoon, Main Beach was almost empty; only a few surfers, some dog-and-Frisbee people—and suntan queen Julia Tulliver.

I dropped beside her and gave my head a little shake. "Check these out." She'd been roasting herself all afternoon, and now she was brown as toast and slick as an eel in cocoa butter.

Julia raised her sunglasses. "Glamour city. Looks like Secret Agent Man did right by you. Where is he?"

"Weeze wanted him to deal with her pre–Lobster Party party."

Julia made a face. "It's like the Burkes are rubbing your nose in it."

"Who cares what they do? I'm just glad I'm sitting with you, same as always." I always had to act like I didn't care about tonight or what the Burkes had done, so that Julia's feelings against Gil didn't get too harsh.

"Catch a few last rays, and then we'll go up."

I arranged myself in exactly her position: arms long at my side, one leg slightly bent, toes pointed in. We lay next to each other, our bodies side by side like cookie cutouts, listening to the surf, the occasional squawk of an overhead gull. It was one of those private games I'd played since I was a kid, right from the first day when my mom drove me to meet Julia after Mrs. Tulliver and Mom had gotten to be friends. I'd seen her in school—she was a grade ahead and already a standout, a girl with a glare, a girl the boys chased, anyway. I ached to be friends.

Julia had been jumping rope in her driveway with a bunch of other neighborhood girls, and without a word, I'd gotten out of the car and jumped right into her game, facing her, matching each smack of her feet on the pavement. She'd barely changed expression, but then we'd jumped together so long that other girls started to get mad that we were taking so much time, using up their turns.

I wasn't as good a jump-roper on my own; even though I had all the endurance, I often lost my rhythm. Julia never did.

It was something I learned about Julia right from that very first day, copying her steadiness, jumping on her beat, staring like a mirror's reflection into her pale silvery-blue eyes, even when girls started to whine and the two rope turners began snapping the rope too fast. I watched Julia's silent, serious face, took her cues, and was better in our pair than I'd ever been on my own.

Maybe I'd never be as chill as Julia, but she had always reminded me to match her groove. I was glad we'd be sticking by each other tonight. As long as I never left her side, I'd be okay.

"It's getting late," she said, finally.

"Nooo . . ." I wriggled my toes in the sand.

"So you know, Oliver thinks it's bogus, too. We both do." Julia stood, stretched, and swept up her beach towel to shake out. She meant Gil, Lobster Party, all of it. She'd been lying next to me, thinking about it all this time. I felt embarrassed and grateful.

"It'll work out," I told her. "Hey, you got some good color."

"I better, I've been baking out here for four hours. My skin *hurts.* Are you still wearing my heinous dress?"

"Yeah, but I've got these earrings now."

"Ha. Consolation prize."

Did Julia mean consolation prize because the dress was so bad? Or because I wasn't sitting at the Burke table—and Jean was?

Either way, Julia was right about the dress. Once upon a time, the red-and-white striped dress had been cute on ninth-grade Julia. On the hanger and on me, it looked stupid, and so gauzy

I had to wear a slip underneath. But I wasn't in a mood to think any harder about this night, with all of its rules and limitations and all the ways I couldn't fix it. Lobster Party needed to happen and be done.

Back at Whisper, I showered and changed in the Tullivers' bathroom. At least the earrings were perfect. I tilted my head this way and that way, staring at myself in the medicine-cabinet mirror. The afternoon light threw a prism across my face, like a church's stained-glass window.

Dot's pounding on the door snapped me out of it. "Hey, Fritz! You gonna let me do your hair like you said?"

"Sure."

She came in with her magazine in one hand and her wire Snoopy brush in the other. I sat on the toilet while Dot went at me, creating two French braids from the how-to pages of her *Young Miss,* using her orthodontic rubber bands, plus a zillion stabbing bobby pins.

"Pretty snazzy," she said when she'd finished. "I should charge you a coupla bucks for this."

"Nice try, Dotty. I feel like I got scalped." Galloping downstairs before Dot could keep demanding payment, I flung myself outside and flopped onto the Tullivers' porch hammock.

Through the kitchen window, I heard Julia's dad complaining to her mom about how his tie was too tight. Mr. Tulliver hadn't been in the army for years, but he still reminded me of my own dad: how he didn't like to wear dressy "civvies"—civilian clothes—and loved his sunrise runs, and sang paratrooper songs about jumping out of C-130s.

When Julia stepped out onto the porch, she gave me a look and pulled a face. "I can't handle you in that dress. It's so not you."

"Don't you think the earrings save it?"

"I don't think so. What's red and white and freckly all over?"

I leaped out of the hammock and started chasing Julia, as she fled with a scream. Laughing and ducking down the worn porch steps, we raced all around the lawn where, as kids, we'd spent summer nights playing kick the can, capture the flag, freeze tag, and whiffle ball.

Running after her, I was hit with a gust of how many years I'd known Julia, how sophisticated she looked this evening in the silver-white dress that she'd restyled with a handkerchief hem, and how long it had been since we'd chased each other around this lawn. Tonight suddenly felt painful, like the end of something, or the beginning of something else.

I didn't know whether to grieve it or celebrate it.

Julia turned on me, as she always did, changing the rules and going after me now, then grabbing me—"*Gotcha!*" Her long arms wrapped around me; her skin smelled like her favorite honeysuckle perfume.

"Girls." Mrs. Tulliver had appeared on the porch. "Ready?"

"Ready," we chorused.

And just as quickly as we had been kids again, it was over.

Halfway up the turnoff to Bay Walk, I slipped on Mrs. Tulliver's thick white wedges, which I'd been letting dangle from my fingers.

"Running like that made me feel like I was back in sixth grade," Julia said, with a glance behind us to the house.

"I was thinking the exact same thing."

"You ever miss us living at Whisper?"

"Sometimes. Remember when we short-sheeted your parents' bed?"

"Or when you broke your arm falling out of the plum tree?"

"After I warned and warned you!" Julia made a mock-serious face, but now I remembered how frightened she'd been at the time. "Remember how every morning, we'd eat Alpha-Bits on the porch and watch the sun come up, waiting for the green herons or whistling swans?"

"We'd get a dime if we got your Grandpa out in time to see them."

"Aw, man. Grandpa." Julia's grandfather, who'd died years ago, had loved those birds. I hadn't even thought about green herons or whistling swans—or, come to think of it, Julia's grandpa—for ages. But I'd always felt at home at the Tulliver cottage. From the patched screens and warped floors, to the iron latch-and-handle door fixtures, to the kinked beach-plum trees by its windows, Whisper's shabby beauty was etched in my brain.

"What if we moved back in next year? Mom said we could if we wanted. She misses us. The Morgue is fun, but it's not home."

"Could be cool," I told her. I'd never hurt Julia by saying that I wasn't sure I wanted to spend my next summer on Sunken Haven. Phoenix's illuminating warning and now this falling-out with the Burkes had been shifting my thoughts about this place. I didn't have the same faith in it. How could I?

Gil had said he wasn't coming back, either. He was hoping to have a paid internship next summer, and we'd talked about how maybe I'd join him in the city, take a waitressing job at one of those fine-dining restaurants, where the bread guy came around with tongs and a basket of rolls.

Would Julia want to come with me? Was she ready to leave Sunken Haven, too? Would she ever be ready? Was this our last summer together?

It seemed almost outrageous, an almost impossible thought.

The dinner tables had been set up by the harbor. White linen tablecloths, weighted down by Mrs. Train's silver place settings, flapped in the bay breeze. Mrs. Train herself stood at the drift line, her tomato-red pants rolled above her blue-white ankles as she told people how to heat the stockpots using the outdoor burners.

Mrs. Train was the lady who made sure nothing happened any different from the year before at Lobster Party, right down to using her personal place settings that could serve over a hundred people and were kept stored in a gun safe at the yacht club. I wondered if Mrs. Train knew the Burkes had banished me from the host table. She had never been expressly mean to me. Just ignored me, mostly. Did she dislike me, too? Had she talked against me after I'd won the Junior Cup, or thought my jean shorts meant that Sunken Haven's standards were lowering?

Tonight, all of the old guard seemed tarnished, capable of harsh thoughts and strong words. Every moment was overlaid with all my doubt.

Gil and Tiger were sharing a smoke while they waited for us on the library steps. From a distance, seeing them together, I was startled by how perfectly Sunkie Gil looked. It stopped me. He hadn't had his hair cut since he'd been here, and it had grown out to the same tousled shagginess as Tiger's, with the same side part, the same longish sideburns. In his checked cobalt-blue shirt, red rep tie, navy blazer, khakis, and boat shoes, Gil could have stepped out of an advertisement for an East Coast boarding school.

"I promise we'll get through it," he'd told me. "Six hours and it's done."

As if Lobster Party was just an event, not a way of life. He'd had me believing it. When I'd slipped on my dress, when I'd allowed Dot to play hair salon, all I was really doing was thinking beyond Lobster Party, to when Gil and I would be together again. I hadn't given much thought to tonight, other than knowing I had to endure it.

But Gil was different. He wanted it, though maybe I had never realized till now just how much. What I did know was that in the short time that he'd been here, Gil had been relentlessly revising himself, learning absolutely everything about fitting in. Now he'd done it, he did fit in; nobody could have known the behind-the-scenes, furious effort it had taken to bury that Alabama boy. All that was left was the polished surface. It all hit me so forcefully now; while I'd been focused on staying me, Gil had been absolutely focused on changing—and his new identity was flawless.

I stared at him, the gorgeous summer colors of him, the way a kaleidoscope image suddenly sharpened into its final, exact pattern. *Of course* Gil saw tonight as a way of life.

Of course Gil was coming back to Sunken Haven next year.

"Did you know they cook the lobsters in the same water they catch 'em in?" Gil asked me as the guys stood up. He dropped and stubbed out his cigarette in the sand.

"No. I didn't." Even his voice sounded a little different to me—more high class. Or was I being extra insecure tonight? After all, it wasn't wrong for Gil to learn how to succeed here—was it?

"Yep, it's a centuries-old tradition." He reached out to tug one of my braids. I almost flinched; my hairstyle seemed so dumb now. "You okay?"

"I guess."

"Arright, then." He gave me a quizzing glance. As we took the stairs, he waved and called out a good-bye to Mrs. Train, whose face melted into a smile.

"I'll do my best to see that you're served a nice big lobster!" she called to him.

"Thanks, Mrs. T!"

"You've sure got everyone eating out of the palm of your hand," I told him.

"Ain't no one can touch my Burke charm."

"Most people didn't know there was such a thing as Burke charm, till you."

"Maybe that's why I'm a necessary asset to my family." There was a note of hope in Gil's voice. I wanted to shake him for it. For valuing them like he did.

"Listen, Fritz. I've said it before." He pulled me nearer as we got to the top of the stairs. "But I want to say it again. How much I appreciate this."

"Let's leave." The words popped out before I could stop them.

"*What?*" His stare was doubtful, maybe even slightly annoyed. "Come on. You really want to bolt on me *now?*"

"I only meant . . . no, I'm sorry," I said. "Flight impulse."

He took my hand and squeezed. "It's okay. I get it."

But as we entered the library, I could feel that same impulse smack me backward, because it was the last thing I'd expected.

Jean Custis looked absolutely beautiful.

It was an image so overwhelming that I couldn't hold in the entire picture of her all at once; even the details hit me like shards of glass.

She was wearing a leafgreen, silk sundress that must have come from one of those Madison Avenue department stores, with straps as thin as Christmas tinsel, and she'd paired it with silver ankle-strap sandals that added a hip, city flair. Her hair was styled high on her head, so sophisticated, like a girl on a Grecian urn, and she'd gone for some shimmery, barely there makeup. She hardly even seemed like herself, the way she was standing with her shoulders back and her chin tilted. Who did she remind me of? Someone. She looked so poised and sure of herself. Like she'd been waiting all her life for this moment.

Her sister. Daphne. That's who she reminded me of.

Of all the things I'd never liked about cheerleading, I'd most dreaded those final, gut-knifing pregame minutes, standing at the edge of the tunnel, when I could hear the loudspeaker and see the blinding field lights. As we all waited for our squad captain to give us the signal, the fear would hit me all at once, and I'd think *No way. I can't. I'm gonna look like an idiot out there. I'm gonna fall on my face, split my shorts, crack a rib.*

This was happening to me right now.

Gil kept a light touch on my waist as we met up with Oliver at the circulation desk. Tonight, it was stocked with ice-filled buckets of wine, rows of goblets, and plastic trays heaped with traditionally unfancy cheese cubes, salami, grapes, and crackers.

"I'm not hungry," I said.

"Me, either," said Julia. "Ollie, bring me a wine, please? How are you doing?" she whispered, as we edged away from the bar crowd, over to the juvenile book section, where there was more room to breathe easy.

"Why didn't I try to look like a knockout tonight?" I asked.

"I feel like I got set up for some kind of girlfriend competition. I mean, check out Jean, would you?"

"Fritz, you can't sweat this for a second."

"My logical brain knows this wasn't some evil Jean-masterminded plan, but it feels really messed up."

"Oh, please. Don't even bother about her." Quickly, Julia pulled a book from a shelf. "Remember our very first summer together, when Hurricane Camille hit and we curled up on those bean bags and read a million Nancy Drews? Look, here's *The Secret of the Old Clock*! Fritz, stop looking over at her."

"Okay, okay. I'm not." Jean's nails had been polished the most delicate shell pink. Her toenails matched. Wow, even the toenails.

"*Clue of the Tapping Heels*," Julia continued, reading the back of the book. "*The Secret of Shadow Ranch*."

"The Sign of the Twisted Burkes," quipped Oliver, as he appeared between us. "They just came in." His jaw lifted, indicating them. I only glanced over for a second; I didn't want to meet Weeze Burke's eye.

There was something about this deeper protectiveness from both Oliver and Julia that made the whole scene worse. I could feel myself all wrapped up in their care. Since when was I the fragile one? The one in need of protection? How had Jean Custis gotten the upper hand?

Why was this night so much wronger than I'd anticipated?

"I'll see you later on." Gil, veering up behind Oliver, gave me a smile that seemed to reach all the way to the bottom of my heart. "Are you cool?"

"I'm okay," I said. But I wasn't. I wanted Gil to see me, to really get it, to see everything I was up against, how small I felt, how rejected. Because if he did, then he'd reach out and grip my hand in his, and he'd lead me out of this library, all the way down Bay Walk and to the dock, where we would wait for the very next ferry and jump on it without even a word exchanged, because we'd both completely understand that if we wanted to stay together, we had to get the hell out of this place.

But Gil stayed oblivious, choosing not to hear my unspoken wishes, hanging out for a couple more moments. As the Burkes moved deeper into the party, he went to join them. I watched Gil work his space, shaking hands, saying hellos, the perfect gentleman.

He stopped at Jean and spoke to her politely, though at a distance—I knew he could feel me looking at them. But in the seconds since he'd left me, I felt like a bell had rung, signaling tonight's new agreement—the one where, for six hours, we officially mattered less to each other. As in, Gil wasn't going to stop talking with Jean because it made me feel uncomfortable, and I wasn't going to stop staring just because he didn't like it.

Together Gil and Jean seemed to agree on what to do next, as they began to move toward the Burkes. I watched as Weeze spoke to Gil, moving in and placing her hand on Gil's forearm in a way that took me by surprise. Whoa, I'd never seen so much warmth radiating from Weeze Burke. She'd really thawed on Gil. It was as if, over the past few weeks, he'd passed some sort of loyalty test, and she'd decided he truly belonged with her family now.

That was it. She had accepted him.

Junior, at Weeze's side, also seemed to catch a wisp of their moment. He said something and motioned toward the bar. Weeze shook her head. She wanted Gil, not Junior, to fix her drink. Junior's face went stony.

But Gil was happy about this victory. I saw it in his closed-mouthed smile, his alert and cheerful turn, the way he strode over, pitched his palms against the desk as he spoke to the bartender, one of the local Bay Shore boys, a new kid who looked at Gil respectfully and stepped to the side as Gil moved behind the bar himself to pour out Weeze's usual—a glass of white wine with a splash of Perrier.

When Jean's parents circled in closer to start chatting with Carp, and Gil rejoined Weeze and Junior, their group coziness pained me. I felt like I'd fallen so far outside of their ranks that my very presence was an intrusion, maybe even a disgrace.

But then Jean suddenly looked up and glanced over at me, and her eyes got all wide. Like I'd done something to shock her. What was it? Was she surprised to see me here at all?

All these years that I'd been coming to this island, all the books I'd read in the Sunken Haven Library, all the games of tag

I'd played on the dunes and Great South Bay, all the Punch Nights and Lobster Parties, all the sunsets and thunderstorms—it all added up to a tonight where I was nobody, a zero.

"Be right back," I told Julia and Oliver, though I wasn't sure if that was even true, I had so little desire to stay; but the only place where I could safely escape was the ladies' room, a quick trip down the library stairs and around the corner.

Thankfully, the restroom was empty. I ducked into the last of the three stalls and stood there for a moment. My shoulders pressed against the cold wall, listening to my heartbeat.

It wasn't until I was finished peeing that I heard the door swing open, and I heard voices I recognized as the girls came barging in.

"She can't help if she's stacked," Sara Train was saying in that whiney way of hers, "but if she's going to put them out like that, people will talk."

"Did you see her in her tube top the other night?" Rosamund Wembley chimed in. "Were we at a barbecue or a disco?"

They were talking about Deirdre Poe, who was Tiger's brick house of a visiting college girlfriend. Her huge chest, no matter how she covered it up, had been making a catty kind of news all week.

"When you have boobs like that, you start to rely on constant attention," said Sara knowingly, although in that department, she herself only had a pair of mosquito bites. "You should have seen her pushing them out for Gil Burke the other day at the club."

The cool delight that usually splashed over me whenever I

heard Gil's name froze with Rosamund's next remark. "Gil better watch it. He's got plenty on his plate as it is."

This comment was followed by laughter.

I kept quiet as two kittens, waiting.

But I'd never have been prepared for what came next.

"Do you think it's really true what Junior said about Gil and all his shady meetups with Jean Custis?" asked Sara. "Or is that only Junior telling his usual tales?"

Okay, I hadn't heard that right. Sara had said something else, something innocent.

"Between us, I highly doubt it." Rosamund's voice was smug. "I mean, we've all known Jeanie our whole lives. She's such a prude."

"Until she's wasted on gin and tonics. Then she might be capable of anything," reminded Sara. "And you have to wonder what Bertie thinks about all this secret romance, since the story on Jean and Bertie is they haven't gone all the way yet."

"I don't get why Gil'd need to go sniffing around Jean. You don't think Fritz puts out for him?" asked Rosamund.

"Why choose the fries or the salad, if you can have both?" Sara sniffed.

"Junior swears it's been going on all summer. He said she came sneaking into the house one night all the way back in June, easy as you please, and Gil took her right up to his room. Also, Lindsay Hasty said once she saw the two of them scurrying into the von Cott house, and they didn't come out. That house isn't even being used this summer."

Now there was some giggling, followed by a sharp silence. One of them must have seen my shoes.

Someone turned on a faucet, so I couldn't hear more, which was probably a good thing. I wasn't sure I could stand listening to them for another second. My mind was on fire.

Was this true? Any of it? All of it?

I wanted them to leave, so that I could leave, too — but then Sara's patent-leather bow-topped Minnie Mouse feet clopped into the stall two over from mine.

"Go on, Ros. I'll catch up," she said, which sounded like a command for bathroom privacy. I heard the door swing as Rosamund took off. I counted to twenty before I flushed and followed. Mrs. Tulliver's ugly wedges had saved me. The girls thought I was just another indifferent mom.

I went back up to the library, my body zinging with shock, my mind an eruption of chaos. Where was Julia? I had to tell her. If I had Julia with me, I could leave.

Sara and Rosamund had joined up and were hanging around Fred Hasty and Chip and Tiger and Deirdre and a few of the others, over at the bar. What did they know? Most of it? Everything? Questions crammed my brain. I needed Julia, my lifeline. I needed her shoulder to cry on, or maybe to scream on. Had she stepped outside for a smoke with Oliver? Did she know about any of this? Who knew and who didn't?

Watching Gil chatting with Jean in that courtly Southern way, I'd never felt so bitterly, stupidly confused. I studied them for clues, as my memory scrambled through time like a rat through trash. When had it happened, where had it happened, did it even really happen, why had Gil wanted it to happen? *And who else knew about it?*

Warm, loud bodies pressed into my space from all sides as I made a dazed circuit of the room. One of the mothers, Mrs. Corey, was having an "exhibit" here tonight. Her mournful, broken-glass pictures were hung crooked over the bookshelves. I saw Bertie by the science and nature section, under a broken-glass painting of his own father.

Who knew more? Me or Bertie? I'd never thought of Bertie as plugged into gossip and rumors. He always held himself a little bit removed, a kid who already seemed like a dad. But there was only one way to find out. I moved directly. My body was shaking through to my center. Could anyone see that? I pressed my hands together to steady myself.

"Hi, Bertie."

"Hey, Fritz. Having any fun yet?" Was he being sarcastic?

"Oh, I don't know. It's not fun to be here stag, right?"

Bertie's wide-set gray eyes narrowed. "This isn't strictly a couples night."

"I guess not. Unless you're already a couple."

"Are you talking about Gil and Jean?" Bertie gave a flick of his shoulder. "Believe me, that's not real. You have my word."

"I guess she told you she was sitting with the Burkes because they asked her specially, as a favor."

"Is there another reason?"

"Maybe that's what I'm asking you?" Though it was becoming pretty obvious that blank-faced Bertie hadn't heard the gossip.

Bertie sighed. Like he had to explain something to a second grader, and didn't much want to. "I don't mean to sound rough, Fritz, but Carp and Weeze aren't wild about you. Everyone knows that. Even you know it. And Gil's a stand-up guy. Everybody, including Jean, wants him to do well tonight. There's no reason for us not to be civilized."

I'd never noticed how much Bertie looked like a shark. Besides his wide-spaced pebble-gray eyes, he had that flat head, that dent of mouth. He was always so publicly mushy around Jean. Now he struck me as a more evasive, sharper person. But I couldn't read that face. And if he didn't know about Gil and Jean, I didn't want to be the one to break it to him.

"Right." I turned to go.

"Fritz." He caught my hand as I began to move away.

When I faced him again, Bertie's expression had changed. "I won't lie," he confided softly. "I've heard . . . things. It's impossible not to hear things, you know? But when you're in a relationship for the long haul—and maybe you and Gil are, too—then sometimes the best thing to do is to look away."

The strangest part of that comment was how much Bertie believed in it. Look Away: Bertie Forsythe's secret, sad life motto.

"Okay," I said. It seemed cruel to do anything but agree. Basically, what Bernie was saying was that he'd decided to play along.

But I was finished standing here, in this steaming-hot library, trying not to flip out.

Finally, I spied Julia with Oliver, out on the side balcony—between us was a crush of people. I was closer to the exit than to the two of them.

And I really wanted to get to her before I started to cry.

In my hurry, I bumped up against Mrs. Walt at the stairs, and I accidentally jostled her white wine, causing her to jump and squeal.

"Oh my gosh, Mrs. Walt, I'm sorry!"

"Get me some napkins!" Her mouth made a grimace of effort, as we both started patting at her front in a flurry, using the cocktail napkins I'd snatched off a tray.

"Fritz?" Gil's voice carried from all the way across the room. Then louder. "Fritz?"

Crap. Why did I do it? Why did I look up? But I did, and I met Gil's gaze so squarely that my eyes heated, and I knew the pain in my face was so raw and naked that he could see it.

No. No way could I handle this. I felt too exposed, and I had no control over it.

I dropped my handful of napkins and bolted.

Outside, I gulped down the fresh bay breeze. Kettledrums were bubbling with fish chowder, and the air smelled delicious, a salty summer mix of brine and butter. Dinner guests were beginning to gather around the bay. A few strollers bayside were watching the sun go down. Picture perfect, as ever.

I started to run.

Not to Whisper. Not the Morgue. Not the beach, not the club. I hit the ridge hard, making no choices. Just straight, on and on, tears striping my cheeks, trying to outrun my thoughts, and by the time I'd stopped, I was at the center of town, sweating, out of breath, and totally confused about what to do next.

The candy store was closed but not locked. I slipped inside the icy-sweet darkness. The cogs of my brain weren't even working, tears brimmed and burned and spilled from my eyes, and I had no idea why I lit on making a milkshake—other than the fact that it was the simplest thing I could do.

Vanilla and chocolate.

Ice, milk, tears, syrup.

I dug into the hard-packed tubs of ice cream, dropping each scoop in snowball globes into the blender, then tossing in clumsy handfuls of ice, a messy squeeze of syrup.

I wiped my eyes, turned the blender to PULVERIZE.

Three summers ago, Julia and I had been the ice-cream queens of the candy store, our very first paying job at Sunken Haven. It was a real score to work a "real" Sunken Haven job, and we were so proud. I could still see the ghostly print of that summer, the two of us in matching pink shirts and braces on our teeth, inventing mixed-up ice-cream flavors, giggling and lightheaded and always paying attention to whatever might happen in a single shift—a cute guy, a new couple, a herd of Minnows. Each innocent customer was a brand-new chance for us to laugh our heads off for reasons that escaped me now, except that it was all vaguely connected to our seventh-grade Awkwardness.

All these memories of me and Julia—and there were tons of them—would they all be tarnished by this summer?

Liar liar liar. The word pounded in my head, hard as my heartbeat. Gil's lie made every part of me shiver with shocked disbelief. My hands were still unreliable as I drained the shake from the metal cup.

I'd finish this shake, and then I'd be out. First upstairs to pack up my suitcase. Next, I'd write Marcy Pency my notice and slide it under her office door. Marcy Pency was one of the few people here who could receive a private note and not broadcast it all over the island.

I'd have to swing by Whisper for some stuff. That meant another note, asking Julia to pack and send me the rest of my things. I didn't want to leave her, but she'd understand when I told her. She'd know exactly why I had to run through that gate and catch a ferry to Bay Shore. At least I'd had the smarts to save my tips all summer. I hadn't saved tons, but there was enough.

"Fritz!"

I looked up—I hadn't even heard the bell jangle. I'd been thinking so hard, and Gil had come in so quietly. I set down my empty cup and wiped my eyes, wiped my ice-cream mustache.

"Fritz, what the hell?"

"Is it *true*? About you getting together with *Jean*?"

He didn't say anything. In the terrifying void of his silence,

I could feel the drop in my body temperature. So it was true. Oh my god, it was true.

"How long?"

"It was once, a one-time thing, a while ago."

"A 'one-time thing!' That sounds like sex. Was it?"

His yes was in his eyes. He let me see that. "Fritz, everything that went on with Jean and me happened the first week I was here. Before, even." He spoke tiredly. "You and I weren't even really together."

"What are you talking about? Do you think I'm stupid? Practically *nothing* had happened between the two of you. And you and I have been together practically since the day you got here."

"All I meant was that stuff started up with Jean before I met you, and then I didn't end it the right way, and I think it caused her a lot of pain."

"I don't even know what to say. I feel like you think I should understand this. What kind of pain do you imagine I'm in now? Never mind as your girlfriend, but as a human being? As someone who thought you were my friend?" My voice was going wobbly, but I hung on and made myself keep talking. "What do you think I should feel about the two of you making your secret plans and creeping off, and me believing everything between us was so real, me thinking I was your only—"

"It wasn't like that." Gil reached out to take my hand; I stepped back. "I couldn't up and confess something like that. Give away what happened between Jean and me. It wasn't just my secret. It was only half my secret."

"Always so protective of precious Jean. What about me? What about my feelings?"

"How can you even say that? You're everything to me. You've been what holds me up here, especially when I'm dealing with my aunt and uncle. You know me better than anyone."

"I don't think I know you at all."

Gil reached for me; I stepped away again, but this time, he caught my wrist. "Fritz, listen, in a way I'm glad you know—"

"Let me go!"

"Not till you listen—"

"I don't need to listen to you! I don't need to listen to how you're *glad,* or *relieved* or whatever, that I know what you did! It's the worst pain I ever felt, to know this!" I wrestled away in one hard wrench, then ducked past him, out the door.

I started running. Heading nowhere, really, since the only straight path was to the harbor.

Gil was right behind. I could hear his breath and the hard pounding of his feet right behind me, and it wasn't a minute before he'd overtaken me. With one strong arm, he cinched my waist, yanking and twisting himself right up next to me. Forcing me to slow down, then walk in lockstep with him, even as I kept moving toward the harbor and the dock.

He couldn't completely stop me, and so we didn't stop. Not

until we had reached the end of the slip and we couldn't go any farther.

A rowboat was tied there. As soon as he let go of me, I stepped into it and unlocked the oars. It was an impulse. All I knew, forcefully and absolutely, was that I wanted to go.

"You should get back to them," I said. "Go back to your family, and to Jean, to Lobster Party. Go back where you belong."

But Gil stepped into the hull. "Cut it out, Fritz. What am I supposed to do, wave good-bye while you row away into the sunset?"

"Get your foot out of this boat."

"Tell me where you're going."

"It doesn't matter! Leave me alone!"

"I'm not gonna leave you." As soon as I tried to push off, Gil got in, hunkering down, his weight solid and immobile. "You want to go somewhere? Fine! Where to, Fritz? You're free to go anywhere. Problem is, I'm coming with you."

"Jump out. Go. I don't want to be around you. The least you can do is give me some space to be by myself."

He didn't answer me. We lapsed into silence.

Gil's face was tight, a mask. He wasn't letting up on this.

I stared past him. Rowed us out in sure strokes. Stared at the space just past him. My face was hot and puffy and tearstained. The gentle, sinking sun felt good on it. The farther away I got from Lobster Party, the more my muscles seemed to unlock naturally, as a deepening, welcome calm melted through my body.

After a moment, I said, "Jump out here, why don't you. Swim back, change your clothes at Snappy Boy, and you'll be in time to catch dinner."

"You can't get away from me that easy, Fritz."

"I already feel miles away from you." My eyes instantly stung with more tears as I said it, but it was true. He could come along with me, but I had already left him.

We were leaving the harbor. Heading out into the ocean, with no plan, and rowing to nowhere.

JEAN

I hadn't prepared myself for the hurt.

Where was he? I'd seen him go but hadn't alerted anyone to it. He'd followed Fritz down the stairs. That was half an hour ago.

The thirty minutes crawled their way to forty-five, and Gil still hadn't returned. At seven o' clock, everyone began to trickle over to dinner, down the stairs and through the doors into the cooled summer air. The Lamplighters had kicked off the evening; there was a general feeling of readiness. The night was beginning in earnest. But no Gil.

"Where's our boy?" Weeze asked, as I circled the Burke table in search of my name card.

"I think he went off to have a cigarette," I lied.

Weeze was no fool. She knew something was amiss. Her eyes continued to scan the bay for him, and I knew it wasn't lost on her that Fritz was gone, too. Still, she bequeathed a good ten more minutes of hostess natter with various guests, before she signaled to Carpie in a gesture of helpless bafflement.

Gil had vanished.

Carpie, thin lipped, indicated that we should take our seats.

I settled in between Weeze and the empty chair on my left, all set with a bowl of cooling chowder and a tender, warm dinner roll. My chin was up, my shoulders back and spine arched, on alert for any sign of him.

As seats filled, I felt as if I were sitting next to a ghost.

Where *was* he?

After a couple of minutes, Carpie stood and tapped his water glass. Thirteen tables went quiet. I could barely concentrate on Carpie's words, as he boomed a lordly welcome. He made the first toast to his wife, Louise, for all her hard work; this was followed by a toast to the incomparable Mrs. Train, who had helmed so many parties past.

Then I saw Carpie's eyes land briefly, irritated, on the empty chair next to me. He'd carved out room for Gil in his opening round of toasts. It was almost palpable, the feeling of Carpie angrily tamping over this part of his speechmaking.

Good lord, where was he?

Carpie closed his talk with some remarks about rebuilding the church, giving a gentle nudge for generosity, and then an invitation to relax and enjoy the evening. There was a smattering of applause and clinking glasses. Carpie sat down.

The sky was tassel-threaded in fading reds. Dusk was closing in.

My brain kept replaying the last moments before Gil had left. We'd all been standing together upstairs in the library. Gil and Dad were discussing the Karen Ann Quinlan case. Gil was impressing Dad the way he could impress anyone: with the cadence of his storytelling, his face so broadly animated, his feet planted solid as a politician's, his hands open and gesturing. I watched him adoringly and I hoped that my feelings didn't show up too plain on my face.

Our whole evening, fat and buttery and blossoming, lay in front of us.

And then he was gone.

No excuses. He hadn't informed anybody that he was leaving or when he'd be back.

I took a shaky spoonful of soup. A few drops spilled onto the napkin on my lap. I set down my spoon. It was pointless to try to eat.

Almost an hour. Had Gil meant to leave us this long? Or was it all an accident? Had the two of them been plotting for a while? Or had Fritz acted alone, and done it on purpose, creating a crisis so that she could sabotage my evening?

Fritz's place next to Julia stayed empty, too. After a while, I saw Julia's sister, Dot, plop herself in Fritz's chair. When Julia got up to go to the bar, I followed.

"Have you seen Fritz and Gil?" I asked.

Julia regarded me in her usual, inscrutable way. "When I saw that they were both gone," she answered, "naturally I assumed they ditched Lobster Night together. Which, in my opinion, was the right thing to do." One eyebrow rose. "Are you spying for the Burkes?"

"Of course I'm not. And you don't have to be rude about it."

"Why not?" she asked calmly. "You've been rude about a few things, don't you think, Jean? Sneaking in from the sidelines, with all your big plans and schemes."

"I didn't come over so that you could pick a fight with me."

"I guess you put me in a fighting mood." Then she took her root beer from the bartender, thanked him, and left me.

Taking a glass of ice water, I stood at the bar alone, sipping to soothe my stomach. It hadn't occurred to me how angry Julia would be about Lobster Party—and, worse, I could see how she was justified. I'd risked so much for this night to work. It made me feel queasy to think how much. But ultimately, ordering my new dress and shoes with Mom, overnighted from Bonwit's, or, earlier tonight, getting Mrs. Otis to do my hair from a magazine picture, my imagination had danced only with optimism. I hadn't prepared myself for the hurt—mine, or anybody else's.

With every moment that passed, the night was shriveling, becoming something shameful and sour. It reminded me of last summer, stepping out onto the tennis court, feeling that harsh force of Fritz's serve. I'd thought we'd have a good game. She had dismantled and humiliated me in minutes. But perhaps I should have known better. After all, tonight had even come with its very own bad omen. Fritz had shown up at the library wearing those very same Christmas earrings that I'd tried to make disappear by giving them to Thriffaney's.

I couldn't throw them away. But I'd hated owning them, too. So I'd donated them. And I thought I'd seen the last of them. It had been a thunderclap shock to rediscover those earrings on Fritz. I'd stared across the room at her, and she'd looked right back at me, and it had been one of those disturbing mirror moments, as we'd tried to judge each other across the rift.

Lobster was being served now, along with salad and grilled corn on the cob and potatoes. Wine glasses were refilled, talk got loose, and a few couples stood up to dance. It was half past seven, and still Gil hadn't come back. I felt tricked and stupid, like in that *Peanuts* cartoon when Lucy snaps the football away from Charlie Brown so that he lands on his back with his head in a spin.

Weeze, talking on her other side with Dr. and Mrs. Bird, one of the New York couples who'd come to Sunken Haven especially for tonight, now turned to me. She kept her face a careful mask. Her anger was only in her voice.

"He's gone off with *her*, hasn't he?"

"Mrs. Burke, I really don't know."

"It really wasn't much to ask him." Her words were warmly wine slurred. "One night. He'd been doing so well with us. That girl has some cheek."

I was conscious of Junior, across the table, listening.

"I'm sure he'll be back soon," I murmured.

"I opened my heart," said Weeze. "The least he could have done was respect my wishes. I'm surprised that hanky panky would be the order of the night. Aren't you?"

"Well, we don't really know . . ." My voice trailed off.

Mom, seated one table away with the Forsythes, was looking pointedly over at Gil's vacant place next to mine. Obviously, she'd noticed that Fritz was also gone. Who hadn't? I lifted my shoulders—I had no answer for anyone. But my cheeks burned, because obviously Mom had lit on the same conclusion as everyone else. Gil and Fritz had rejected Lobster Party—which meant that Gil had rejected me, too—so that the two of them could be with just each other.

That day in the Coop with Weeze, I should have been stronger. I should have said no. I should have said thank you, but no, thank you. I should have said please leave me out of it, I was coming here with dear Bertie.

Instead, I ran as fast and clumsily and unheedingly as I could toward my same old fate, hoping for a different outcome. I'd even told Bertie that my date with Gil was "socially important for the Burkes." And I'd watched his eyes cloud with hurt, and I hadn't cared.

Over at the Forsythe table, Bertie's back had been to me all night. It shamed me now, maybe because there was something so vulnerable about the back of Bertie—the thin bird bones of his neck and that slight bend in his one ear. It depressed me that I wasn't right next to him, listening to his compliments, accepting his offers for how to make me more comfortable and happy.

I'd hurt Bertie. I'd hurt everyone.

Junior had been staring at me for the longest time. When I looked up and let him catch my eye, he picked up his wine glass and made a sweeping gesture in the air. Careful to speak quietly enough so that his mother didn't hear.

"To rematches," he toasted.

FRITZ

"How could you have spent one easy day?"

"I'm sorry, Fritz." We'd been drifting out for a while, past the place of conversation. The hurt between us felt as wide as the ocean that surrounded us. The words he offered sounded so small.

Jean Custis had always been the little itch lurking in a place that I couldn't find to scratch. It wasn't only that Gil defended her whenever she came up in conversation. It was the way he did it, with genuine affection and maybe even a little awe. It had never struck me as more than a bother that Jean represented so much about Sunken Haven—including, and mostly, Carpie and Weeze's approval—that I couldn't give him.

Now here we were, slap-bang in the middle of all of this blue sea and sky and silence and overwhelming truth. Maybe I hadn't wanted to see the power of what Jean had. And I sure hadn't wanted to see the piece of Gil that craved it.

After a while, I set back the oars, letting the boat drift, looking at him. "Talk to me," he finally said.

"There's not much to say. I've never felt so bad in my whole life." The emotions felt wrung out of me. "I thought you were mine. I know I was yours. I was sure we'd picked each other. Somehow, it seemed that simple. But I guess I was stupid and naïve and wrong to believe in it."

"You're not wrong. It's always been you. Christ, I'm here with you right now. Do you know how much I've screwed things up with the Burkes, by leaving their party?"

It bugged me that he'd even bring up the Burkes. I leaned forward, gripping my elbows. "Here's the thing I care about the most. Now that I know you've been lying to me all along, how do I trust anything you might say? You'll figure out your future with the Burkes on your own. I'm not part of that. But how do I figure out a future of us?"

"I don't know. I don't know how you trust me again, after this. All I know is that I want you. I love you. And I've always, always chosen you."

"But you've never chosen me *enough*." I didn't say: *You've never loved me enough.*

He went quiet. "I messed up," he said. "I completely messed up. I never, ever meant to hurt you."

Tears began to seep from my eyes again, rolling fast and

warm. "But you did. How did you imagine I'd feel about you and Jean? How would that not hurt? How could you look me in the eye? How could you have spent one easy day? How could you have told me that you loved me and ever felt happy about it?" My voice was undependable, trembling all over the place. I stood up. "To be tricked like this—it feels so mean, Gil. Like maybe you hated me all along."

The boat wobbled dangerously beneath my feet. But it felt good to stand above him. To catch my balance and then to use it to rock the boat, as I shifted my weight from one foot to the other. Creating just enough tip that he had to hold onto the hull.

His eyes never left me. "That's insane—how could you say that?"

"And do you love her? Even a little bit?"

"Fritz, sit *down!*"

"Do you love her, too?"

"It was more like I wanted to protect her."

"Protect Jean Custis? She has *everything*! Did you love her?"

"I might have felt . . . something for her. Even if it was only, I dunno, an envy or a wish for everything she had. Is that unforgivable? To want more than what you've got—Fritz, can you sit down, you're acting all kinds of crazy."

I'd edged up to the bow of the boat. He might have loved her, even. I wanted to jump. I wanted out. I wanted to clear my head. "You shouldn't have needed more than me. So yes. I guess I think it *is* unforgivable, in a way."

"Fritz, don't you even dare—"

The boat tipped hard as I went for it. Gil cried out, grappling for balance, and I sensed the slide of an oar as I was quickly submerged in deep, dark, tugging ocean, boundless and real. I popped to the surface, to hear him yelling in my ear.

"Fritz! Enough with this hissy fit, get in the boat, you're putting yourself in danger—grab hold of my hand!"

But I couldn't. Even with the shock of water on my skin, even with the voice in my head telling me *girl don't be dumb,* my hurt trumped my fear.

No. No way was I taking Gil's hand. Not a chance.

I started to swim away from him. Maybe it was dramatic, but it wasn't dangerous. I had visible land on my left and we were less than half an hour out.

Behind me, I heard Gil's oar splashing clumsily at the water. "Look, quit your fuming so we can talk for real. We need to get this worked out between us. Climb back in the boat. There's nowhere to go, and we lost an oar. Let's just row in, and go somewhere safe and nice, please? Just us?"

"Row yourself in." I could hear all that Southern charm in his talk, buttering me up, but now it felt like a trick. And I knew Gil, who hadn't grown up around the ocean, was shy about it in a way that I wasn't.

My breaststroke skimmed the water, as I began to swim away from him.

"Arright, then, have it your way. I'll meet you at the shore, okay, Fritz? Are you fixing to swim into Ocean Bay Park? You just tell me what you're doing! You owe me that, at least, Fritz—look around or raise your hand that you're leastways acknowledging that you hear me. Ain't you even listening to one thing I say?" The deep South that Gil had been taming in his voice all summer was pushing its way through in his panic.

"I don't owe you so much as a plug nickel, Gil Burke!"

"Fine, fine, but you've gotta come in! Jesus, Fritz, I can't keep up with you! You're going over into Ocean Bay, right? I'll meetcha there, okay? Ya hear me, Fritz? *Fritz?*"

"Yeah, I hear you." But I didn't look back. I kept swimming.

"Meet me at Ramps!" Gil's voice was more distant; he was making himself hoarse. I was a much faster swimmer than Gil was a one-oared rower, and I was pretty far away from him now.

"Ramps!" he called.

"Yeah . . ."

Or maybe I'd swim all the way to Seaview. I'd swum that much distance before. Maybe I'd make Gil sweat it out at Ramps, and then loop back to him. Or maybe I'd walk all the way to Sunken Haven without him.

I needed to get my wallet, anyway. Pack a small bag, call my parents, and explain everything to Julia.

The ocean was doing what it needed to do. Swimming was restful. My head and my plan were both steadier.

"I'm going in . . . I can catch up . . . going to shore, Fritz . . . turn back . . . safe." Gil's voice tuned in and out.

Soon the pounding of my heart and the sound of my breath became all I needed.

With the water so flat, I probably could swim past many more towns than Ocean Beach. I could swim all the way out to Lonelyville, if I wanted.

Past the reef, the ocean was a liquid embroidery of warm and colder currents. I closed my eyes. My voice was sore from shouting, my body finally emptied of tears.

I only needed to swim.

I didn't look back.

Gil was receding, dealing with his hobbled boat.

It wasn't for another few minutes that I became aware of a problem. A cross-current, no matter how hard I swam against it, was moving me farther from the left-hand strip of sandbar. Treading, floating, actively pushing in a crawl stroke toward shore, still I couldn't reorient.

Another five minutes and I was even farther out.

My breath shortened. My nerves tightened a notch, my muscles kinked with effort on each new stroke. I had to stay calm. Because I knew what this was. This was a deep rip current, and I was caught in it. And now a flood of panic rushed my body. I'd made an impulsive, dumb choice, jumping out of that boat—and now I was face-to-face with its consequences.

JEAN

Or maybe I* had *seen her?

Something was wrong. I knew it as soon as I saw Gil brake his bike, then toss it against the side of the boathouse when he saw all the bike stands were crammed full. Dusk was washing soft blues over the sunset. Through the shadows, I could see that every muscle in Gil's face was locked, though his eyes were roving. He was in his same clothes, but they were sodden, and he was barefoot. I felt a moment's flash of relief that he wasn't with Fritz—but where had he been?

My stomach was a leaden weight of dread.

What had happened?

Throughout dinner, everyone had been on Gil Watch. But now dinner was over, and The Lamplighters had changed over from playing their usual oldies to covers of hit songs, to get more people out on the parquet dance floor, which had been specially assembled for this night. It was a successful strategy, as a few couples were now bumping around, smiling, fumbling, occasionally going into a dip to show that it was all in good fun.

Along with the gathering darkness, the noise of the crowd and the music had swelled, so at first, nobody noticed Gil's return.

Gil didn't sense me observing him, as I sidled out from behind my untouched plate of corpse-cold lobster. My cup of drawn butter had hardened with a top layer of waxen fat. I skirted the other tables, people lingering over their berry crisp and coffee, though many of them had left their table to dance or mingle.

I approached Gil where he was pacing on the far side of a dessert buffet table. His gaze was fixed in concentration on the bay.

"Hi, Stranger." I reached across the table and tapped him gently on the arm. "Dinner's over. Where've you be—?"

"Have you seen Fritz?" he asked on top of my question. "Is she here? Did she come back?"

"Fritz?" I repeated. I hadn't ever really been looking for Fritz—only Gil.

There was sand stuck to Gil's pants' legs and chest, his neck and jaw. I saw a welled, dark crescent of blood at the base of his thumb that thinned to a scratch down his forearm—a recent cut.

"What happened to you?" As I reached for a stray napkin, the song ended, and the tempo changed as the band shifted into another tune.

Oh! *That* song! The dark cave where I kept my precious memories of that night was suddenly lit by the torch of this song, as past and present collided. My heart began racing with a kind of elated madness. Did he hear it, too?

"Listen, Jean, I don't think Fritz has come back to Sunken Haven. But I can't think where else she might have gone."

"Oh my gosh, Gil, they're playing 'Young Americans!'" I practically shouted it over his words, as I darted around the table and quick pressed the napkin to his cut. "Do you hear it?" My fingers tightened to a clamp around his wrist.

"Hear what?"

"Our song!"

The humiliation of this night, Junior's smugness, Bertie's distance, my mother's and Weeze's dismay, my complete and utter failure—and now *our song*. It was spinning above us in the air like a reminder of everything I'd sacrificed for this night, while marking the possible promise of another chance.

Gil looked down at my fingers locked around his wrist, as if surprised by my pressure. "Jean, I'm not kidding—have you seen Fritz tonight? She was supposed to meet me in Ocean Bay Park, at Ramps. But she never showed. She's really upset with me. We took out a boat and she jumped in the water. I haven't seen her anywhere on shore, it's been a while now, and I can't think where else—"

"Yes, she's here!" I interrupted.

I wanted to stop his worry. That's all I knew for sure when I thought about it, after. It wasn't about my own profit, and it wasn't about a trick. It was a white lie, and I'd meant only to soothe him. That's what I swore to myself.

"When?" He was immediately, visibly relieved. "When did you see her?"

I made a face of thinking about it. "Oh, about fifteen minutes ago?" Or maybe I *had* seen her? In a wet dress, barefoot, her hair unraveling from those terrible, zigzaggy braids. There was so much room in the space of my memory as I'd sat alone all evening. All those happy couples on the dance floor, and all the kids running by. Surely I could remember her, if I needed to! Had I seen her? Had I? Hadn't I? "She's around."

Gil exhaled a long, pent-up breath. Then he looked at me with eyes like bullets. "You sure?"

"Yes yes yes! Let's dance to this one, please, Gil? Remember this song? From Hollander's?" And in my imagination, in my molten desire, I could almost see Fritz streaking past us, calling for Julia, her hair and dress sopping wet, upset over whatever silly thing she was upset about. It wasn't my problem.

Not this one, Fritz. You can't win every single game of every single match.

I pulled him by the hand in the direction of the floor. "I'm sure she's with Julia. We'll go get her right after this song. Gil, you abandoned me all night!" My voice plaintive, semiteasing. Because I wouldn't mention Carp and Weeze's fury yet. He could deal with them later.

"Listen, I'm all wet . . ."

"One little dance."

He took my hand, but he continued to seem dogged, shadowed by his doubts. His eyes combed the darkness.

"Young Americans" sounded so marvelous live. It gave the song an extra-nifty little kick and warmth. As Gil swung me out, I could feel him trying hard to click into the moment.

"I'm super-glad you didn't miss the dancing! It's my favorite part." I spun in and pressed close against him, the front of my dress dampening against his wet clothes. His body felt warm and strong beneath.

Gil nodded. "Yeah."

"You've been gone so long, I thought you weren't coming back at all."

"Sorry, Jean. I've sure got some apologies to make tonight."

"Oh, it's all right. You're here now. And this song! It's strange, isn't it? Of all the songs!"

"Yeah. It is strange," he said. Then he seemed to take it all in, with a new readiness and attention to the details—me, the dance floor, the lit lamps and the band. He looked down at me, and I could feel him weighing my remark. "Maybe—maybe it's a sign of something."

It was the first real encouragement he'd ever given us since New York. I didn't even know what to think, I was so dazzled by all the things he might mean by it, and I knew I'd never forget anything about this moment. The clean-cut, trustworthy handsomeness of

Gil's face, the heat in his hands, the long shadows we cast in the blue evening, the chill of the bay breeze light against the backs of my legs.

Oh, but here it was again, the body-lurching, wobbling lift of a roller coaster, that airborne sensation of once again being so near Gil, and also knowing how easily I could fall, spiraling, into the shameful emptiness of losing him.

Because, after all, tonight had not been *our night*. Gil had barely shown up for it. Fritz—even in her absence—had broken this night into a hundred fragments.

And then, out of the corner of my eye, I saw Weeze and Carp move onto the dance floor, attempting to work through the beats of an old-fashioned dance they both seemed to have mostly forgotten. Weeze looked up and caught my eye. Not knowing what else to do, I gave a little wave—*everything's fine now, look, I found Gil*—but it wasn't another moment before Carp saw us, too, and detached from Weeze to stride toward us, his face rigid.

"Young man." Carp clapped a hand on Gil's shoulder, putting a stop to everything. "You've got some explaining to do."

"Uncle Carp, I'm so sorry." Gil was the picture of calm politeness, his fingers still light on my waist. "I never thought I'd be gone that long, and know I've disappointed you . . ." In the next instant, they'd both stepped away, moving swiftly to stand on the sidelines, apart from the crowd.

Gil's back was turned, shutting me out of his apology and explanation.

In the next second, Weeze had joined them, and their conversation closed into a tight fist of privacy.

Awkwardly, I edged off the dance floor. One step closer to them, then another, until I could hear Carp's voice, saturated with frustration. "But why in God's name would you leave at *all*?" His voice, loud, clattering up the space so that other people turned, as Weeze put her fingers to her lips and shook her head.

Gil kept his own tone quiet when he answered. I strained to hear. ". . . and Fritz was upset . . . when I followed her . . . the ocean . . . lost an oar, couldn't get to her . . . but it's okay, Jean saw . . ."

"*I* haven't seen Fritz tonight," Weeze declared emphatically. "And I've been watching. How upset was she? Would she do something dramatic, like go to Bay Shore?"

Gil glanced over at me. "Jean saw her . . ."

Heated prickles worked down my spine. This would be awful, but I had to say something. How could I not? And the quicker I confessed, the quicker it would be over. I stepped forward.

" . . . but the bottom line is you let me down," Carpie was storming. "What are we supposed to think, when you're gone for hours and you haven't met *any* of my guests who've come in *specifically* for this evening!"

"And what does Fritz have to say for herself?"

Carpie waved off Weeze's words. "The girl is none of my concern. We need to figure out if we can repair some of this night, and introduce—"

I broke in. "Excuse me, but I think I should say that I *didn't* see her." My voice felt as if it snipped sharp and ragged into the conversation, just as "Young Americans" ended and the band stopped to take a break.

Gil looked at me. "What?" His voice was incredulous. "You *told* me."

"I mean, I can't be sure . . ." Three pairs of eyes were suddenly fixed on me. I'd only wanted that one moment. That one dance. A single hallucinatory flashback to that perfect New York evening. Was it really too much to want?

My rib cage hurt with each breath. But I stepped closer, into my guilt.

"Jean, you *said* you saw her," said Gil. "You said you were *sure*."

"I know, but I can't help but wonder, now, if it wasn't one of the younger girls I saw? Because some of the Minnows did a dock jump earlier tonight. They were all running around in wet clothes, and Melinda Hasty always wears French braids and tonight Fritz had French braids in her hair and . . ."

"So—wait—you *didn't* see her?" Gil looked aghast. "But you *told me*. You *said* that you did!" As if his repeating it would make it true.

"Yes, I know. I'm not—"

"We've got to call the Coast Guard." Gil's voice turned forceful. "Uncle Carp, she might be out there in the water. This is an emergency."

"The *Coast Guard*?" I repeated. "Why? Was she out too far? Was there a problem? Was she hurt?" Questions I maybe ought to have asked ten minutes ago, when I'd first seen Gil. I didn't want to think about it.

"I'll go find Marcy," said Weeze, slipping away.

"Jean, I *did* tell you that I never saw her come in!" Gil practically barked the words at me. His face was ashen but scathing. "For God's sake, you gave me your word!" His hands gripped his head, as if forcing himself to think it through. "Okay, okay. We can radio this."

"Yes, yes." Carp nodded. "We're right by the bay. We'll send a distress signal from one of the boats."

"I don't think I realized . . . ," I began, but everyone had scattered. I had a needling sense of being stared at; when I looked behind me, it was only Bertie. I shook my head; if he'd been a cat, I would have shooed him. As it was, my ignoring him wasn't enough.

"Jean, what's going on?"

"Fritz O'Neill's gone missing. She and Gil went out on a boat earlier, and she jumped off, and he couldn't get to her, and he doesn't know when she made it back to shore, or if she did, or where she is now."

"When she made it or *if* she made it?" The frankly panicked look that crossed Bertie's face scared me.

"No doubt she's fine," I snapped.

"But Gil thinks she might be out on the water alone? Still?"

"He was hoping she came back to the party." Explaining it, I could feel the oxygen in my body shorting out a little. Would I be directly blamed for this? My only known crime was confusion—I'd thought I'd seen her! I was sure for a second I'd seen her! I just maybe hadn't spoken my doubts soon enough. But I was only accountable for what I hadn't done when I should have done it. "They were supposed to meet up at Ocean Park, but she didn't show. Funny thing, you know, I thought she was around, earlier."

"Really? *I* most certainly haven't seen her," said Bertie, "and I've been on watch for her ever since she ran out of the library and Gil took off after her."

Of course Bertie had been on watch for everything that had happened with Gil and Fritz and me tonight. Everyone knew how Bertie felt about me. I knew it, too. Even if it had been easier to pretend I hadn't understood or hadn't been aware.

"What happened? Did they get separated on the water? Why were they out there, anyway?"

"Bertie, how would I know?" Bertie winced at the slap in my voice, but he stayed on my side. I was slightly relieved—Bertie had been upset with me all night, and now he'd melted back to his usual support role, right when I needed him.

If Fritz had gotten lost in the ocean, it would be Bertie who would assure everyone that it wasn't my fault. Maybe a little tiny bit my fault, but not in a malicious, terrible way.

Gil was everywhere at once. The story caught like a fire, burning through the party. It wasn't long before panic had set in, curling and smoking up the edges of all conversation, the danger of possible catastrophe more real by the moment. I wished I could block my ears and run home to safety. I felt trapped, like the chained monkey in that awful story, forced to endure the whole night through to its disastrous end.

I had really, really thought I'd seen Fritz! I could hear my own voice, defending myself. But nobody was asking me about her. Not yet, anyway. Search parties were being assigned, areas divided. I stayed near Gil, who seemed to be the center of everything.

"How are we looking, boatwise?" asked Mr. Tulliver. "If she's out there, every minute she doesn't show up here is another minute lost."

"Oh my God. If she's out there." Julia sank, deflated, against her mother.

"Coast Guard's got four boats in now," said Gil. "They're twenty minutes from putting a helicopter up. They want us to keep searching land."

"Remember that it's Fritz," said Tiger. "She's a sensible chick. If she knew the tide was changing, she'd swim back to shore immediately. Maybe she went the other way, to Cherry Grove."

"Maybe." Gil looked so unsure.

"We're gonna check all up and down Bay Walk." And because Bertie and I were standing right there, and because it seemed as if that's what Tiger had meant by "we," it felt natural for Bertie and me to tag along with Tiger.

"Fritz wasn't in any frame of mind to just go hang out in Ocean Bay tonight and see a movie," Bertie said, as we all found bikes. When I looked down, I saw that my dress was crushed and watermarked from dancing with Gil. I was like Cinderella after midnight, my ball gown magically changed back into a messy, mottled-green watercolor painting.

"How do you know?" I slid off my sandals—I'd never wear them again, either; not if they reminded me of tonight, what a waste—and stuck them in the basket.

"I spoke with her in the library."

"Well, whatever she decided," I said, "nothing *bad* has happened to her." But Bertie's comment, and the darkly sidelong look he'd thrown me as he said it, quivered in my heart.

What had Fritz and Bertie been speaking about? About Gil and me? How much did Bertie think he knew about Gil and me, anyway?

We hit the end of Bay Walk, where we dropped bikes. We searched the Watching Stile and the ferry harbor. The moon, low and heavy in the sky, brushed a glaze of light on the lapping water.

"Deserted," I noted.

"Everyone's at the party," said Bertie.

"The bay tide is always less than the ocean. It's a shame they didn't take the boat bayside," said Tiger. "Ocean's a whole different animal."

"Nobody's on the water now," I said.

"Anyone know what they were fighting about?" Tiger asked. "What would have got her so pissed?"

Neither Bertie nor I answered.

"Oookay," said Tiger. "Guess not. Let's search around."

After a few minutes of swooping our flashlights and calling Fritz's name, the excursion seemed futile. We doubled back to check in with the others.

In the time we'd been gone, the mood of the evening had become grim. The band was packing up. Nearly everyone was armed with a flashlight, and groups of five or six prowled the night, calling her name. I could hear Julia's voiced raised above the others, so desperate and pleading, it made me feel sick inside. The few older people who hadn't taken off to look for Fritz seemed disoriented by the disintegration of Lobster Party into these nervous search parties. They stood around, softly talking of plans to go home and make tea and wait for word.

When I finally slipped Bertie and reclaimed Gil, he was corralling some of the youngest kids, telling them to stick together, commanding them to stake out specific assigned areas.

"Gil," I began, reaching for his arm. "It was a mistake."

He sidestepped me. "Don't."

"I've been thinking, Fritz's so athletic, and I remember from when we taught Minnows classes together a few years ago, that even if by some remote chance she got caught out here, she can tread water for a really long time. I mean, until the rescue boats come. I remember how she could do that for so long."

Had that been the right thing to say? His face was empty, staring at me.

But when I stepped nearer, Gil put up his hands as if to physically block me. "If you really want to help out with this night,

Jean," he said, "then leave me alone. Join the search. Be useful. Arright?"

Wounded, blinking, nodding, I retreated.

In all the times I'd ever said something foolish or silly or awkward, Gil had rescued me. He'd always made me feel less regretful about my blunders.

Not tonight.

"Folks, I have some updates." We all looked up to where Carpie was standing on a table. His bullhorn voice forced our attention. "We're going to make Whisper our Base Camp. That's the most likely place Fritz will return. Bay Shore has dispatched two officers to take our statements. So I'm headed over there now, with Mike and Patsy." Then he said, almost as an aside, "But I'll bet that girl's creeping back through the gate by midnight."

"Carpie, you're in no position to bet anything!" Mrs. Tulliver's warning rang angry in the darkness.

"Listen, Pats, I know you're worried," said Carpie. "I know she's your ward and responsibility. But this is very likely a runaway situation."

"You don't know what's likely! You don't know anything!" Mrs. Tulliver's sudden bold words scared me fresh. "A missing child, out of reach and possibly in danger? Nothing is *likely*. Nothing is a *bet*. Tonight's about as goddamn serious as it gets!"

A murmur rose up in the crowd, mostly because swearing was discouraged at Sunken Haven, and Mrs. Tulliver did not tend to be mouthy.

"I understand," Carpie said, sounding more hurt than anything else. "But let's not waste more precious time arguing." Now his voice boomed twice as loud and bossy. "Let's get out there and find this girl!"

One of the mothers mentioned that if Fritz had intended to spend the night off Sunken Haven, she'd have returned for money and identification. This prompted Julia and Oliver to shoot over to the Tulliver cottage.

They came racing back, minutes later, bearing the baby-blue plastic wallet.

Something about seeing it, and her driver's license intact, caused the conversation to explode into a pileup of horrible theories and conjecture. My own panic welled—what in the world would Fritz do in Ocean Bay Park without money and identification? Until then, I'd made a picture of her, smirking and strolling down a boardwalk, imagining all of us here caught in our foolish handwringing. It was so hard to see Fritz in any role other than victorious.

"Oliver and I are going to trace the walk from Ocean Bay Park and hope we run into her," Julia said, as she came over to where a few of us were standing. "I keep holding onto the fact that Fritz's too smart and too strong not to know how to rescue herself."

"That's what I keep thinking, too," I said.

Julia ignored me.

"We'll do one more sweep," said Tiger. "And maybe the bird blind. We'll be back at Whisper for when the police get here."

"See you there." Julia didn't like that I was standing so near her. I knew she thought I was pushing in where I didn't belong.

Since Tiger didn't care if we stayed with him, and because Bertie and I had already established that we were part of Tiger's search party, we remained together. Then Tiger's girlfriend joined, and so, as a foursome, we hit the dunes and the bird blind. Circling with our lights, calling for her, before we doubled back to where Mrs. Walt was overseeing Lobster Party's final, dismal pack-up.

Hardly anyone was there now. But as I went to collect the purse that I'd left at the host table, I saw that Junior and a couple of his friends had never moved. They were playing quarters by the flickering votive candles.

"Why aren't you helping to search?"

Junior looked at me a long moment. His face was illuminated by candlelight. "Kinda feels out of our hands," he drawled. "You're all looking around here to make yourselves feel better. If she turns up, she turns up. Or she doesn't. She's not hiding."

His friends sniggered agreement, as Junior must have hoped they would.

"You shouldn't make such dark assumptions," I said. "But more important, Gil's your own cousin. He's never been anything but kind to you. You ought to be ashamed that you're not out there helping him."

"So crucify me. But I can't look for Fritz if she's at the bottom of the ocean." Junior bounced a quarter and sank it, bull's-eye, into the shot glass.

"You're a snake, Junior. You always have been. It's why you're one of the worst things about Sunken Haven."

He flipped and sank another quarter. "Takes one to know one. And if you don't think that fight between Gil and Fritz was about you, you're a dumber cluck than I thought." He turned over the shot glass and scooped the quarters. "But we both know you're not dumb at all. In fact, you're pretty sly. Right, Jean?"

I didn't have to listen to that. Wordless, I left him, dodging Bertie as I ran all the way to Whisper. I didn't want to go there, but it seemed worse not to. Would the police ask me questions? Would I be part of their "taking statements"? How would I answer?

As I approached the house, Julia jumped off the porch as if she'd been in wait. Quick as a spider, she sped out to the lawn, moving in on me. Seeing her up close gave me a strange, frightened feeling, remembering when we'd been friends, all the fun we'd had when we were young.

But we weren't close anymore. That friendship had perished, and with her nearly white hair and in her long silver dress, her pale blue eyes so icy on me, Julia reminded me of a vengeful ghost.

"I know what you did."

I stopped in my tracks. "What do you mean?"

"You know what. Pretending you saw Fritz. Even if Gil's

officially making excuses for you. I saw you out there dancing. Let me guess what you thought."

"Julia, tonight is upsetting enough, please don't— "

"You thought, 'Oh, if I say I saw Fritz and I say she's here, it's cool, then Gil will stop looking for her, and he'll stay with me. Nothing will happen if I say I saw her. Because nothing ever happens when I do something stupid and selfish!'"

"That not true, that's not— "

"And now that you've doubled back, now that you're all 'Gosh, I guess I didn't see her!' you think you're off the hook. But this, Jean?" Julia used every inch of her height to look down on me, to push me as low as she could. "This was so much worse than stupid and selfish."

"I understand that you want to blame someone, and that I'm as good a patsy as any. But Fritz jumping in the ocean like an airhead and swimming off to where nobody can catch her, if that's what she did, is *not* my fault, Julia."

"I suppose you think you can make mistakes all day long," Julia continued as if she hadn't heard me, "and none of them will count. But if this turns out to be our worst nightmare, and we learn there was any chance that Fritz could have been saved— " She paused, making sure every word counted. "—then, Jean Custis, I will make sure you pay for it. I will tell everyone, and I mean everyone, exactly what you did. You will never be forgiven. And you will never come back to your precious Sunken Haven again. Never."

FRITZ

Rip currents are a change of the ocean's heart. They're when the sea looks totally beautiful but, underneath, it isn't your friend. Then you realize, maybe too late, that it never was. It doesn't want you to be safe, doesn't give a crap if you live or die.

My voice was hoarse from calling for him, but Gil hadn't heard me. He didn't seem to be anywhere. Getting so far away from him was my mistake. I'd thought I could swim out past Ocean Bay Park, to Robbins Rest. On another current, I could have done it.

He'd only had the one oar, and he'd told me the plan. Then he'd stubbornly stuck to it. He'd given me his word, and he'd played by his rules.

Now I couldn't see land, and I wasn't sure where I was going.

Eventually, I began to wriggle out of my waterlogged dress. I couldn't control everything, or even anything, but I would not go down in this dress.

I kicked and squirmed until I was free to my slip.

As the dress got bogged down and slurped under the water in a candy-cane swirl, some long-ago Minnows class advice returned to me.

If you ever get caught in a rip current, swim gently alongside the current. Never against it.

That tip had always seemed like such an abracadabra. One of those magical promises that didn't count when life got real. Because what dummy would be out performing a stunt like swimming in a riptide?

Me, so it seemed. A dummy with a death wish.

My pulse pounded like the surf in my ears. I held my gaze locked ahead. I kept my head in line with my spine. I made my arms into rudders, each one a perfect mirror and balance of the other. One easy breath at a time.

And do not think about Jaws *for even one fucking second.*

Gil had broken my trust. Maybe he'd even made me lose my mind temporarily, if that's why I was out here. But now the thing was, facing it, I knew one fact for sure: I really, really didn't want to die.

"Alongside." I spoke the word out loud so it would sink into me.

If I was going to swim along the current, then I also had to calm down. I'd have to split in two Fritzes, and betrayed-Fritz needed to sit this one out while survivor-Fritz kicked in.

Survivor-Fritz was the one I trusted to save my own life. If I breathed evenly, and as slowly as I could, then I'd have a better chance of not short-circuiting my lungs. Slow and careful also meant I wouldn't burn up energy every time the water lifted and resettled my body farther, farther, and farther from the strip of sandbar that I was almost losing sight of.

Was Gil waiting for me on shore? Was he panicking? It probably never occurred to him that I wouldn't do exactly as he said and head to Ocean Bay Park, so that he could sprint right on back to Sunken Haven to play perfect nephew again. Make his apologies, clean up his mess, accept his punishment. But there was nothing more the Burkes could do to me. I was free of all of them.

I pushed toward shore. Gently, gently. I couldn't figure out how to break out of the current. I'd really screwed this one up. Was there even some tiny, remotest chance Gil was still out here? Could he have gone in and then gone out again?

"Gil!" I heard the saw of desperation in my voice. A cry like a baby. My lungs spending precious force.

He was nowhere. My course had been diverted so wide that I couldn't even see around the inlet where Sunken Haven's boats were kept.

Last summer, when Julia was dating Tiger, the three of us had gotten into an afternoon habit of swimming in the ocean until we came to Ocean Bay Park, where we'd then swim in to shore, follow the boardwalk until we hit a run-down old beachfront bar on Evergreen Walk that served fifty-cent taps plus burgers and paper twists of the best greasy shoestring fries we'd ever tasted.

All we'd ever needed for those swimming field trips was the key to get back into Sunken Haven, along with Tiger's waterproof wallet, which held all our fake IDs plus fifteen bucks for lunch all around. We'd be dripping wet in our bathing suits, of course, but the bar was exactly the type of joint that didn't mind kids with no shoes and hilariously phony drivers' licenses. We'd gorge ourselves, play some pool, then trudge back by land to Sunken Haven a few hours later, buzzed on Schlitz and feeling lazy as bears.

I kept my brain floating on those easy, summery thoughts. Trying to hold on to serenity there. I had to. I swam in a steady burn. I thought about myself like a movie, a girl swimming on the TV screen, while the real me sat in the kitchen at Fort Polk, eating a big bowl of Cheerios and telling Mom and Dad how it happened, pointing myself out, a tiny speck in the ocean. Watching Dad's slow smile lift his blond mustache—"See, and that's why we named you Fritz! Look at you go! You're tough as any soldier in the marine corps!"

I made myself banish the fatigue as it pushed from inside my lungs. Every stroke became a stitch, and then a gnawing ache, until, finally, I was living the nightmare, the total horror that I might be really, truly losing this one.

Don't drown, Fritz. I whittled myself down to this one command. To give up, to drown—that would be a total defeat.

Julia had always been downright terrified by my impulses. She'd never come out and say it; she wasn't the type even to let her fear show in her face. But my chair jump off the pier, or when I'd climbed to the top of that plum tree one summer—even the way I did a backflip or sped my bike along the ridge—unsettled her. She'd be so mad at me right now, if she knew.

No, I wouldn't let her be right. I'd get back home to her.

I focused my willpower. Stayed in control of my terror.

The current dragged at me like a claw, and then when it finally released me, I felt so lightheaded with exhaustion that it was hard to hold on to my point of orientation. I wavered, kept going, sunburnt, dry mouthed. I felt the sun turn chilly in the sky.

All I could hear was the hush of the water, the strangely comforting animal sound of my pounding heart. I was all out of options. I kept going.

JEAN

If he were more blamed, then I'd be less blamed.

I ached with Julia's words, even after she'd turned away from me and stole inside the house. She seemed so sure that she had accused me rightly of jealousy, of sickness and greed. Awful things, and I knew she mostly said them because she was petrified. Still, any exchange with Julia made me feel tired—the same old worn-out, empty tired I felt every time she made me stare down the hole of our abandoned friendship.

I didn't want to follow her, so I lingered outside on the lawn, hoping for Bertie to show.

"Were you waiting for me?" he asked, as he appeared on the walk.

"I was."

He looked quietly pleased. It felt wrong, that I could make Bertie so happy when I offered him so little.

Whisper was packed and stuffy with people sitting or standing around in a state of wait and worry. I hadn't been here in years—not since I was a little girl. Julia and Oliver were together, their bodies dipping the middle of Mrs. Tulliver's old maroon loveseat. I saw that the cotton curtains were faded, and the pine-green kitchen linoleum had gone bald in patches. Still, the familiarity depressed me, reminded me of when this house had been a happy destination for Julia and me, once upon a time, after lunch or swimming

Weeze and Carpie and some of their New York friends all stood in the kitchen, mostly not drinking the Genesee cream ales that Mr. Tulliver was passing around, whether anyone wanted them or not. A shortwave radio was out on the kitchen counter, but it didn't sound like anything had been tuned in.

Carpie kept checking his watch and commenting on the lateness of the police, who were supposed to be at Whisper at any minute.

"When did they say they'd get here?" he'd ask the room in general. Or, "Saturday night, I bet you most cops have been dispatched to the Pines. They've had to go break up, you know, all those homosexual orgies."

Nobody was paying much attention to him. Nobody had any more information than Carpie about what kept the Bay Shore police force preoccupied on Saturday nights.

Someone had turned the television to the Olympics, but few people were watching except Junior and his friends, who'd eventually come in from the bay to sprawl on the floor in front of the set.

"Check it out. That's Bruce Jenner," Junior said, at one point, leaning forward and pointing. I glanced at the screen. The papers had been filled with pictures and stories of the buff sports hero from California, but I hadn't seen him on TV yet.

"Two solid days of decathlon competition," Junior went on, though nobody had asked for more information. "What a stud, that guy."

Gil strode to the set and snapped it off. "Not helpful."

"Then what do you want me to do?"

Julia lifted her head from Oliver's shoulder. "We want you to shut up, Junior."

"Nobody could survive out there this long," I heard Weeze say, softly, a moment later. This was the general, whispered theme of conversation—that Fritz had no chance. I tried not to hear it, not to think about what that meant.

When the phone rang, everyone jumped—but it was only Mr. Wolfe letting Mrs. Tulliver know that his grandson, Bennett, had seen Fritz at the candy store, where she'd been making a milkshake.

"That was three hours ago," Gil said impatiently. "Before we went out on the boat."

"She left the party to go make a milkshake in the candy

store?" Mrs. Tulliver's forehead was flexed, working to piece these events together.

"Yes. She did," said Gil. "I was there, too."

"But . . . *why*?" asked Mrs. Tulliver. The open, connecting rooms of Whisper went quiet. Everyone was listening.

"She was upset," said Gil. "And she went there, and that's where I found her."

Some of the mothers were exchanging looks all around. I felt tugged by the sense that Gil's story sounded strange. Horrible as it would have been to admit, the vague recklessness of Gil's and Fritz's argument put me slightly at ease. If he were more blamed, then I'd be less blamed.

A timer pinged. Mrs. Tulliver shifted her attention to remove a deep-dish apple cobbler from where it had been warming in the oven. She placed it on the kitchen table along with a stack of paper plates, and Mr. Tulliver set out a platter of grilled cheese sandwiches—which some of the little kids had decided they needed, earlier. But once it was presented, smelling thickly of Velveeta and butter and greasy toasted bread, hardly anyone touched the sandwiches. Nobody really wanted food or drinks at all.

"I'm not going to call them just yet," Mrs. Tulliver would tell one of her friends, usually Mrs. Flagler, every five minutes or so. Everyone knew "them" meant Fritz's parents in Louisiana. "I need to let the Coast Guard do their job. We have no information. No need to panic anybody now."

Their friends would nod agreement, and then Mrs. Tulliver would make another round of the kitchen. Opening the fridge or setting something in the oven or on the stovetop, occasionally glancing at the telephone on the kitchen counter, and trying generally, like all of us, to hold her hopes high.

Nothing bad ever happens to anyone here. My parents often said that, when I was younger. But unhappy things did happen at Sunken Haven. Like, when old Mr. Todd's cottage had burned down two years ago, Mr. Todd had burned up right with it. This summer, Tracy Gibbons-Kent was gone, and nobody—not even her parents—was telling us a story that anyone believed.

Gil and Tiger moved in and out of the cottage like restless animals. Sometimes when they slammed outside, I could hear them on the porch, as they thought up new places where Fritz might have gone and then, with voices raised, they ordered other kids to check these hunches. And while Gil knew I was right here, he never looked my way.

Of all the awful things I felt, of all the fear that permeated this night, in some ways the very worst part was that Gil wouldn't look at me.

But I stayed where I was, chained to my little space with Bertie, on the living room windowsill. Gil hated me now. It was awful, but my heart clenched in defensiveness, resistant to all that he might want to heap on me. What had happened tonight wasn't all my fault. I had been coerced. Dragged back in by the Burkes, after I'd made a point to stay out of Gil's way. After I had found my new life at the Coop.

I had been a good sport, and I had been a good loser.

In fact, I was the very definition of a gracious loser, considering I wouldn't have had to be a loser at all if it hadn't been for Fritz.

What if Fritz had never come to Sunken Haven? What if I'd held on to my friendship with Julia, and hadn't told everyone about her being adopted, accidentally trading our friendship for gossip? Julia had brought Fritz to Sunken Haven the very next summer to replace me. I had been shocked when that happened, despite the fact that the entire school year before, Julia had cut me off. I'd written her four letters back in fifth grade, and she'd answered none of them. But I'd hoped it would all blow over. I'd certainly never thought she'd find an outsider to replace me.

What if I hadn't betrayed Julia? Hadn't shared her private story with everyone? What if there'd been no fight, no falling out between us? What if there'd been no Fritz O'Neill that first summer?

Then there would have been no Fritz O'Neill this summer.

Gil and I would have shared that night at Hollander's, and then shared this summer, including Lobster Night, and it never would have ended like this.

The noise of crackling radios and calls of greeting outside signaled that the police were finally here. My heart was thudding, my palms slick. What kinds of questions would they ask me? Would they be angry, would I be in trouble? Had my lie about seeing Fritz broken the law in some awful way that I didn't know?

In the next minutes, two male officers in blue uniforms had laid siege to Whisper. Their bulky presence, their unfamiliar voices, their shiny boots and stiff caps instantly pulled the throttle on everyone's attention. Police were a rare sight. The officers were only from Bay Shore, but neither of them—skinny, popeyed Officer Plano or beefier, older Officer Novack—had ever been here.

As Mrs. Tulliver got them coffee, Carpie spoke for all of us. "Strange to see you boys. We never get police visiting."

"Will you hear news on the water immediately . . . from that?" Mrs. Tulliver asked, indicating their walkie-talkie.

"Yes. We're in direct contact with the Coast Guard," answered Officer Plano.

Officer Novack asked the questions, while Officer Plano took the notes on Fritz—her height, her age, her hair color, what she was wearing tonight. Dot mentioned the French braids, Julia knew her exact weight, and the Tullivers had week-old Polaroid pictures ready to offer.

I couldn't figure out exactly when it began, but sometime during the volley of questions and answers leading up to her disappearance, both of the officers started focusing in on Gil. And it wasn't long before they were targeting him, and the questions become pointed.

Gil's answers stayed simple.

"She left the party because she was angry at me."

"You left the party together?" Novack asked. Plano's pencil hovered over his legal pad.

"She left and I followed her. I chased her down."

"Why?"

"Because she was so upset."

"Either of you drinking? Drugs?"

"No, neither of us."

"He was drinking water," Tiger said.

"Not even a little pot?" Officer Novack had one of those kindly voices that the nice adults used on those *ABC Afterschool Specials,* but he didn't fool anyone.

"No, sir."

"You two get physical at any point? How bad was this fight?"

Gil looked unhappy. "In the candy store, I held on to her arms—it wasn't a big deal. She broke away, and I followed her to the harbor."

"So you were still chasing her?"

"At first, I chased her. But then I caught up. And we walked together."

"Who got in the boat?"

"She did first. Then me."

"And in the boat? Did things get physical?"

"She kind of kicked at me in the boat."

"This wasn't a little fight. You push her out of the boat? By accident, I mean? Cause her to fall out?"

"No, no, I didn't. Not at all. She jumped."

"Pretty angry, I take it. Why'd she do it?"

Gil ran his hands though his hair. "She wanted to cool off."

"How'd you get that cut on your hand?"

"Trying to save the oar. It went in when she jumped."

"Coast Guard says in your initial radio, you told them the two of you were about twenty minutes from shore."

"Yes, that's right."

"Outside of the oar, was the boat compromised?"

"When Fritz jumped, she tipped the boat. There was some water in the hull."

"You follow her in the boat?"

"I did, but she'd swum so far out, and I only had the one oar. She was faster swimming than I was rowing."

"So what'd you do next?"

"When I realized I couldn't overtake her, I kept calling for her to come in. I told her I'd meet her at Ocean Bay Park."

"She say she would?"

"She didn't say she wouldn't. She was getting away from me so fast. I had this boat to deal with. So when she went around the inlet, I turned in. And I towed the boat in, tied it up, and I ran right to the bar—Ramps, it's called—where we agreed to meet."

"In the water, she heard you say Ramps?"

"She did."

"And she agreed?"

"She did."

"Did she injure herself, jumping? Would her swimming have been impeded?"

"I don't think so. No. She didn't say that she was injured."

"Why didn't you jump out after her?"

"I knew I wouldn't be able to catch up to her. She's fast. She's a better swimmer. All I could do was shout for her to meet me. I didn't like the plan, but the water was calm at that point. I went right back in the surf, at Ocean Bay Park. I swam out, but I didn't see her. I had the whole shoreline looking. She'd vanished. The only thing I could think was that she'd come in."

"After Ocean Bay Park, what'd you do?"

"I came right back here. My uncle and I called it in immediately."

There was a silence, as the officers jotted notes. I waited for Julia to chide me. But she didn't. She stood next to her mother on the other side of the room, staring at Gil. Maybe I was in the clear.

But then Junior broke the silence. "Well, wait a minute. First you had a dance with Jean," he said. "I saw you two. Out there twirling on the dance floor."

"That was my fault," I said quickly, before I lost my nerve. "I told Gil that I thought I saw Fritz at Lobster Party. He'd asked me first thing."

Here it was. Both officers shifted, eyes on me. Expressionless faces, but fully focused as they took me in. I slid off the windowsill, my hands in a knot.

“What made you think that?” Officer Plano held his pencil in the air like a magic wand. It spooked me to stare into his pale, froggy eyes. I looked down.

“Well, the thing is, I thought I had seen her. But then I wasn’t exactly sure.”

“Yes,” Gil said. “You were confused. I’m sure you weren’t aware of the danger Fritz was in.” He spoke slowly, deliberately saving me, but he was also letting me know that he didn’t believe me. Not for a second.

I couldn’t even look at Julia.

“Yes.” I nodded. My clasped hands and the spaces between my fingers had gone sweaty.

“How much time passed before you realized your mistake?” asked Officer Plano.

“Only a few minutes. Three, four minutes.” My voice was just above a whisper. I knew what everyone was thinking. In the ocean, every minute counts.

“So, what next?” asked Mrs. Tulliver. “What else can they do?”

“We’ve got the chopper out there,” Officer Novack answered. “It’s getting dark now, which works against us. But if she stays put and she can tread water . . .”

Suddenly Officer Plano’s walkie-talkie beeped and crackled. Past the hissing, a voice broke through.

Without a word, he handed off the pencil and paper to Officer Novack, then stood and stepped outside through the screen door. And while Novack continued to ask us questions and jot down facts as we answered, every ear was tuned to what Plano might be learning, out on the Tullivers' porch.

A few minutes later, when he came back inside, his face was grim.

A white-hot flare of fear shot through me.

"That was the Coast Guard," said Officer Plano. "A boater picked up a dress. It matches the description."

FRITZ

Not my style.

So this was the end of my story. I would die out here. I was pretty sure of it. I was dying now. My body was giving up. I could feel the current winning, pushing at me. When I got too tired to swim, I floated on my back.

Fritz O'Neill, you lost this one, girl. You lost big.

In my mind's eye, I saw myself rising up from the sea almost mystically, carried on a wave, all the way back to Sunken Haven. And when I got there, a survivor, I knew that I wouldn't hide. I wouldn't scurry away to the Morgue to pack my suitcase and then catch the morning ferry. Because I had some things to say before I went.

First, I would tell the Burkes what snobs and phonies and

generally uncool people they were. Whoa, and how satisfying it would be, to look into their eyes and let them know that I wasn't fooled by any of their games. And then I'd tell Jean Custis she could have Gil. I'd tell her that they were meant for each other.

"Take him," I'd tell her. "I'm done with him. He wasn't worth my heart. I don't want him anymore."

The whole vision was unexpectedly thrilling, like a slow shower of sparks inside me. It sent a surge of energy through my body. And the thing was, if I held on, floating, I could also let the tide drive me this way and that way until I was washed up onto shore like a mermaid.

It was scary to let go of my control. But wasn't the whole idea to stay alongside a current, and not to fight it? The journey might be longer, but eventually I'd get there.

Besides, this didn't seem like my right death at all.

All alone in the middle of a dark ocean? No. Not my style.

What I didn't like was how the sea had turned, getting choppier. Maybe I could shift tactics, do that facedown float they'd taught kids at Minnows—another lesson that I'd never thought I'd need.

Funny how the Minnows never really prepared kids for any real fear. I'd taught Minnows a few years ago, and I'd made a couple of little kids cry by accident, telling them stories of drownings that I'd heard about from army lifeguards at the YMCA—how it was one of the leading causes of death in kids under the age of fourteen. I told those stories and that lady—what was her name again?—she'd taken me aside and asked me to go a little easier with the warnings. "And don't call the Minnows 'ya little boogas,'" she'd said. When I'd asked her why not, she'd explained it was "too rough."

When I'd told Gil that whole story, we'd laughed and laughed and repeated *ya little boogas* back and forth, flicking the words at each other, loving the grossness. He knew just what it felt like, to be ashamed of seeming "too rough" here.

Keep thinking. Keep remembering stories, that's how you stay awake and alive.

But I was getting too tired. Too tired even to think. I scooped a breath and relaxed and allowed my body to pitch and roll so that I was facedown.

Marcy Pency, that was her name.

I could feel myself being tugged under slightly, like my dress.

Stay calm . . . one scissor cut to surface, one breath, and return.

I closed my eyes and felt the enormous darkness all around me. Darkness and motion, that jerking forward rhythm, like being on the sleeper car on a train. I'd done that once, a family vacation. Nothing was safer than that, the whole family snug in bunks on a Silver Star Amtrak, rolling down to Florida. The tide would bring me in eventually, as long as I stayed patient, as long as I kept calm and suspended, and held on, as long as I didn't give up hope.

JEAN

We were all a little bit to blame.

Fritz's dress had been found on the beach at Seaview. This wasn't good news.

The officers didn't even pretend to be polite to Gil anymore.

"Listen, this girl was swimming away from you. *Anywhere* in the Atlantic Ocean seemed better than being with *you*," said Officer Novack. His words were weapons, all aimed at Gil. "So in the heat of the moment, what was she thinking? Enlighten me."

Gil's voice was even. "I don't know. Fritz has a temper."

"And do you?" asked Officer Plano bluntly. "Do you have a temper?"

"No." Gil made a helpless gesture with his hands. "I'm not known for having a temper. But tonight . . ."

"But tonight what?" Plano rolled back his head in a semicircle, loosening the tension, before fixing his concentration on Gil again.

"Tonight we were upset with each other. We were . . . emotional."

"You want to say why?"

"I'd rather not go into it in front of all these folks."

The officer didn't press it.

But then Julia spoke, her voice lifting clear above the conversation without seeming to be overly loud. "Gil, you know this is about Jean. Everyone does. You might as well tell them." Her gaze swept over me. Judging me. "When you got pushed to invite Jean to the party instead of Fritz, you did what you were told. Maybe you didn't think it would hurt Fritz as much as it did. But whatever happened with you both tonight—you made her feel absolutely terrible. Her judgment might not have been her best because of it. And everyone should know that."

"Julia," said Mrs. Tulliver warningly. "Honey . . . take a breath."

"How can I? My best friend might be dead." Julia's voice didn't change, her focus on Gil didn't falter, but she was trembling.

"No, no, no. Don't say that. She's not . . ." Then Mrs. Tulliver quickly went to Julia and held her, while we all stood there, stupidly watching in the dry, rustling silence that held us.

Across the room, Weeze Burke was staring, her mouth hanging open like a trout's. She was plainly shocked by Julia's accusation.

"Look, there's no point imagining a specific scenario." Officer Plano gave Gil a look like he'd already imagined plenty. He stood and slid a pack of cigarettes from his breast pocket, then tapped one out. "You people need to be braced," he said, as he and Officer Novack prepared to go. "Be braced, and pray."

A murmur rippled through us. Some of the little girls began to cry. I thought about comforting them; after all, I knew them all from the Coop. But my legs felt like they were made out of glue.

After the policemen had left, every pent-up, private conversation broke out.

Weeze was first and loudest. She began telling anyone and everyone what spunk and strength Fritz had, what a sweetheart she was, how she had a real fighting chance out there in the ocean because there was no athlete on Sunken Haven better than Fritz! And she hoped nobody thought the invitation had been a command performance, because the situation only was that Jean is Carpie's goddaughter—practically family—and she, Weeze, truly had thought Fritz wanted to sit with Julia tonight for Lobster Party! Just like always! But if only someone had spoken up, she could have done something! Oh, but adults were never privy to any of these teenager dramatics!

On and on Weeze went. She reminded me of my own parents, the way she reached for all the easiest justifications. She reminded me of a lot of people here, maybe even me. Maybe the workings of Weeze's heart were not so very different from my own. Maybe we were all to blame for Fritz's leaving. The idea was a spike of guilt inside me.

In the living room, some of the younger kids began to deal out a hand of crazy eights, to keep awake.

Bertie sidled up. "You want to walk somewhere?"

"Where?"

"Anywhere. Fresh air."

I nodded. I did feel suffocated.

Outside, we walked around to the Tullivers' backyard, where the grass was kept long and soft to the touch. We sat down next to each other, shoulder to shoulder. I stared up at the night sky, with its winking stars. So beautiful. Was Fritz out there somewhere, staring up at this same night?

"I know there's a lot going on, and everyone's kind of half out of their minds, and this night isn't about us," said Bertie quietly, after we'd sat in silence for a few minutes, "but I want you to know, Jean, when this is over, I'm always here for you."

It was such a sweet thing to say, that I wouldn't have even needed to answer him. All I'd need to do was to lean a little deeper into him. To show him how much I appreciated him. And that I'd be happy for things to continue as they had.

But would I? Did I want things to continue as they had?

As chaotic as the entire evening felt, I could feel my mind wrap around my answer, a single point of clarity, sharp to the touch.

No. I didn't want to be that girl, the girl who Bertie kept making excuses for. Even though I was also selfishly afraid of life without him, afraid of Bertie propelling forward without me foremost in his mind. I'd always been Bertie's best, most important thing. Even if he wasn't mine. And I didn't want to lose that role, even while I knew it wasn't any good for either of us. But if I didn't end it, he never would.

I plunged. "Bertie, I've treated you badly this summer," I said. "And I really want to stay friends with you. But it's gotten so hard for me to see us."

"I thought we'd been doing fairly well, finding private time, but I understand what you mean," he said, "with you always off at the Coop, teaching art to those girls. Would you ever think about cutting back hours?"

"See us as a couple, I mean. I don't want to take advantage of your hope anymore."

"You haven't ever—"

"Because I know that's what I've been doing. I'm sorry for that. I'm really sorry, Bertie. I do want to stay friends."

He was hurting. I knew that. It hurt me, too, as I waited for his reaction. Which wasn't much, outwardly. But then again, Bertie wasn't the type to expose his innermost feelings. He held on to his elegance before everything and anything.

Now he pushed the heels of his palms into the sockets of his closed eyes and let go of a long breath. "Okay," he said simply.

After a moment, he reached his arm around me. I leaned against him.

We stayed like that for a while.

FRITZ

She was the one I'd come back for.

It had happened. I had washed up on shore like a mermaid, after all.

Gingerly, I turned over and stared into the night sky.

Stars sparkled in the clean blackness like pebbles in a magic kingdom. My body felt run over, burnt up, and crushed in on itself. The pain was so deep, like a fire had gone out in me and left only a charred, broken shell on this night-blackened sand.

But I also knew I'd never loved a night so much as this one, the night I hadn't thought I'd get to see.

I saw the stars and the sky and my life. And maybe, for a moment, I'd even seen my own death.

It was late, wildly late, one of those hours you never stayed up till or woke up for, which made it even more stunning. The steam in the air had lifted, and the tide had gone out. I couldn't even hear the stray sound of a barking dog.

I knew I had to get back to Sunken Haven. Everyone must be a little bit out of their minds, wondering what had happened to me. I needed a phone, and a dime to call.

Something had happened to my shoulder. We'd better wake up Dr. Gamba tonight. But all I really wanted to do was go back to sleep.

It took so long before I could get myself to stand up. On overcooked, rubbery legs, I began the trek along the beach to the pitch-dark stiles.

In the distance, a bike swizzed past. Other than that, nobody was out on the boardwalk. I had no sense of this night, outside of an instinctive twinge that I was locked inside a strange, sleeping hour.

From far away, I saw a sign for Pier 60, Fair Harbor.

I'd never been to Fair Harbor before. Sunken Haven kids almost never went there, because there wasn't anything here that we couldn't get in Ocean Bay Park. Was I heading in the right direction? One way would take me farther out, to Saltaire. The other direction would take me closer, to Dunewood. Both directions had their advantages. Leave or go home.

I picked one and began to walk.

It felt like it had all happened to another person, a girl so scrambled up inside herself that she'd risked that jump into the sea. My head had been a blaze of anger and betrayal and disappointment. But now the quiet inside me matched the cool night. The air felt good on my sand-crusted skin, and the unlit walk gave me peace.

I saw the glow of hibachi embers on second-story porches, or caught a friendly scent of beer and burnt hot dogs, along with a sweet odor of onions and bug spray. Just enough to remind me that even if I was a stranger, I was not alone. People were here and they were close. It was nice to know, especially when I was so weak with exhaustion, too tired to borrow a bike even if I'd seen one.

Weathered brown or gray cedar beach houses banked the boardwalk on both sides, with the occasional break for dunes, a general store, or a bar. I was relieved to see that the next town was Dunewood. Then Lonelyville, then Robbins Rest.

"Depend on me," George had said. I should have depended earlier, when Weeze and Carp had imposed their restrictions. I should have left Sunken Haven weeks ago, and found my right people—with or without Gil. They'd always been here. Should I go find George now? Wake him up, get him to call over to the Tullivers? Who were surely scared to death. They'd probably got the Coast Guard involved, my parents alerted, all of it.

The detour was peaceful and uneventful. When I got to George's house, I saw a light on upstairs, but nobody answered my knock. I leaned my head against the door and let memories of the Fourth float through me. Those divas with their sequins and pumps and sprayed-up hair, their defiant celebrating, their willingness to let Gil and me be part of that evening's closeness. I could feel the smile on my face, my hands stretched out, my heart full. It had been the best night of my life, and if this dark hour depended on having lived that bright one, it had been worth it. Love was always worth it.

Walking had eased my mind as I slowly closed the distance to Sunken Haven. As my hair dried, I'd occasionally pick out a bobby pin and flick it to the ground. Like a reverse trail of breadcrumbs. I could feel my hair unraveling loose and soft. My feet were light on the boardwalk's wooden slats.

As I approached, I saw that the gated door stood wide open. I could have picked the lock with my last pin, but I didn't need to; I passed through easily, without another look behind me.

The small hours held a scent of pine and juniper. My sense of smell seemed extra sharp, as I cut across the grass. The dew was cool on my feet. As I crossed along the bay and cut up the ridge, I didn't see another soul—not that I thought I would.

It was only once I got to the big, dried-out old hemlock that stood in front of Whisper that I stopped. The lamplit glow of the cottage through the tangle of forest was sweet and comforting. Through the windows, I saw everyone, and I knew they were all here on account of me. There was a tense listlessness, as if the whole entire party had been placed under a sleeping spell that had only halfway worked.

And now I would be the one to break it.

Mr. and Mrs. Tulliver were sitting with the Burkes at the kitchen nook. Behind them, Gil was leaning with Tiger and

Deirdre against the counter. There was a larger, older group seated in the dining room area. Most of the kids were in the living room; a few were sleeping.

I crept near, slowly, until I stood at the top of the porch steps, taking it all in.

From the porch I moved to stand in the doorframe.

Gil saw me first. We stared at each other. He blinked once, long. I could see in his face all the hard hours of the evening, and I could see that all he wanted was to cross into this dark space and hold me.

But too much had happened between us. Too much was broken.

Silently, I buried all of the things I wanted to tell him. We had nothing to live for together, and nothing between us mattered anymore.

The room's awareness of me caught like a slow flame licking a curl of paper, and they appeared almost as strangers to me, maybe because now I knew what I didn't know then: that all they'd been was kindly tolerant of me, Julia's little friend, scooping ice cream or taking lunch orders right next to her. My single moment of Sunken Haven visibility, when I'd won the Junior Cup, had not been what many of them had wanted from me. I hadn't understood the rules. It all seemed so silly now, though of course, in a way, those rules were deadly.

Now you see me, I said. Ya little boogas.

It was hard not to be kind of amused by the whole thing, the way I always felt when I'd completed a dare. It was the whole point of a dare, really, to show your triumph over the moment just after it. They all came at me at once, a flood of voices, everyone speaking in a tidal wave of relief and confusion. And of course I forgave them, all of those tolerant Sunkies — Walts, Trains, Forsythes, Knightleys, Tingleys, Custises, Wembleys, Todds, Hastys, and Burkes — because Sunken Haven had given me the Tullivers, and most especially Julia, and in the end, she was the one I'd come back for.

Julia, who was at me at once, a bright column of skin and silver. Her face as calm as the sea itself, because she'd always known that I would return to her. Her pale eyes unblinking as I approached, facing me just as she had that very first day, when I'd jumped into her game and never jumped out.

I'm so sorry, I told her. You know how much I love you. Her eyes closed; a terrified shudder seemed to pass through her body, and it was only when she opened her eyes again that I saw the sting of her bright tears, and I felt the force of the sea inside me. I lay on the cool, damp beach, my lungs swollen with salt water, about to burst; but I also held on to Julia, my most precious thing, the sea finally pouring unstoppered out of me, as I stared up at the clear, beautiful night of black sky and silver stars. I held on to Julia. And then I let go.

JEAN

We could not doubt our guilt.

They found Fritz's body all the way over in Fair Haven.

Later, whenever people spoke of that night, there was speculation and rumor with regard to just about everything. Some said she'd done it on purpose, a silly girl's dramatic impulse. Others whispered that she'd fought long and hard, and if that call to the Coast Guard had been radioed a tiny bit earlier, it would have made all the difference. If only she'd done this. If only he'd done that. There were stories about drinking and fighting and love gone off the rails.

It was the usual gossip. You couldn't pay attention to it.

On Sunken Haven, we had a few more details, but that didn't stop our own guesswork. Julia was sure that ten minutes could have saved Fritz. That's what she told everyone, probably mostly to make good on her warning that I'd have to pay for swearing I'd seen Fritz come back, when I hadn't. But Julia was so broken up, so out of her mind and undone in anguish, that nobody could take her seriously. She even swore that she'd known the exact moment Fritz's soul had passed on, hours before the Coast Guard had radioed.

The helicopter took the body to Bay Shore, and from there it was flown back, accompanied by the Tulliver family, to the O'Neill family in Louisiana. Two days later, Gil went out for the funeral. Nobody came back to Sunken Haven—the Tullivers stayed on with the O'Neills so they could help one another through those first, grieving weeks, while Gil returned to New York City, where he resumed his job at his uncle's firm.

I'd thought Gil and I would speak again after that night, but speaking again turned out to be too difficult. I would have had to call or write him, and over the next months, while I often looked for him in restaurants or down city streets, once school resumed, we were completely out of each other's orbit.

It was probably for the best. How could Gil not always think of me as the girl who traded a last dance for Fritz's life?

And so, it seemed the only thing for me to do about that night was to close it, lock it up, and keep it hidden, pretending as best I could to walk away from it.

What I didn't know then—Gil Burke and I would never again be in touch, though I'd hear about him sporadically over the years. While he returned to Sunken Haven that next summer, I got a job as camp counselor up in Kennebunk, Maine, and later that fall, I moved out to Berkeley, to attend school in a state that suited me surprisingly well, although my original intention had been only to get as far away from home as I could.

My mother would speak of Gil in passing; that the Burke boy had transferred to Columbia, or that he'd graduated magna cum laude, or that he was in law school, or in Europe or Newport with his family. At NYU, Gil apparently moved with a fast, glamorous set of friends, some of whom were also friends with Daphne. Occasionally she'd mention seeing him in South Hampton or at a disco or a wedding.

"Oh, that handsome Gil Burke," my mother might say, if Daphne brought him up. "Remember all that awful business?" As time slowly unstitched Gil's direct connection to that night, Fritz O'Neill was generally evoked more as an accident he'd been lucky to walk away from.

But once, I'd known his heart. And I knew that Gil Burke had not escaped that night unscathed. We could not doubt our guilt, either of us, no matter how hard we worked to live apart from it.

But I had none of this knowledge when, the following weekend, much to my parents' delight, I beat Pepper Hale to win the Junior Cup. Pepper hadn't been here for June or July. Her parents had divorced the year before; she'd spent most of the summer up in Vermont with her dad's family. She'd attended a tennis clinic there, she told me, and she had been practicing hard at her game.

But I'd been practicing all summer. I had to keep reminding myself that I had earned it. I beat Pepper slowly and charmingly, the Sunkie way. I used a lot of friendly eye contact, happy-go-lucky shrugs, and a gracious smile whenever a set was called.

It was a magnificent trophy, and I hated to look at it. My parents tucked it up on a high shelf in the pantry, so I wouldn't have to.

A couple of nights later, a severe flash thunderstorm left the Coop flooded and without electric power. The flooding was pretty bad, and the Association decided to close the Coop temporarily. That's when I realized—there was absolutely nothing else for me here on Sunken Haven.

I waited for the right afternoon, later that same week, when my parents had left for an afternoon of playing bridge with the Burkes. The Burkes had gone into retreat since that night, but were slowly putting out feelers that they were ready to be happy and entertained again, though only by their closest circle.

And so once my parents were gone, I packed a small bag and wrote them a note that I was going off the island to spend time in the city for a while. I'd never done anything so disobedient before. They'd be surprised and upset. I'd worry about their reaction when the time came.

Before I took off, I walked through every room of Lazy Days for what, even then, I was sure would be the last time. Out the front door, I wished silent good-byes to the American holly, the two red cedars, the black gum. August was always so beautiful on Sunken Haven. The fruits on the sassafras were turning from green to blue—a feast for robins and jays, calling and chattering at one another.

It was a blessing to have spent all the summers of my childhood here. It was another blessing to know it was over.

The minute I came out of the subway station at Eighty-Sixth and Lexington, on the 6 connecting from Grand Central, I was hit with a dozen smells, lingering in drifts of garbage and gasoline. Steamed heat stuck to my skirt, to my neck and knees. Rooftops and water tanks looked like they'd burn my fingers at a touch.

I'd had an idea that I'd go get a job for August, and that this job would give me a reason—at least a reason that I could legitimately explain to my parents—to stay in town. On the way to the apartment, with vigorous purpose, I filled out applications in places I frequented regularly, like Peterson's Pharmacy, the local diner, and the dry cleaners. Every application came with a phantom life attached, as I saw myself handing over boxes of crisp, pressed shirts, or locating a particularly off-brand mouthwash, or rattling off the pancake specials. It was exciting to me, this prospect of a new identity, a different Jean Custis, who understood things not taught in country clubs and tennis clinics.

I am ready to be anybody, just as long as I change.

The afternoon exhausted me. Inside, the apartment was hot and stale.

I turned on the air conditioner and stood in front of the living room window. The sun was going down, picking up the floating dust motes in its rich gold light.

Would I ever see a setting sun and not think about what I should have done differently? Doubtful.

On the street, Mikhail Baryshnikov, in sunglasses, jeans, and a T-shirt, was walking his small black poodle up the street. My heart leaped; I touched my forehead and fingertips to the glass, watching him—it was such a direct and personal glimpse. There he was, so close that if the window weren't sealed shut, he'd have heard me call his name.

I wished I could ask him things. Real things. Had there been a getaway car when he defected? Had there been bodyguards and passwords? Did he regret what he'd had to give up, or did he love this country the way only a person who feels saved by it can? Did he know real freedom, or was he always looking over his shoulder, waiting for someone to pin him to his history?

Moving from window to window, I trailed Baryshnikov as we both moved uptown, from the living room to the dining room and through into the study, a corner of the apartment that we rarely used. When he disappeared around the corner, I lost my project and, with it, the surprising lightness of its distraction.

I dropped into Dad's leather wing chair and curled up. His bookcase took up the whole wall. A glint caught my eye. I leaned forward. Resting on the second shelf, right where I'd put them, were my earrings.

The ones I'd been given for Christmas.

With a lurch in my heart, I remembered. I'd had them on since Christmas morning. And then Christmas night I'd hidden in here to escape my parents' party and all those guests. I'd taken the earrings off and put them right there, on the bookshelf, and forgotten about it. But these earrings looked so different from the other pair, the pair I'd stolen from Daphne—the pair I'd seen Fritz wearing, that night.

I took the earrings and held them in my palm for a long time before I put them back where I'd found them. In the sun's last light, I stood on shaking legs and went to the kitchen, where earlier this summer Daphne had taped the number of her Spanish host family to the fridge.

I messed up twice and got an operator's recording, before I'd correctly punched the long sequence of country and city codes into the wall phone. It was almost eight o'clock here, which meant it would be one in the morning in Spain.

But I didn't care. I had to hear her.

A man with a voice like a growl answered, in words that I didn't quite understand.

"Daphne!" I called. "Please? I need to speak with Daphne. My sister."

I heard the *clonk* of the receiver being set down. I waited, every second wanting to hang up. Minutes later, when Daphne picked up, her voice sounded far away and frightened, the call of a girl lost at sea. "Jean? Is that you?"

Light-headed, my heart pounding, I slid to the floor. Just to hear her, I felt ruptured, drowning on the inside from all that I hadn't confessed, like a poison contained and leaking inside me. My hand held the receiver in a death grip.

"You were right, Daphne," I whispered across the ocean, into the static, and only now did I let tears slide, unstoppable, down my face. "I made a mistake. I made a really stupid, horrible mistake here, and there's no way I can take it back. And I am so, so sorry, and I'd do anything to fix it, to make it right again, but I can't, Daphne. I went too far, and I can't."

ACKNOWLEDGMENTS

Quite a few wonderful people gave their time, thoughts, and advice during the writing of this book. Many thanks to Jenny Han, who was so intrigued by a novel set in the summer of '76 that she created a spellbinding Pinterest board even before I'd set down my first word. A big thank-you to Julia DeVillers, who read that messy landslide of an early manuscript and gave me the encouragement I needed to keep going.

For her scrupulous attention to each step along the journey, many thanks to Emily van Beek. This book is infinitely better because of your ability to deliver fresh insights on every draft—and there were many. Thank you, Siobhan Vivian, for your humor and enthusiasm during what is not always an easy process, and thank you Courtney Sheinmel; I can't think of one instance when you didn't say "Yes! Send it!" whenever I asked you for a read.

To my other, fellow hardworking writer pals whose work and

company I love, a shout-out to Melissa Walker, Micol Ostow, Sarah Mlynowski, Morgan Matson, Elizabeth Eulberg, Michael Buckley, Jen E. Smith, Robin Wasserman, Lynne Weingarten, and Bennett Madison. I couldn't ask for a more creative crew.

I am profoundly delighted that *Be True to Me* is an Algonquin book; what a joy to be here. I'm extremely grateful for the insight and wisdom of my editor, Elise Howard, who guided this story with seasoned clarity and confidence. It has been an inspiring process. *Be True to Me* and I really lucked out.

Finally, I'd like to thank the MacDowell Colony for the solace of my fall 2015 residency, where I mostly took walks, but where I also stuck my landing. A magic moment; I think about it still.

Read on for a sneak peek
at Adele Griffin's new YA novel,

tell me no lies

The new girl arrived at Argyll on the Tuesday after Columbus Day weekend, a month late for the start of school. Not that anyone was expecting her, late or ever. I'd slumped into the art room after lunch, my brain burnt out on physics and history but reorienting for the one subject where I could lose myself.

We all saw her right away, an elegant stork over by the stereo system, painting her nails with a bottle of Wite-Out.

Who's that? I mouthed to Gage and Mimi, who shrugged in sync.

But seriously, who was that? None of us knew. Could you be a new girl *and* a senior? The two facts scraped against each other.

She had on a navy school kilt, too new and baggy on her hips—upper schoolers wore our kilts short, faded, and (if you looked close) doodled on with Sharpie pen. But the rest of her style was a middle finger to the uniforms section of the Argyll handbook, from the pair of men's boxer shorts that drooped below her hemline to her conspicuously wrinkled, untucked button-down to her beat-up pink espadrilles that she wore with heels crushed like bedroom slippers.

We shuffled around her, retrieving our projects from the flat files, watching as she jiggered a cassette tape with one hand while blowing the nails of the other. She held herself in that alert, pose-y way of someone used to compliments. I couldn't see her face full-on, but her hair was black and glossy as a doll's. Tendrils fell soft to brush the pale nape of her neck.

What was her story?

AP Art was taught Tuesdays and Thursdays by the Custis-Browns, our husband-and-wife art teachers. The rumor was that lurid nudie pictures of her by him hung in galleries in Philadelphia—Maggie Farthington had sworn she'd seen one last fall, and it was a complete and total gross-out. But at least it wasn't *him* naked, we all agreed, with his woolly beard and woodchuck's overbite.

For the first few minutes of class, Mrs. Custis-Brown made long-distance calls in her office. She'd fling herself into the main room eventually.

Once the new girl had snapped in her cassette, she slid nearer to one of the long metal tables where Mimi, Gage, and I had spread out. My quick, shy glance proved my hunch that she was pretty, with dark eyes and delicate bones. She moved in a sort of purposeful trance, her fingers trailing the edges of easels and shelves.

Last week, Mimi, Gage, and I had chosen our "concentration" to submit for AP portfolio credit. We'd had the summer to think about it. Mimi, who liked designs, had decided to focus on "Patterns." Gage, the maverick, had gone with "Water." I'd picked "Hands," which had seemed like a clever challenge—or at least, Mrs. Custis-Brown had been pleased.

"Hands are technical, but expressive," she told me. "I think you could do something interesting there."

So far, I hadn't.

The new girl dropped at our table, resting her chin on its surface, her heavy-lidded gaze fixed on nothing, clicking her jaw and singing lyrics she knew by heart. The song was in French—an old man's pervert voice, sometimes joined by a whispery girl-woman. It sounded nothing like what we loved, the British techno bands fronted by guys who sounded like they'd drive Vespas, make out with you in nightclubs, and know all the slang words for drugs.

Mimi plunged in. "Are you new?" she asked. "Are you a senior? Are you in AP Art?"

Without lifting her chin, the girl nodded a yes that answered all the questions.

"Mrs. C-B will be out soon. Or I can go get her." I sounded too helpful, which girls said about me. Teacher's pet. Kiss-up. But it just came naturally, like preferring mint chip or being a good babysitter.

"No, thanks."

"I don't mind."

"No." The girl lifted her head, then raised herself higher, arcing her back and stretching her arms. As she glanced at me, I stared. Popcorn-pale skin dusted in freckles. A beaky nose balanced by her wide, kohl-smudged eyes. Knobby cheekbones, lips on the thin side. She had looks people got in arguments about, where some called her beautiful and others said no, too racehorse, too freakish, too harsh—a haunted face that was closed to me, to everyone, and yet I couldn't shrug off the sense that any moment she might cry.

"I can get you some sketch paper," I said, "while you wait?"

"Lizzy . . ." Mimi didn't like when I got too eager-beaver.

But the girl just shrugged. "Sure."

I jumped to tear a piece of butcher paper from a roll on the other side of the room, then slid it in front of her like a waitress providing a place mat.

With a suggestion of thanks in her nod, the girl took a pencil from the coffee can of chalks and pencils I set down. She pulled a mirrored compact from her sling bag, opened it, propped her chin in her hand, and began to draw herself.

Right away, the sketch captured an enhanced, Hollywood version of her, with a pouty mouth and swooping eyelashes. It was almost comic—if she'd been a friend of ours, we'd have laid right in:

Hey, in love with yourself much?

Oh, I didn't know you were secretly Isabella Rossellini!

Mimi, Gage, and I were now trading so many disbelieving looks around the table that we couldn't even concentrate on our own work.

When Mrs. Custis-Brown finally appeared, I could tell she didn't think much of the sketch, either.

"A portrait!" she said, and nothing else. "Are you Claire? Claire Reynolds?"

"That's me." *Claire Reynolds.* As she stood, we all buttoned her into her name.

A normal name. Almost plain, but pretty.

Claire made a sophisticated contrast to Mrs. Custis-Brown, who—in her bright, shapeless smocks and clogs—looked like someone who worked at a Swedish day care. But Mrs. Custis-Brown was smiling, her blue eyes crinkling. More delighted by Claire's artsy style than with her actual art.

"Great! I've just read your transcript. Welcome to Advanced Placement Art. I teach the first semester and my husband takes over in January."

Claire was half listening, the way you hear a stewardess do the safety talk.

"I don't know if the girls filled you in that we submit AP portfolios come spring?" Mrs. Custis-Brown chirped on. "The panel judges between twelve and fifteen pieces on breadth, quality, and concentration. Technically it's called a 'sustained investigation,' but that sounds so detective show, right? You don't have to decide—" Mrs. Custis-Brown broke off, startled by the music, the woman's voice saturating the room with gasps and animal breathing.

"My mixtape," said Claire.

"Okay!" said Mrs. Custis-Brown. "I'm not familiar! And I'm from New York, originally—but we never get in to see the new acts anymore."

"But this song is old," said Claire. "I'd have thought by now Serge Gainsbourg's got zero shock value."

"Oh, *Gainsbourg*!" Mrs. Custis-Brown batted a hand. "It's been so long since I heard him. Fine by me. It's everybody's art room." She threw out a nervous laugh.

Under the table, Mimi pushed her leg against mine. Gage rolled in her lips. I looked down—to start laughing would be to make the worst noise possible.

"And I already know my art concentration," Claire said.

"Oh? Wonderful! What is it?"

"Myself."

"Okay, right on!"

The song had melted into liquid sighs and squeals.

Gage was visibly shaking, in the throes of a silent laugh-attack.

"The art room is also open after school, and you'll want those extra hours," Mrs. Custis-Brown continued loudly over the sex music. "As for someone taking you through the nuts and bolts of where we keep art supplies, I nominate Lizzy Swift." She looked at me, knowing I'd be happy to.

"Sure," I managed to wheeze through a laugh-breath. "I'd be happy to."

With a nod, Mrs. Custis-Brown left us, her hands clasped behind her back as she moved to another table. We all exhaled relief.

"My parents play this repulsive guy," said someone at one of the other tables.

I sketched my right hand with my left, watching my fingers shape into a pile of kindling. Nerves clenched in hope that Claire would ask me for the art room tour.

Claire didn't ask me for anything.